HE
FORGOT
TO SAY
GOODBYE

Benjamin Alire Sáenz

HE
FORGOT
TO SAY
GOODBYE

Simon & Schuster Books for Young Readers
New York London Toronto Sydney

SIMON & SCHUSTER BOOKS FOR YOUNG READERS
An imprint of Simon & Schuster Children's Publishing Division
1230 Avenue of the Americas, New York, New York 10020
SIMON & SCHUSTER BOOKS FOR YOUNG READERS is a trademark of Simon & Schuster, Inc.
Book design by Karen Hudson
The text for this book is set in Meridien 11/16.
Manufactured in the United States of America
10 9 8 7 6 5 4
Library of Congress Cataloging-in-Publication Data
Sáenz, Benjamin Alire.
He forgot to say goodbye / Benjamin Alire Sáenz.
p. cm.
Summary: Two teenaged boys with very different lives find that they share a common bond—fathers they have never met who left them when they were small boys—and in spite of their differences, they become close when they each need someone who understands.
ISBN-13: 978-1-4169-4963-3
ISBN-10: 1-4169-4963-1
[1. Fathers—Fiction. 2. Emotional problems—Fiction. 3. Interpersonal relations—Fiction. 4. Family problems—Fiction. 5. Mexican Americans—Fiction. 6. El Paso (Tex.)—Fiction.] I. Title.
PZ7.S1273He 2008
[Fic]—dc22
2007021959

For Gabriela and Adrian
(two very seriously beautiful people)

ACKNOWLEDGMENTS

There are always people to thank after a book has been written. After all, no author can claim to have written a book without help. I thank Bobby and Lee Byrd and all the good people at Cinco Puntos Press who encouraged me to become a writer of books for young adults. I thank all the young people in my life who have come in many forms and have always been a great blessing and who have continually reminded me that adults do not have a monopoly on the word "hurt."

I thank all my students who keep language astonishingly alive and who constantly keep me on the lookout for new ways of seeing the world. I thank my father, dead four years now. I thank him for the ways in which he was present and for the ways in which he was absent—and thank him especially for the ways in which he continues to shape my imagination. I thank my mom who reads all my books and who I'm sure wonders where I came from. Without her steadfast love, I would not have become a writer.

I thank my agent, Patty Moosbrugger, who is a credit to her profession. I do not know where my career would be without her. I thank my editor, David Gale, for his careful reading of my work, for his professional, respectful and gracious manner—and for the great faith he placed in this novel.

Finally, I thank my wife, Patricia, who has graced my life with her voice, her laughter, and her steadfast love.

HE
FORGOT
TO SAY
GOODBYE

Someday I'll be a father. A real father. And I'll make sure all my kids know everything about me, so they won't have to go around guessing who the hell I am. I mean, a son or a daughter should know who their father is. And not just the superficial crap like his name or what he does or what he looks like but *who he really is*. I've lived my whole life guessing. Guessing makes a kid tired and old. I don't want my kids to be old and tired. I want them to be happy.

—Ramiro Lopez

Sometimes the idea of being a father enters my head. I'm not exactly in love with the idea. I mean, what would I do? You know what I'd do? I'd just hang out with my kid—that's what I'd do. I'd read to him. I'd just hold him and kiss him and hold his hand. And when he was old, and I didn't touch him anymore, it wouldn't matter. Because every time he looked at me, he'd remember how it was when he was a boy. And the memory would be seriously beautiful. And we would be father and son.

—Jake Upthegrove

ONE

Me, Ramiro Lopez

My mom says I need to stop and think about things. I think about things all the effen time. Think and think and think. You know, it's not like all that thinking has gotten me places.

Him

Sometimes I think of him. And when I do, I start to draw a picture. Not a real picture. I'm not an artist, not even close. I just draw this picture in my head.

Of him.

My dad.

It's easier for me to draw a picture of what he looks like than to imagine his voice. I mean, I don't know what he would sound like. He would use a lot of Spanish. But his voice, I don't know, I just don't know what words he'd use. He'd be angry, but that would just make him normal. A lot of fathers are like that—especially fathers who've gone away. I think of their anger as a wind. And that wind took them away. From me. And all the others like me.

So I draw a picture in my head. *Of him.* Not of his voice but of his face. He has dark eyes and thick, wavy hair that was once really black—*really* black. But now his hair is more white than black because that's how it goes when men get older. Their hair begins to get old too. That's the way it is and there's nothing we can do about it. And he has lines on his face, more from working out in the sun than from laughing. He doesn't like to laugh. He looks tired because he's had to work so hard. With his body, not with his mind, not like a teacher or a doctor or an insurance guy or a computer geek. You know, like construction. Working in construction—it makes you old and tired. It kills your body because you have to work out in the sun every day, in the heat, in the cold, every day. It's not like working out in a gym and hanging out with other jocks that have nothing better to do than to muscle up—it's not like that. If you work with your mind, then working with your body is just a hobby. But if you work with your body, then, well, your only hobby is to rest.

"Your body is nothing but a money machine." That's what Uncle Rudy says. "That's the way it is. We're all just prostitutes." My aunt hit him when he said that and told me not to pay any attention to him.

But listen, when you work in construction, your body is the car *and* the road *and* the destination. No, no, I'm getting all tangled up in my own words. That's not right. Look, I don't agree with Uncle Rudy. I get the part about using your body to make money. But the body's not a machine. When you work with your body every day of your life, well, your body's more like a punching bag—it gets hit all the time. All day. Every day. And it's never going to stop. Not ever. I know. I hear men talk—and they say things about their tired bodies, things like: "Ya estoy pa la patada." Mexican working guys, they talk like that. My dad's one of those guys. I know. He didn't go to college or anything like that. He didn't even graduate from high school. My Tía Lisa told me that once. She likes to tell me things I'm not supposed to know.

In the picture I've drawn in my head, my dad looks sad. Tired and sad and maybe mad, too. Definitely mad as hell. That's not a good combination. You don't see the anger in his body or his face. But if you look into his dark eyes, that's where you see all the anger—they're like a bomb about to go off. You can almost hear the *tick tick tick*.

Yeah, he's mad as hell.

Mad at the world.

Mad at himself.

Mad at my mom.

Mad because he was born a poor Mexican. Mad because he never finished high school. Mad because he got a rotten deal. He thinks the world cheated him. *And maybe the world did cheat him*. But I don't think he helped himself out. I mean, my Uncle Rudy says, "If you know a man's gonna cheat you, then why the hell are you lending him twenty bucks?" No, I don't think my dad helped himself out. See, the way I picture him, he has so much anger in his eyes, that he's half-blind. He can't see straight. He can't see the leaves on a tree. He can't see the fact that some dogs know how to smile. That's what happens. When you get too angry you can't see the world anymore.

My dad, he looks down at the ground more than he looks up at the sky. It's like he doesn't even notice the birds anymore. He's just looking down at things that crawl. That's how I draw him—his eyes never looking up.

He's crooked now. He's all dented up. He's a car that's been on the road too long. Too many accidents. The paint's all peeled off.

He used to be handsome. Real, *real* handsome. Girls used to look at him, praying he'd look back. And his walk was like a dance. I guess we always want our dads to be handsome just like we want our moms to be beautiful. But now I'm thinking he's changed and he's more than just an ordinary handsome guy. Now he has the most interesting face in the world. Maybe interesting is better than handsome. But interesting doesn't mean happy, and I mean he looks beat-up as an old, chained-up dog. And disappointed, as if somehow a part of him is missing. *Me. It's me that's missing.* He's thinking of me and he's missing me, and sometimes he looks out at the sky and whispers my name and tries to imagine me just like I'm imagining him.

Look, I don't know what I'm talking about. It's not as if I really know what he looks like because I've never seen him. My mother once said he was beautiful. "He was like an ocean—beautiful to look at." The way she said that, right then she looked soft as a cloud. And then all of a sudden she turned real hard. "I almost drowned in that ocean." I knew she wasn't about to go near another man ever again. All men had become oceans she might drown in.

Once, when we'd gone to my cousin's wedding, my mom looked at me and said. "I ripped up all our wedding pictures—and then I burned them." She looked at me like maybe she was sorry she'd blurted that out, and she gave me a look like I wasn't supposed to be asking her any questions about him. *Him.* I don't think she blurted out that piece of information to be mean. I think sometimes our minds get so full of something that we just have to empty them out. I think that's what happened to her. Sure. That's a good theory. I mean, she sounded so mad when she said that. Really, really mad. Not mad at me, but mad at the way things had turned out—and well, sad, too. It's as if some of my dad's anger and some of his sadness rubbed off on my mother every time he touched her. And I know she carries his face somewhere inside her (and for all I know, somewhere in her purse). I mean, you can't rip up all the pictures you carry in your head. You can't. Even if you want to. I think sometimes she cries for him. But she doesn't cry in front of me or my little brother. My little brother, Tito, wasn't even born when he left. He was still inside her. And I was almost two.

I sometimes try to imagine him on the day he left. I see him packing all his clothes. I see him looking around the room—trying to figure out what else he should pack in his suitcase. Maybe he thinks he should stay, but he knows he has to go. I picture him with a confused look on his face and I picture my mother sitting in the kitchen. Saying nothing. Just waiting. Waiting for him to leave so she can have herself a good cry. I wonder if he said good-bye to us and said something to us, you know, like fathers do, talk to their sons, tell them things.

Important things like *I'll miss you, I'll think of you every day, I'll come back, you'll see, I'll come back, and don't ever forget that I love you, hijito de mi vida.* I don't know. Maybe he just left. Maybe he didn't say a damn thing.

My dad must have held me in his arms when I was a baby. He must have kissed me like I see other fathers kiss their babies. He must have done that.

His breath might have smelled of cigarettes and garlic.

His breath might have smelled like cilantro.

His breath might have smelled like too much anger and work.

But there might have been something sweet on his breath. He might have taken me to the grocery store or to wash his car at the H & H or taken me for a ride to get ice cream at the 31 Flavors, and he probably took me to the El Paso Zoo and to the swimming pool at Memorial Park and to Western Playland and to get empanadas at Gussie's and to get tacos at Chico's—places like that. He might have taken me to watch the Diablos play baseball or to a Miners football game. He might have. Just because I don't remember doesn't mean it didn't happen.

Me, Jake Upthegrove

All I'm trying to do is talk to you. Are you listening? See, the thing is, *I don't think you are listening*. Okay, see, we have a problem. You don't think I want to talk and I don't think you want to listen.

Me
(Jake Upthegrove)

"Hey, Upthegrove! Someday you'll be sent up the river." That was the first joke I ever heard about my last name. I don't even remember who said it, and back then I didn't even know what the expression "being sent up the river" meant. I was five years old. Okay, it was supposed to be a joke—but I just didn't get it. All I remember was that some guy was barking a joke at me. I mean, c'mon, let's get down to it, people are like dogs. Let me tell you something, if a dog acts like a dog, well, that's a beautiful thing. That's very cool. I can dig that. I can really dig that. But if a human being acts like a dog, well, that's not a beautiful thing. Definitely not cool.

Another time, a girl in second grade called me "Up the Street." Got a real laugh out of that one. I mean, I was so destroyed. And if that wasn't enough, the next day she accosted me with "Down the Road." That girl was real stand-up material. There's something about my name that people just can't leave alone. It's like a kitty they have to pet or a shoe they just have to try on. People always fall into calling me by my last name. It feels like I've always been in the Army. Everybody's a drill sergeant. And me, I'm permanently assigned to be in boot camp all my life. Okay, look, maybe that doesn't qualify as abuse but it doesn't qualify as affection either. People just destroy me.

When I was a freshman in high school, I got into my first fistfight. "Hey Upthegrove!" Some guy was yelling my name. I turned around and there in front of me was this guy named Tom. Hated him, that guy. I mean guys like that really destroy me. He was one of those kinds of dudes that dressed down in ratty clothes, torn T-shirts, ripped jeans, and had tattoos all over the place. He liked to make out like he was poor and lived in a tough neighborhood. But who the hell could afford that kind of body art if you weren't fucking rich?

"Upthegrove!" he taunted, singing my name like it was a piece of wadded-up paper he was swatting around in the air. "Upthegrove," he sang, "what kind of shit name is that?" I turned around, my fist closed tight, and pounded him right in the face. Didn't even know I was going to do that.

When I pulled back my fist, I could see blood pouring from Tom's face. Blood is more real than any tattoo, I'll tell you that. It sort of scared me at first—but then the thought came to me that he wasn't exactly going to die on me. Maybe his nose was broken or something—but he was going to be just fine. See, in situations like this, it's always best to take the long view of things. In the short term he was bleeding and hurting. In the long term he was going to be just fine.

So, there's Tom holding his bloody nose and looking like maybe he was going to cry, and there was red all over his ratty shirt. I wasn't about to let go, though, no sir, I was in this and I was going for all the marbles, so I just looked at him and said, "Fuck you. And fuck your rich dad, and fuck your expensive tattoos, and fuck your rich bitch of a dog." I don't know why I said that. I mean, I don't think dogs know anything about being rich or poor and I have a soft spot for dogs, especially girl dogs because they don't go around screwing up the world and they tend to be loyal and sweet, and the part about his dad, maybe I should have left that out—I mean, I'm not exactly living in squalor. On the other hand, his father didn't get to be where he was by being the world's nicest guy—so maybe I was glad I'd dragged him into the whole discussion. Not that any of this qualified as a discussion.

Anyway, not a second later, his loyal, boot-licking, dumb-ass sidekick, John, jumped in swinging. I mean, the guy was ready to party. His fists were a pair of shoes on a dance floor—and me, well, I was the dance floor. I'll spare you all the pretty details. It was over quick. That was the good part. I had to have stitches above my left eye, and I don't think my lower left rib will ever be the same. And believe me, I saw stars—the big dipper, the little dipper, and some constellations I didn't even know existed. Stars. Shit. I mean, can you dig that? I suppose I should thank the guy for showing me a universe I didn't know existed.

That was my first and last fight. The one thing I learned on that day was that I was better at using words than using my fists. Live and learn, you know? I mean, even if you can't dig the fact that I popped a guy right in the nose, you *can* dig the fact that I learned something.

I was in deep trouble at home and at school. We're talking seriously deep trouble. Profoundly deep trouble. No video games. No television. No movies. No going out. No allowance. No reading e-mails, no downloading music, no hanging out with people I liked. No leaving the house without being accompanied by an adult. I told my mom I didn't think she qualified as an adult. I got in even deeper. She looked right at me and said, "That's it. Your life is ruined."

"Sure," I said. "Wow. Ruined. I'm so destroyed."

"I hate that expression," she said. "I wish you'd stop using it."

"Okay," I said, "Make a list, okay? Just list all the expressions I use that you wish I'd stop using. I'll take the list, read it over, and take it under advisement."

She pointed her finger—which meant I should go to my room. She walked in behind me and confiscated my iPod and took away my laptop.

So there I was, alone, with no electronic devices to comfort me. For a whole month.

Well, at least I read all those books I was supposed to be reading. I didn't mind. And then there was the whole thing of talking to counselors and my mother asking me for days at a time, "What's wrong with you? Don't you know you could wind up in jail? And you don't even know Spanish." I tried to keep from rolling my eyes. See, I actually *do* speak some Spanish, and I'm always translating for her—*her* (my mother, the woman who just told me that I didn't speak Spanish)—when she wants Rosario, our housekeeper, to do *this* and *that*. This fact was apparently lost on her. But see, the point here is that my mom happens to believe that jails are full of Mexicans who don't speak English. She has these ideas—though sometimes the things she says don't actually qualify as ideas. She destroys me.

And then I smiled and said, "Hey, Mom, they have special sections in jails for gringos." And then she gives me this look—that don't-interrupt-me-don't-mock-me-have-some-respect look. She patted her chest (her favorite gesture) and finally said, "You're very glib."

I decided it was best to just zip it up. And my mom, just as she stopped patting her chest, she let it rip, and she's going on and on about rights and responsibilities and I swear her little lecture even had something in it about the Constitution—and my stepfather is shaking his head but also trying to calm my mother down and trying to smile at me—and he has this stupefied look on his face like a fish who's caught in a net, all pained and confused—poor guy, and he keeps telling me that this is not easy for him and I want to tell him that really the whole thing has nothing to do with him, but I don't say anything because, well, I'm already in a helluva lot of trouble, and the truth of the matter is that I just don't see things their way. They weren't even there when I decided to rearrange Tom's nose. I mean, what did they have to go on except hearsay?

Look, all they have is this parent perspective thing. They have this image of themselves as having a more global view of things, like they really see the big picture. Right, right, sure. I mean, can you dig that? Let's look at the big picture by all means. Let's put it this way: *I am not responsible for all the chaos in the world.* I am not responsible for dudes with attitudes and the twisted, grotesque things they have in their screwed-up heads. Please. Someone help me out here. And even though there's no excuse for going around hitting people so hard that you draw blood, there's also no excuse for bullshit bullies with pedestrian names like Tom and John. And when we all grow up to be forty, who the hell do you think is going to be screwing people over? Me? Or Tom and John? Now you're getting the picture. I'd say my long-term perspective is pretty global.

So, the whole thing about punching Tom got really involved and complicated. Of course it did. I mean, there were adults involved. We know what happens when adults step in. They have to be in charge. They have to have a plan. They like plans. Not that they ever work—but coming up with a plan feels like they've done something. You know, I don't see that the adults around me have done such a hot job of running things. Nope, not in my opinion. Adults, they really destroy me.

The thing is, just because they all go to work and bring in some cash, they figure they know how to run the world. Well, take a look around. Global warming, pollution, poor people without health insurance, bad schools, bad streets, underpaid teachers, overpaid insurance lawyers, and gasoline prices that are as high as Katie Scopes at a party. (Katie Scopes, I like her, but, hell, she's always stoned—probably due to the fact that adults are running the world). Look, I could get a list going here that could get really long—I'm talking seriously long. Dig it? So, anyway, without asking my opinion, the adults took over "the situation." That's what the principal said when he called my mom: "We have a situation here." The principal, he really destroys me.

In the end, the adults proposed a "solution" to "the situation." There were apologies from me and apologies from Tom and John, none of them sincere, though no one seemed to give a damn about sincerity. See, I get criticized for being glib and ironic all the time. Well, when I try sincerity, you want to know what happens? I get stepped on like an ant. Like a worm. Like a cockroach. Bring on the irony, that's what I say. I'm sure you can dig that.

So, of course detention was part of the solution. We had to write essays about how we wound up there. I had to write mine again because I was told that the "tone of my essay lacked a genuine sense of remorse." *I see*, I said to myself, *we can live without sincerity but we cannot live without remorse.* I told Mr. Alexis, the principal, that if the president of the United States could start a war in Iraq on false pretenses of WMDs and didn't have to apologize for his big fat lies, then there was no reason to expect more from a worthless, out-of-control anarchist like me.

Mr. Alexis put on this stone face and looked right at me. He told me I hadn't earned the right to speak that way about the president of the United States who was a decent, Christian man. And, in addition, he informed me that I didn't have a nickel's worth of knowledge about the serious philosophy of anarchism. I explained—disrespectfully, I'm sure—that my opinions of the president were at least based on something that resembled reality, and even if they weren't, I was entitled to them *and would he please keep his well-intentioned but small-*

minded lectures defending our nation's political leaders to himself. I didn't stop there. Of course I didn't. I just felt I had to add that I probably had a better idea of the serious philosophy of anarchy than a man like him whose addiction to order seriously undermined his feeble attempts at engaging his imagination.

He returned my remark by reminding me that he remained unimpressed with my shallow intellectual demeanor and that nothing could disguise my obstinate, disrespectful, and undisciplined attitude. He said being a smart aleck didn't actually make me smart. And then he said it again: "Despite your extensive, if aggressive vocabulary, you're nothing but an angry, disrespectful young man who needs a little discipline." You see, the thing with adults is that respect is just a word they use to guilt us nonadults into doing what they want us to do. But did Mr. Alexis leave it at that? Of course not. He reminded me and Tom and John that it was a privilege to attend a premed magnet school and if we weren't very careful, well, we just might be sent back to a normal school. That's how he put it. A normal school. That guy, he destroys me. Where in the hell was he going to find a normal school? How can schools be normal when they're run by adults like him?

I could make the exchange between me and Mr. Alexis as long as it actually was. But it's pointless, really. He did warn me about my politics which I thought was totally out of line. "Apart from the fact that you're a completely unmanageable young man, your politics are offensive to the thinking people of this nation." I told him pretty much that I didn't think he— or anybody of his ilk—qualified as a thinking person. He tried to say something at that point but I just kept on going. I told him that as far as being unmanageable, well, I came to school to be taught, not to be managed. "I'm a person, not a portfolio." And then I really got myself into trouble by telling him that if he wasn't careful, I was going to make his nose look like Tom's.

He said he could throw me out of school for that threat. I said to take it up with my stepfather, the attorney (not that David would have sided with me). I eventually agreed to put more remorse into my essay. I even started to refer to him as "sir." He wasn't smart enough to pick up on the fact that I was mocking him. Look, he won the argument. I put remorse into my essay. But seasoning my essay with remorse was not the final solution that the adults around me had concocted. That was just the beginning. To put some à la mode on top of the apple pie, I was forced to attend *anger management classes*, where the only thing I really learned to do was to keep my mouth shut and my hands to myself. Maybe that wasn't such a bad thing to learn. *And all of this because of my name.* There's a lot of irony here, of course. Irony—that's my favorite word. Look, I live in a seriously ironic world and if there *is* a God, I've decided irony is his favorite word too.

And to layer irony upon irony, I don't even know the guy whose name I own. I mean, *I really am destroyed.* I don't mean to play victim here, but c'mon. People get to make fun of me because I have a last name that got stuck on me like a permanent bumper sticker? Look, my mother left that guy—*my father*—when I was about three. In my seventeen-plus years of living, I've talked to the guy only once.

And he has never, never, never tried to communicate with me directly. Sending advice secondhand through my mother doesn't qualify as paternal involvement. Not in my book, it doesn't. I don't talk to him, I don't know him, and I don't even remember his face. What do three-year-olds remember? Ducks in a bathtub, that's what they remember. Red wagons with wheels. Books made of cardboard you could bite.

I'm not happy about any of this. Look, I'm destroyed.

Me, Ramiro Lopez

Look, just because you don't have a girlfriend doesn't mean you don't know anything about love. I know more than I want to know.

Her

Mom is a pretty lady. Even without makeup.

She's not even forty yet. I mean, that sounds old, but it's not. I mean, fifty, that's getting old—but she's thirty-eight. She's younger than a lot of my teachers. And her sister, Tía Lisa (who's even younger) is always trying to fix her up on a date. When she brings up some guy's name as someone that might be on the market, my mom shakes her head and says things like "I've already dated a man like that once, remember?" or "I'd rather work at the Dollar Store than go out with a man like that."

Once, my Tía Lisa invited this guy over to a backyard barbecue at my uncle's house. At first, I thought it was her boyfriend. But pretty fast I got the whole scene in my head: This guy named Steve was there because my Tía Lisa met him at some party and thought he'd be perfect for my mom. All the women at the barbecue thought he was really fine and all that. They called him a "fox." Sure. I mean, women can be as bad as guys when they see good-looking guys. Believe me, I've listened to enough of that crap. This business of women falling all over themselves over a good-looking guy, nothing original there. Nope. And guys? They're the same. Hell, they're worse.

So, anyway, everyone thinks this guy, Steve, is the star on a Christmas tree. Even my Great Aunt Chepa said he was *bien chulo*, and she never says anything good about anybody.

But my mom wasn't that impressed. "What would I do with a man who spends more time combing his hair than I do?" My mom doesn't trip over herself for anyone.

Well, to me he seemed okay. I thought he was a gringo, but really he was mostly Mexican. You know, my uncle Rudy, he calls people who are half Mexican and half gringo "coyotes." I don't know where he got that, but that's what he calls them. He called Steve a good coyote. And you know, that guy, Steve, spoke Spanish and everything like that, and he seemed to be a regular Joe. And I think he really liked my mom, the way he looked at her when she talked which really made me a little bit, well, you know, I didn't like that. Look, she's my mom. I know she had to have sex in order to have me and my brother, Tito, but I don't think it's a very good idea to think about those kinds of things. I mean, it's not normal. Not that I know that much about normal. Look, I don't know anything about normal. But I know what's *not normal*. So, when this guy is looking at my mom in a certain way—you know which way—well, I didn't like that much. Not much, nope, just didn't like that.

But look, the guy was decent. He had a job and didn't seem like a pervert or anything like that, and he didn't give me the creeps, and he even asked me all kinds of questions, like where did I go to school and did I have a girlfriend and what kind of music did I like. He was trying real hard. He wasn't so bad. And he liked to say "cat," which I liked. I mean, he'd refer to people as cats. This cat did this. And this cat did that. And when he was talking about the Beatles, he said he really liked those "cats." And I thought that was a very cool way of talking. My Tía Lisa said it was "fantastically retro." But, you know, retro's not necessarily bad. Yeah, that cat was okay.

But I got to thinking that maybe that cat might start hanging around a lot. I wasn't sure what to think about that. I mean, it's not as if I want a father. I *have* a father. It's just that I don't know who he is or where he is. But I have one. I didn't want any proxies. Proxy, that's a cool word. That's what my friend Louie says about girls he takes out. "They're all proxies," he says, "cuz the real one, she won't go out with me." He's funny. He's always in love with girls who don't love him back.

So, the poor guy is stuck with proxies. I'm not like Louie. I don't do the proxy thing.

I know that if my mom ever got interested in another man, well, that wouldn't necessarily mean she was looking for a father for me and Tito. Maybe it would only mean that she still had a heart and that she wasn't dead and that she didn't like being alone. Women don't like being alone. I hear them talk. But sometimes they'd rather be alone than be with a real creep. Creep, I like that word. It's been around awhile—that's why I like it. You know, maybe I'm a little bit like that guy Steve. I like retro. Anyway, like my Tía Lisa says, "Creeps are a dime a dozen. *Mejor sola que mal acompañada.*" But my Tía Lisa also says: "Everybody needs to be loved—even mothers," and then she bops me on the head. I'm crazy about my Tía Lisa.

But, you know, I don't think I need to worry too much about my mom and other men. She's just not ready. "Your dad left her wounded." That's what my Tía Lisa says. When I think of wounded, I think of dogs that have been run over. But a dog doesn't always die when he's been hit by a car. Sometimes the dog recovers and lives a normal dog life. I've even seen dogs with three legs hop a fence.

Mom never says much about what went wrong between her and my dad. She just says, "He left us one day." I know a part of her wants to talk about it—about everything. But a part of her is used to being quiet. Not talking about things is an addiction. I didn't make that up. I heard some woman say that to her friend at the Big 8 grocery store as she tried to decide which avocado she wanted to buy. She said, "*Dios mio*, these avocados are terrible, and my good-for-nothing husband, he's addicted to television and to silence. That husband of mine, he just doesn't talk. *Así son*, that's the way they are. They won't talk." And her friend says, "It hurts men too much to talk, so they just sit there and watch television. But just get them into a bar with all their no-good, beer-guzzling *boracho* friends, and hell, they talk so much their lips get sore." They both nodded at each other as they picked just the right avocado.

But the thing is, it's not just men who are addicted to not talking. It's women too. It's like the flu. Everyone gets it—and then they just pass it on. My mom, she has that flu. Maybe she's passed it on to me. For sure she's passed it on to Tito. He'd rather be hit by an effen hammer than to tell you what he's thinking. He's seriously addicted to not talking.

Mom works as an assistant nurse to a doctor. "We do okay," she says. That means we have enough money to get by. And we have a good doctor because her boss, Dr. Gómez, he'll always see us for free. Or close to free, anyway. "And that's a lot," my mother says. "There's a lot of people in the world who never see a doctor because they just don't have the money." She's proud. But she can be hard, too. She says if you didn't earn something, well, then you just shouldn't have it. With her, you have to earn everything. It's like life is a job, and you don't even get paid for it. But she's soft too, my mom. I like that about her, she can be hard and she can be soft. It makes her interesting. I never know which part of her is going to be in the kitchen—the hard Mom or the soft one. Sometimes, I get tired of trying to guess which Mom is going to show up.

"Life is up and down," my Tía Lisa says. She's the kicks. I mean the real effen kicks. She's about ten years younger than my mother and sometimes she looks like she's still a girl, and she's always smoking a cigarette and she's always talking about life. Life is this and life is that, and life, life, life, life. I never heard anyone talk about life so much. "Be good to your mom," she says, "life's been hard on her. You know, your dad was never good to her. She didn't deserve that." I think she wants to tell me all sorts of things about them, but she always winds up changing the subject. Usually, the subject she changes back to is life. Life this and life that. "Life is always better with a cup of coffee." She likes saying that. I wouldn't give you a dime for a cup of coffee. Not a dime. Not a nickel. Tastes like a pigeon crapped in your mouth. I pretty much stick to orange juice. Cherry Cokes sometimes.

We have our own house on Calle Concepción. It's a white house that my mother wants to paint another color. She just can't seem to decide on the color—so it's kind of stayed white by default. I got that expression from Mrs. Herrera, my English teacher. She loves to say that. She says things like "Mr. Lopez, you're the best student in this class *by default.*" Which means that she thinks we're just a bunch of dumb-ass Mexicans good for nothing but flipping burgers and making breakfast burritos at Whataburger, and that I'll grow up to be one of the better burrito-makers. Yup, that's what she pretty much thinks, we're all a bunch of burrito guys. Well, hell, I *do* work at Whataburger. I flip a good burger. But that's only a part-time job and it's only temporary. Screw Mrs. Herrera.

Our house is pretty close to Thomas Jefferson High School—but we just call our school "La Jeff." That's what we say, "I go to La Jeff." And our rival school, well, that would be "La Bowie." We're foxes and they're bears, and, hell, my friend Lalo, he says we're just a bunch of animals. And then he starts laughing his stupid animal head off. I like Lalo. He scares me, though. He takes drugs and drinks and cusses like a drunk man in a bar and does everything he's not allowed to do—and he tells me I'm too straight and that being straight doesn't do me a damn bit of good because I'll never be good enough anyway, not for the teachers and not for anyone who's in charge of anything in this hellhole of a world and who in the hell ever told me I was ever gonna make it. I don't know. Lalo, he can be mean. I don't know why he likes me but he does. He comes over all the time and eats with us. My mom's nice to him—but when he leaves, she shakes her head. "Poor Lalo," she says, "His mom and dad just don't give a damn." My mom gets real mad at parents who don't care. That's one of the things that make her cuss. That and drunks. And memories of my father.

I'm a senior this year. Next year I'm going to college. My mom, she says I knew what a verb was when I was six. She knew it was a good sign. She says I was born with two strikes against me—I was a poor Mexican and I didn't have a father. But this summer she took me aside and said, "You've done a beautiful job, *hijo de mi vida*. You're on third base, now." My mom, she loves baseball. I don't know where she got that, because a lot of girls don't like sports, but my mother, she loves baseball. She likes the Dodgers and the Cubs and secretly she likes the Yankees but they win too much, and she normally doesn't like people and teams who win more than their fair share of the time. So now my mom says I'm on third base. It means I'm about to score. It means I might be going some- where. Father or no father, I might be going somewhere.

But where? What happens after you reach home plate?

I worry about my mom. I don't know if she'll be all right when I'm gone. I worry about my little brother too. He's gotten into smoking pot. Other stuff too. All that stuff that messes with his head, he thinks it's the effen kicks. Yeah, sure, I tell him, the real effen kicks. I tell him all that crap is gonna beat the holy hell out of him so bad that he'll never think straight again. Tito just smiles like I'm full of all that leftover grease from the grill at WhataBurger. And then he says if I tell Mom, he'll kick my ass all the way to Denver. I laugh. I mean, I don't even think Tito knows where Denver is.

I keep an eye out, and I drag Tito's good-for-nothing ass home when I need to. And every day I tell him to cut that shit out. And every day he gives me those looks like he'd really like to hurt me. Those eyes are stone. And they hate. But I'm not afraid of those eyes. And I tell him that it's him who doesn't know his skinny brown ass from a store-bought tortilla. Tito, he goes through my closets and asks me which shirts I don't wear anymore, so he can take them and sell them and try to score some dope. He takes my shoes even when they're still good and my pants—anything he can get his hands on. And sometimes he steals other people's old clothes too. I followed him once to one of those places that sell used clothes by the pound. The border's full of those places. And pawn shops and loan shops that screw people. So my little brother, he's learned how it all works. He's become a regular little entrepreneur so he can score some pot. A regular little capitalist trying to make the most of whatever capital he has. Capital. It's a new thing for me. I'm studying basic theories of economics. My brother, Tito, doesn't have to take that class. He knows all the basic rules already.

My mom took me to one of those loan shark places once. It was called Border Loan Company. Their motto was "Money for the people." She said it was time I learned a few things—so she took me there and pretended to want a loan of five hundred dollars. She took the paperwork as some guy who was wearing way too much cologne was trying to make her sign. She said she wanted to read the contract. He said he could tell her what it said. She looked at him and said she'd like to take it home.

When we walked out, she looked at me and smiled. "Never trust a man who smells nicer than your mother." We both laughed. I liked to do that, laugh with my mother. When we got home, she showed me how she would've had to pay three times the amount of the loan because of the interest they charged. And then she took me to a real bank. She got a real loan there. A home-improvement loan. She said she could redo the bathroom and the kitchen, get a new stove and a new refrigerator and new cabinets, and paint the house with that loan. She took me through the whole thing. It was an education all right. I asked her how come those loan shops were allowed to do stuff like that to poor people. She said that half the rich people in the world got rich off the poor, and that was the God's honest truth. And since those same rich people ran the world, why on God's good earth did I think the whole messed-up system was going to change? My mom gets really angry about things like that. But the thing is, she's not angry at me and my brother.

She's great, my mom. Even when she's being strict, I know she's keeping her eye on the ball. I know a lot of guys, and they're always pissed off at their mothers. Not me.

I wish my dad would have seen what kind of woman she was. He wouldn't have left her. He'd have stayed with her forever.

Me, Jake
(you know, Upthegrove)

I don't think anybody really knows where anybody lives.

Him
(Upthegrove)

You see, the Upthegrove whose name I inherited happens to reside in the state of Florida. Miami. He has a house on the beach, or near it—like I really know. According to my mom, "Your father was neither remarkable nor reliable." (I take it he was good-looking. My mother likes to stare at nice-looking men. Don't think I don't notice). "He was born rich and he'll die rich, and he'll go from job to job and place to place, and the minute he gets bored, he'll move on. He has the attention span of a black crow." I don't know anything about the attention span of black crows—and to tell you the truth, neither does my mother, but she always says things like that. I'll give my mother one thing—she believes everything she says.

Right when she came to the part about black crows, that's the part where she crossed her arms *and* rolled her eyes. "When he walked out on us, he wrote out a check and handed it to me. It was as if he was paying me off. Which is all he's ever done. It was no different than buying a new car or paying a call girl for a well-spent evening." And then, at that part of her story, she clenched her fists and laughed. "Sorry about the call-girl business. I shouldn't have said that. Anyway, since me, well, your father's gone through several other women."

The thing is that my mother always fails to mention one of the most important parts of the story: *She took the check.* Look, let's just move on. But my mom was probably right about Upthegrove going through several other women. I wondered if he'd gone through several other sons, too.

My mom hears from him sometimes. I know she does. It's not that he's really interested in her. I think he just gets lonely sometimes, and my mom, well, she likes to listen. Even to him.

Not that she says that much about their conversations. He always asks her to give me some kind of useless message: *Tell him I said to keep studying. Tell him I said that he shouldn't get side-tracked by girls. Tell him I said that it's not good for him to continue down the road of all that political nonsense he gets all hot and bothered about—and tell him that anarchy thing he has going in his head will only get him into trouble.* I mean, the guy only knows about me through my conversations with my mother. He knows what she tells him. For all he knows I'm gay. I'm not. But I could be. For all he knows.

Well, at least Upthegrove wants to make sure I have a good life even though he's not very interested in seeing me. I even called him once. I made my mother give me his phone number. I was twelve at the time. "Hi," I said, "it's me."

The guy on the other end of the phone, my father, said, "Who's *me*?" His voice was deep and he sounded like he was distracted. Maybe he was with some woman.

"Me. Jake."

"Jake?"

"Yeah, Jake."

"Jake who?"

"Jake Upthegrove."

"Oh," he said. And then he said it again, "Oh." And then there wasn't anything coming from the other end. Nothing. And then finally, he said. "Is your mother all right?"

"She's fine," I said. "And me, hell, I'm fine too."

"I was getting to that," he said.

"Sure you were," I said.

And then there wasn't anything coming from the other end again. Nothing. And then he asks: "She still married to that guy? What was his name?"

"You destroy me, Dad." That's what I said.

"What's that supposed to mean."

"It means you're killing me. In a complete kind of way."

He didn't say anything. And then he asked me again what my stepfather's name was. Okay. I was getting the picture that he wasn't real big on talking. At least not to me. "David," I said. "His name is David."

"Yeah. He still around?"

"Yeah," I said.

"She happy?"

"Yeah." I had no idea whether she was happy or not.

"He's good to her, then?"

"Yeah."

"And this guy, David, he's not mean to you or anything like that, is he?"

"No. He's nice," I said. And David *was* nice. He just wasn't my father.

"You're sure?"

"I'm sure."

"And you like him? I mean, he doesn't destroy you or anything?" Then he laughed, like he was really amused because he'd used my expression.

"Nope," I said. "He doesn't destroy me."

"So you like him?"

"I didn't say that. Right now, I don't like anybody."

"Well, that's normal," he said.

"Does that make you happy, that I'm normal?"

"Every man wants a normal son."

God, he really was destroying me. "Yeah, well, every son wants a normal father."

I could tell he was lighting a cigarette.

"Guess so," he said. I could tell he was puffing on his cigarette. "Look," he said, "is that why you called—to fight with your old man?" And then I think he felt bad for scolding me, and he mumbled something, and finally, he just said, "You need money?"

I was twelve. What would I need money for? He knew damn well that Mom and I weren't exactly living in South El Paso. He knew that. And I knew that *he knew* that David was, as my mother put it, "an extremely sought-after and successful attorney." I hated that he'd asked me about money. I really hated that. I didn't say anything for a long time. Finally, I said, "I just wanted to talk."

"About what?" he said. And then, well, I just hung up the phone.

I think I cried. I think I cried for a long time. Days maybe. Destroyed. Completely destroyed. I think I was sad all that summer. Well, hell, I was twelve and that's what twelve-year-olds do, they mope. And then I wasn't so sad after that. But sometimes I still want to call old Upthegrove up. But I don't even know what I'd say to him. Maybe I'd call him by his first name. Maybe I'd say, "Gerald, what do you say me and you go golfing?" Mom says he loves to golf. I hate that crap. White balls and green grass. I'd rather piss in my pants than go golfing. I would. I just don't dig that sport. I'm not playing around, here. Hell, I don't have anything to say to Upthegrove. I don't. I don't have anything to ask him. Maybe I'd ask him for money. At least it's something he knows how to give. But what would I do with it? I have everything. Mostly everything. Two iPods, a BlackBerry, a laptop, a desert bike, a car, five pairs of tennis shoes including a pair of Chuck Taylors, and, well, I could go on and on. Yeah, I have everything. Well, except a father.

Sometimes, I just want to yell at him, "Listen, you roach, you lazy fly-eating lizard, you polluted puddle of rancid rainwater, you spineless excuse for a man, you piece of dog crap in the neighbor's yard, you creep among creeps, you worm in a perfect red apple, you chewed-up piece of gum that's stuck under my foot, you can keep your last name and put it in your good-for-nothing bank account! You just keep the damn thing! I don't want it! I don't! Can you dig it, Upthegrove? Are you listening?"

Ah, I know I'm just sore at him. I get real sore at people sometimes.

I have my reasons.

Look, the thing is there are certain things we're all entitled to. The pursuit of happiness—that's one thing we're entitled to. And who the hell can be happy when you got a father who lives in Florida and doesn't care enough about you to pick up his cell phone and call you on your birthday? Not so much as a text message.

My birthday. I'll lay you all the money you got in your pocket that Upthegrove doesn't have a clue as to when my birthday is. Hell, he doesn't even know how old I am.

Yeah. I get real sore sometimes.

I have my reasons.

You know that summer when I thought Upthegrove had completely destroyed me. I was wrong. He didn't. I'm still here.

Me, Ramiro
(son, brother)

Brothers. They're great. Everyone should have at least one.
Sure.

Him
(My Brother)

I keep a journal. In my computer. I write things in it. Things that happen to me. Things I'm thinking. Keeps me sane. Not that I'm a crazy kind of guy. I'm not. Keeping a journal, it's like talking to myself. Sometimes I think I write in this journal because I think that someday my father's going to read it. Wouldn't that be effen something? My dad reading all the things I wrote? My dad knowing everything I thought— wouldn't that be the effen kicks? Man, that would be effen something. It scares me, though. It scares the living crap out of me.

I know what my little brother, Tito, would say. He would say I was full of Ralphie's dog shit. Ralphie's this mean dog that lives down the street. They keep the poor dog all chained up, and my mom's always after those people. She tells them it's a bad thing to chain a dog up and make him mean like that. "Dogs are like people," she says. "Chain them up, and they get real mean." I sometimes think Tito has something in common with Ralphie. Somewhere inside, Tito feels all chained up. And so he's really mad all the time. The kind of mad that makes you growl and bare your teeth and bite. It seems like he wants to attack everyone who passes in front of our house. I don't know where he gets that, though. Maybe because my mom is so strict. Maybe he thinks my mom is chaining him up. But hell, he doesn't listen anyway, so why's he so damn mad? I mean chains just don't work on that dude. Dude—that's one of Tito's favorite words. Dude and *vato*.

Every time Tito gets into my clothes to sell them, I get mad at him and tell him to knock it off. He just sits there and looks at me and says: "You're fuckin' loco, dude." And he gives me this look—like he wants to hurt me. And I give him a look right back and say, "I'm not a dude, *ese*." And he says, "You sure as hell aren't a *vato*." *Vatos* to him are the kicks. They rock. The coolest. And me, well, to him I'm as uncool as you can get. How could someone so uncool be a *vato*? "Ahh," he says, "you're lucky to be a called a dude." Then he gives me that look again. That I-might-hurt-you look. That stone look. That hate look. And I just keep looking back at him. It's like a game of ping-pong.

I don't know why Tito and I are so different. He's younger, but he's a lot harder than me. He was always harder. Maybe people are just born that way. Maybe there's not a reason, and if we keep looking for reasons then we'll just go crazy. That's what my Uncle Tabo says. He says, "We think there's a reason for everything, as if life was supposed to make sense. It's not exactly math. People aren't numbers. Everybody knows life doesn't make any sense at all, so we just better deal with the whole mess. Have a beer. Have a cup of coffee. Have a piece of cake. Go out to a movie. Enjoy the popcorn." He shrugs and laughs. Maybe he says that because two of his sons are in jail. But he has another son who just started law school. How'd that happen? Maybe my Uncle Tabo is right. I mean, it's like he gets it, and he's all chilled out about it. Maybe it's because he got married when he was eighteen and had four kids in five years and had to learn a lot of things the hard way. But he never ran away from his family. Not like my father.

Look, I'm not my Uncle Tabo and I have my own problems. And I still want to know why me and Tito are so damn different. We don't look different. We don't. We look alike—well, we look like my father, the one we've never seen. I mean, we must look like him since we don't look like my mom. Who knows? I don't know anything about genetics. I'm not pre-med.

I'm just a Mexican who's got a lot of questions.

When Tito was about five, I saw him get mad at another little guy at a birthday party. They were fighting over a toy and he pushed that kid down on the ground—and then started kicking him. I had to pull Tito off him. I mean, that poor kid was just lying on the ground crying. And I made Tito shake the other little boy's hand and tell him he was sorry, and I made Tito give the little boy his toy back. Man, Tito was mad. He went and sat in the car for the rest of the afternoon. When we got home, he told me he wasn't sorry and when he grew up he was never going to say he was sorry about anything he wasn't really sorry about. And you know what? I don't think Tito is sorry about most things he does. I mean, even Lalo's sorry about the stuff he pulls. I mean, sometimes when Lalo gets drunk, he just cries. He cries about everything and how sorry he is about everything. Makes me sad. I hate being sad.

And my brother, Tito, he really makes me sad. But he's not sorry about anything. He says I'm always saying I'm sorry. "What are you sorry about, bro? Give it up, *pendejo*." I hate it when he calls me *pendejo*. And I told him I always said I was sorry when I was wrong.

"Most people think you're wrong 'cause you're nothing but a poor Mexican. And if you're poor, that just means you're stupid."

"Where do you get that shit?" I said. "And you know what? I'm not worried about what most people say."

"You should be," he said. "They'll screw you."

Tito, he thinks everyone's out to screw him. Truth is, it's Tito that's out to screw everyone. Never turn your back on that guy. Not if you want to hold on to what you've got.

The problem is, when you only have one brother, then that brother means a lot. Maybe he means more than he should.

When I hear someone say: "Look, he's my brother, man. What am I supposed to do?", when I hear someone say something like that, I really know what they're talking about. I mean, I really know.

My mom, she likes to hug us. Not all the time. But sometimes. Well, why not? Moms have certain privileges. I don't mind. It's nice, to have a mom who wants to hug you. But, Tito, hell, he just pushes her away. He says, "Don't do that. I don't like that. Just don't do that." And he has this look in his eyes, like maybe he means business. It makes me afraid. Well, not quite. But almost. I'm glad that my mom isn't afraid of him and doesn't let him push her around. Sometimes, moms let that happen, they let their kids push them around—but not my mom. Nope. Last week she kissed my brother right on the cheek. And he got really mad, and he started to say something and my mom stopped him cold. "I'm your mother. I can hug and kiss you anytime I want. I have a license to do that just like I have a license to be a nurse. So you just have to be a man and deal with it." That really got to him—because she brought up the whole business about being a man. And if there's one thing Tito wants to be, it's a real man. He's all about that man stuff— even though he doesn't know the first thing about the whole man thing. My mom, I gotta hand it to her, she knows exactly what she's doing. I don't mess with her, not if I don't have to. Not a chance.

I know that Mom is trying to make Tito into someone decent. I don't think he's going to have a good life—I don't. The other day I heard him talking to his friends. He was badmouthing me and my mom. "Fuck 'em," he said. He said that about us. His only family. I wanted to hurt him. I did. But he's as big as I am—and he's meaner. If he put his mind to it, he could hurt me.

You know, really, I don't understand.

And what I really don't understand is why I love that guy so much—even though I know he doesn't love me. Guys like Tito don't love anyone. It's not personal, I know that. He's just hard as a rock. Some people need and some people don't need. I'm more of a needer than he is. He's not a needer at all. So, it's not really anybody's fault. That's just the way things are. Like I said, it's not personal. *But it is personal*. He's my brother.

Me, Jake
(not finished yet, not by a long shot)

The thing is this: Fathers aren't the only problem. There's always mothers.

Her
(My Mom)

Last year, I was mad at my mom. Mad, angry, sore. I mean for the entire year. Maybe I was going through something. I would just look at her like she was a trash can that needed to be emptied out. I took to calling her Sally. "Sally," I'd tell her, "I just want you to lay off me for a while. Is that okay with you, Sally? Can you dig it?" And she would really lose it. She said she was going to take me to a therapist.

"Oh, like the Anger Management Lady?" I asked her.

"Don't start," she said. "Have some respect." There was that word again.

"Whatever you say, Sally," I said.

And then she just blew up and started yelling at me. I mean she really lost it. I calmly reached into my wallet and pulled out the Anger Management Lady's business card and handed it to her. "You could use her," I said.

It wasn't the best time in our relationship. I'll take my share of the blame. Okay, I'll take all the blame. How's that? No one has to tell me when things are my fault.

Through all of this, David spent most of his time shaking his head. "Stop calling her Sally," he told me one day. He never gave me orders—but that sounded like an order to me. "If you have to call her by anything other than Mom, at least have the decency to call her by her given name." He was mad too. So we were all mad. But I kept it up. I kept referring to her as Sally. Her "given name," as David put it, was Elaine. Elaine Cosgrove Ballard. Ballard—that's David's name. Cosgrove—that was her name before she married Upthegrove.

And then, I'm not sure why, I just kind of stopped being sore at her. Maybe I just got tired of being angry all the time. Or maybe I just decided to get angry at something else. I mean, take your pick, there are so many things to be mad at that when you get tired of being mad at one thing, you can just move on down the list. In fact, I have that list somewhere on my computer.

So after I got over being mad at mom for a year, well, she and I were all right—at least for a while.

And now, it's *she* who's sore at *me*. She says I've gotten an attitude and that I don't talk to anyone and that my politics are just an excuse to bring out the worst in everyone. She said, "Not once do you ever talk about something you really feel." Not true. Well, maybe I didn't talk to Sally because I didn't think she cared to hear what I had to say. And really, what was the point in talking all the time? Talk, talk, talk. Talk's overrated. All you have to do is listen to all that buffalo crap on talk radio and you'll see exactly what I mean. Listen to talk radio and tell me I should respect "adults." I mean, can you dig that crap? Who can? Who?

Look, I know my mom's a good person and a decent human being. She's a little flawed, and she can't think her way out of a paper bag, but she's very decent. Okay, not very. Look, I'm of the opinion that we should be realistic about things. Parents should be realistic about their kids (they're not). And kids should be realistic about their parents (they're not). But on the whole, kids fare better than parents on the realism thing. Trust me.

Realism aside, every day I try to think of something to say to my mom when I come home—*something I really feel*. So yesterday, when I walked in the door, I said, "I think I hate Mr. Moore." Mr. Moore's my English teacher.

"Why?" she wanted to know.

"Because he's a snob."

"Why is he a snob?"

"I don't know. Maybe we should ask his mother."

She gave me one of those looks.

I shrugged. "He thinks anything written after the mid-1950s is trash. He says Kerouac and Ginsberg and Ferlinghetti and all the rest of the Beat writers were nothing more than bad typists. He says that most Americans wouldn't know literature if it bit their noses off. He says things like that. He says Faulkner and a few other Southerners are the exception. He's full of crap, that's what I think. And you know what else I think. I think he doesn't much care for girls or Mexicans."

"That's a mean thing to say, Jacob Upthegrove."

I gave her one of my don't-call-me-Upthegrove looks. "Look," I said, "his sexual persuasion is the only interesting part about him. But I know a racist when I see one."

"You judge people," she said. And then she starts telling me how ungenerous I am, and how I'm too hard on people, and how I have this really superior attitude, and she's going on and on and on. She was really destroying me.

And then I stopped her and said, "You say you want me to talk. And when I do, you lecture me. So don't ask me to talk anymore. I'm not going to engage, Elaine. I'm just not."

"Don't call me Elaine," she said.

"Elaine or Sally," I said. "Take your pick." And then I just walked into the backyard. I thought of having a cigarette—but I didn't have any. Not that I smoked that much because, well, I wasn't eighteen and I was always having to go through a middleman. The logistics weren't simple. But I have to say that there's something about smoking that really helped chill me out. I mean, you can dig that, right? The Anger Management Lady told me cigarettes only made things worse. How? How? Cigarettes were inanimate. Not like airhead mothers who didn't want their sons to think about politics or religion or any other topic that really mattered and not like slacker fathers who lived in Florida, doing nothing but going through women like a chain-smoker goes through cigarettes.

I sat in the backyard for a while—then I walked back inside and told Elaine I was sorry. Look, she's trying to teach me right from wrong, my mom. The problem is we have such different ideas about those sorts of things. My mom happens to like the world she lives in. She thinks everything is very nice. I don't share her optimism about things, and, really, I think the world's all screwed up. It is. *And that is the absolute truth*. But Mom and David, well, they like their nice world, their nice vacations, their nice house, their nice friends. They sometimes vote for Democrats—but only if they know them personally. They mostly vote for Republicans. Well, that's fine. They have their reasons, I suppose, and they're entitled to their politics—but when I ask them about it, they look at me as if I'm from the planet Mexico. And my mom always says stuff like "Well, when you're a little older you'll understand the way things work." This from a woman who has a hard time plugging in the toaster. Okay, okay, I'm being superior again. But tell me, who really understands the way things work?

The thing is, David and Elaine don't like people who ask a lot of questions. And they sure as hell don't like extremists—though neither of them believes that you can be too rich. I listen to them at dinner all the time. I get tired of their voices. I know they think I have an attitude. Well, they have an attitude too. It's just that they run the place. I'm just, well, a resident. Well, that's not really true. I mean, I have a real home and I'm not alone in the world, and hey, I have health insurance. I'm being ironic again. I can't help myself. But look, I have Mom and David. They care about me. I know that. They sure as hell care more about me than Upthegrove.

Sometimes I think my mom would be happier if she got a job. But she'll never do that. Look, she doesn't need the money. And she doesn't know how to do anything except worry about me. I'm her job. Shit. Have you ever been anyone's job? Have you? It's not a cool place for your mind to inhabit. I mean, my mom should have a real job—one that's part of the system. I mean, if she's going to be such a big defender of the status quo, she should at least be a part of it. I mean, the world is about work and buying and selling. As far as I can tell, my mom's just about buying. She's had a couple of garage sales, but I don't think that counts as being part of the selling thing. You know, there's this place called Serena's. It's this place that sells overpriced furniture that caters to people who need to buy things that are overpriced because they make too much money. Perfect place for my mom. She'd be happy working there. I mean it. She could see all her friends, and she could get a discount on the stuff she buys. I'm not being ironic. I'm not. Sure.

Okay, but she's not going to work "outside of the house," as she puts it. I mean, what the hell is she talking about? We have a full-time maid, Rosario (whom I call Rosie), who cooks, cleans, and irons, and my mother complains about her because her English isn't very good, and when I tell her that she could pay for a language tutor for Rosie, she just looks at me funny. Hell, my mom could buy one less dress a month and pay for a tutor. Look, let's not go there. The point is my I-don't-work-outside-the-home mother doesn't even clean the house. And we have this guy who works the grounds twice a week. And if anything breaks down, everything is just one phone call away. So what is there left to do? If my mother works "inside the house" and not "outside," then what the hell does she do? She sure as hell doesn't stay home, that's for sure. Not that I mind. Not that I care.

She does what she does. But she sure as hell appears on the scene when I get myself into trouble. "You could be anything you wanted to be," she tells me. "You're as smart as Albert Einstein." I was impressed. My mother knew who Albert Einstein was. That's something. Maybe I had more to work with than I thought.

Him and Her
(Me and Sally)

My mom looks at me sometimes as if she's searching for that thing in me that really bugs her. So, as I was sitting there, trying to find something to say to her, I noticed she was studying me with that look. So I looked right back at her and told her that I'd decided to become a Catholic. You know, when people have you off balance, well, you've got to do something that makes them even more off balance than you are.

"What?" she said. "You haven't gone to church since you were ten. You threatened to drown yourself in the bathtub if I made you go."

"I'm not ten anymore. And the thing is, I've never really liked the idea of Protestantism."

"What? Where do you get these things? And you don't even believe in God."

"God has nothing to do with it," I said. "I just think it would be interesting to become a Catholic. I mean, I like the idea of all those saints."

"Is this about some girl?"

My mom thinks everything is about some girl. See, it's because in her life everything's about some guy. "No, Sally, it isn't. I don't happen to be like Upthegrove."

"Are we going to start this Sally business again?"

"From here on in, when you say inane things, I'm going to call you Sally."

"Inane? Where did you get that word?"

"From studying you."

She got this I-don't-believe-you're-my-own-flesh-and-blood look on her face and said, "I don't know what I'm going to do with you." She shook her head. "Has Rosario been trying to proselytize you?"

"What?" That made me mad. Rosario had more class than to go around trying to convert a guy like me to her religion.

"Well, you know, Jacob, she's always praying."

"Now, *there's a crime*. Maybe you should fire her."

"Stop it, Jacob, you're being glib again."

"Yes, I am, Sally. Maybe I'll become Jewish instead."

"What is wrong with you?"

"I mean, I'm circumcised. Why not just go all the way."

"Go to your room."

"Can't we just have this discussion?"

"This is not a discussion."

"Of course it is. I'm trying to discuss my future religion with you."

"What you're trying to do is make me angry. You know David and I are committed Episcopalians. You're just mocking us."

"No, I'm not. I'm trying to talk to you. What if I became a Quaker. They don't believe in wars."

"I'm going to take you to a therapist." See, Elaine really believes in therapists. She goes to see one all the time. Of course, she changes therapists every two years or so. And then she just starts all over.

"I won't go. I'll drown myself in the bathtub."

"Now you really are mocking me, Jake. I want to know what I did to make you mistreat me like this? What did I ever do to you, Jacob Upthegrove?"

"Mom, you're getting all Blanche DuBois on me."

"Stop it! Just stop it!" That's when she slapped me. I decided it was best not to say anything. I'll tell you something, Sally can pack a punch. I sat down on the couch and put my head down and took a breath.

So there, I *can* see the world from my mom's point of view. I really can. She wants me to grow up. She wants me to attend a nice Protestant church where the people mostly look like us. See, the thing is, I don't think my mom's all that comfortable around Catholics because here in El Paso most Catholics are Mexicans. And I know that makes her uncomfortable because she says, "Well, if they would only speak English." Speaking English makes us morally and intellectually superior. I get my mother, I do. And because of this doctor thing she has in her head, I go to the Silva Magnet School next to Jefferson High School. I go there to please her. Not that I mind going there. At least it gets me out my neighborhood and into somebody else's. I can dig that. But the thing is, I don't want to be a doctor. I mean, I might want to be a veterinarian and take care of dogs and cats and parrots and other assorted animals. I mean, I think I'd like that. Of course, then I'd have to deal with their crazy owners. Have you ever talked to a cat lover? Or a dog lover? They're nuts. Completely. I mean, we're talking fanatics here. They all think their pets are brilliant. Can you dig that shit? Maybe I won't be a veterinarian. Look, animals are very cool entities. They are the coolest beings. I love animals. But their owners, well, I'm really into mocking them.

And this is the thing about going to the Silva Magnet School. It's not really a part of Jefferson High School. I mean everybody at Jefferson High School is Mexican. Well, technically, Mexican American, but Sally always says Mexican. But most importantly, they're poor. Not necessarily homeless or anything like that. Working-class. Yup, though the word is not supposed to be spoken in my house. David wanted to make conversation one night at dinner, so he says, "So what do you want to talk about tonight, Jake?"

And I said, "Let's talk about class."

He thought I meant class, as in school. "Which class do you want to talk about? How's that class you're taking with Mrs. Anaya? Very inspirational teacher, I hear." David, he's not as plastic as all that. He just tries too hard.

I looked at him and said, "I didn't mean that kind of class. I meant, class. As in working-class, as in ruling-class, as in middle-class, as in leisure-class."

"Leisure-class?"

"Yes. That would be us."

"I work seventy hours a week. What's so leisure about that?"

"Sorry," I said. "So you're working-class?"

"I didn't say that. I'm a working professional."

"White-collar?"

"Of course, white-collar."

He was starting to get mad, I could tell. "How come we have different classes in America, if we're all supposed to be equal?"

"Equal opportunity, Jake." David said that very seriously. "This country affords everyone an equal opportunity. And not everyone takes advantage of that opportunity. And then there's this thing called merit. I mean, some people *do* work harder than others. And some people are just plain smarter than others. And some people are just more gifted."

I nodded. "I see," I said. I wanted to ask him if he worked harder than Eddie, our yard man—but I could see he didn't like the way I said *I see*.

And then he looked right at me and said, "I don't know where you're getting these liberal ideas." He said it like I'd gotten some kind of sexually transmitted disease.

"Look," I said, "I go to a school where I'm not even allowed to mingle with the kids who go to Jefferson."

"We're not sending you to a school for you to mingle,"

David said. "We just want the best for you."

That expression makes me sick. It really does. "What about everybody else?" I said.

"We can't be worrying about everybody else."

"In other words, fuck everybody else," I said.

"I didn't say that. And there isn't any excuse for that kind of language, Jake."

"Actually, you *did* say fuck everybody else. You think because you used nicer language that what you meant was nicer?"

David was angry. He hardly ever got angry. At least not around me. My mother wasn't there for dinner that night. And I don't think he ever told her about our argument that evening—otherwise she would have said something. Anyway, I stopped trying to talk to David after that. I mean, he may be a brilliant attorney, but as a human being, he was about as brilliant as the sun in the middle of a midnight blizzard. He used his mind to think when he was at work. But after that, I think he just coasted. His father handed him a religion, and he just took it like he'd take a dollar bill. His father handed him the political party he was going to belong to, and David just stuck that in his pocket too.

Every time someone asks him a question, he just reaches in his pocket and pulls out an answer—but the guy sounds like cardboard. I swear that guy's never really thought about anything except the law. Well, maybe he thinks about my mother sometimes, and he keeps his car spotless, so I guess he thinks about the car sometimes, but otherwise, he's the most checked-out guy I've ever met. Well, he's less checked-out than Upthegrove, my father—but that's like saying gin tastes better than vodka (not that I'd know). Anyway, Mom always got upset if I upset David—though it never seemed to bother

her if he upset me. Look, I'm not complaining. I never brought the whole class thing up again—but I sure as hell think about it a lot. I do. I mean something's off. I can see that. I mean this straight. I'm not being ironic and I'm not just mocking David and Elaine. I mean, the truth is, they don't need to be mocked. They do okay all by themselves.

"Jacob?"

I looked up at Sally from where I was sitting on the couch. We stared at each other for a while.

"Are you going to slap me again, Sally?"

"Maybe I should," she said.

I looked right back at her. "Yeah. Go ahead. Maybe it will really teach me a lesson." And then, I just sort of slinked into my room and shut the door.

Me, Ramiro
(Again)

Alejandra says people who have everything are really shallow.
Which is a very interesting thing to say for a girl who happens
to want everything. I mean, does she want to grow up and be
shallow? Me, I don't want everything. I just want my brother
and my mother to be happy. And while we're at it, I want me
to be happy too. Maybe that's too much to ask.

Me
(Bad Days)

Today, I had a bad day. It happens. Mr. Cardoza, my chemistry teacher, handed back our lab notebooks and said we had to do them all over again. "They're not worth grading," he said. Not fair. Maybe some of them were really bad, but mine was good. I knew it was good—and so did he. But now I have to do it all over again on account of the fact that the other lazy-asses in the class messed up the whole assignment. So now I have to pick a new project and start all over. I hate that and hate Mr. Cardoza, too. I worked hard. Not fair—just because he hates teaching here. Just because he got laid off of some big-time job and had to come back to El Paso to teach. He hates us because he thinks his life is shit. He thinks we're shit too. He thinks this neighborhood should be flushed down the toilet. So it's a war, him against us. Guess we're the big losers in this war, guess so, but maybe we win—because we hate him more than he could ever dream of hating us. And we'll live long enough to curse his name into history.

It's a big deal to be in this class because there's a pre-med magnet school that they built right next door to our school, and Mr. Cardoza teaches in that school, but he also teaches this *one* class here at La Jeff because it's an AP class. AP. Yeah, yeah, and everybody says we're really lucky to be in this class. AP and magnet school and everybody gets all into that stuff—if they're teachers and parents and kids who don't have a life right now but will probably have one someday, a real good life—real good. Yup, they all love this AP and pre-med magnet crap. But most of us don't give a rat's tail or a frog's intestines about pre-med shit. And big deal, anyway, because all the pre-med students that come from the other parts of town all go to their classes in their nice separate building and have their nice separate classes. Put it this way: The good, intelligent pre-med magnet school students "attend their classes in a separate facility." So we don't even have "contact." That's the word they use too. "Contact." Like they've landed on the moon. I mean, crap, what's wrong with contact? What are we gonna do to those kids, kill them? Touch them? Infect them with Mexican ways of thinking? Make them ride burros? Take their English and put it in between two pieces of corn tortillas until it sounds like Spanish? What? It really makes me mad. So we're all separate. I mean, the only person I know from the pre-med magnet school is this guy named Jake. We both sort of hang out in the same place on the school grounds. We don't say much—we just sort of nod at each other. Sometimes we exchange a few words. That's it. He likes to smoke. Sometimes we talk a little bit. Not a lot. I mean, I'm not sure what to say to the guy. The thing is, I don't think either one of us fits in at school. It's a place we go to because we have to.

School is like this speed bump, and I think we're both in a hurry to move on down the road. So we both sort of hide out just off the school grounds, which is illegal. Well, not exactly illegal, but against the rules. Rules, see, they keep us in line. In line is better than chaos, I suppose. Or maybe not. Who knows?

Anyway, I guess we're different from them—those magnet school students—even those of us who are in the AP classes. I guess most of us are just your average plain old-fashioned barrio kids who just don't understand what the hell good it will do us to know the valence of helium. Okay, I know the valence of helium. I got an A on that test. But I don't have a plan I believe in. Not like Jake who lives on the Oh-Wow West Side. He thinks he's really some kind of fantastic cool animal because he comes to a school in a poor neighborhood. Big effen deal. He only comes here because it's the magnet school. Period. End of story. It's not like his parents didn't fight like hell to put the magnet school somewhere else. Only thing is, our school is right across the street from Texas Tech Medical school. So, like, the whole thing happened because of that. And that's the whole story. And there's Jake with his eighty-dollar shorts and his one-hundred-dollar jeans and his straight-paid-for teeth, and he's always grinning at me. "Hey," he says, "what's up?" The effen sky. The effen clouds. That's what's effen up.

So here I got into this class, and that was hard to do. Yeah, that's right, because it's an AP class and all of that effen stuff. I think I got in by mistake, but here I am. And then, after class, some guy who calls himself Elvis but whose real name is Domingo, decides to pick a fight with me. He says he doesn't like me. I don't like him either. So what? And he takes a swing at me and knocks the wind out of me. Man, right in the stomach. And there I was, lying on the ground. I mean I wasn't really that hurt. I was just more or less wounded—emotionally, I mean. There I was in public, lying on the ground, and I'm trying not to feel sorry for myself, so I'm thinking: "Elvis, I thought you'd left the effen building."

So, there I am making stupid jokes to myself as I lay on the ground and the principal, Mrs. Casillas, walks right up to me and says that maybe it wouldn't be such a bad idea if I learned to take care of myself. She shook her head, and then she smiled, and she told me not to worry too much about it. "I saw what Domingo did to you."

"He doesn't like to be called Domingo," I said. "He likes to be called Elvis."

"I don't care what he likes to be called," she said. "No drugs and no violence in this school."

I hated to burst her bubble, but our school was full of drugs and violence. I mean, this was the United States of America, right? I looked at her and said, "Well, maybe it's better if we just leave him alone. He's kinda touchy."

"No way, son," she said, "I'm on to him." So now Domingo's gonna have his brown *cholo* ass in a sling, which means my brown not-so-*cholo* ass is gonna be in a sling too. Look, you can't win. All you can do is try to stay out of the way. I was born in the middle of the effen freeway dodging cars. Well, maybe I'm just feeling sorry for myself. I hate that, when I feel sorry for myself. Anyway, it's not such a bad thing, trying to make yourself invisible. Monica, this girl I really like, she said we're all anonymous anyway.

"Anonymous?" I asked.

"Yeah," she said.

"It's a big word," I said, "hard to spell."

"Hard to spell? It's hard to get up in the morning. So what? And, really, it's not such a big word." That's what she said. And then she smiled and said, "It just means we don't matter. What's so big about that?"

"We do matter," I said.

"Yeah. We matter. Okay."

"You matter," I told her.

She sort of rolled her eyes. "That's a line."

"No, it's not a line."

"I'm not a fish you can catch," she said.

I didn't know a damn thing about fishing, but I knew her father went fishing every chance he got. And she knew I kinda liked her, and she was smarter than me, so I didn't know exactly what to say. "Look, I don't own any fishing rods." That made her laugh. "We can be friends, can't we?"

She looked at me like I was a rat she was trying to get out of her house. "I'll think about it."

I nodded. So as I walked home, that was what I was doing, thinking about Domingo taking a swing at me and thinking about Monica who thought I was a rat, and thinking about Jake who liked to smoke and lived on the Oh-Wow West Side of town. Yeah, Monica was right. Anonymous wasn't such a big word. Right now, that's all I want to be. Then I made a joke to myself and laughed: "Ram, what do you want to be when you grow up? Who? Me? I want to be anonymous."

Her
(Alejandra)

Sometimes I just want everything to be the same. I don't want any of this up and down crap that my Tía Lisa talks about all the time. I know that sounds boring as hell. Alejandra, this girl who lives two streets down and is always hanging around, sort of agrees with me. Sort of. She tells me that consistency is a good thing for human beings. Con-sis-ten-cy. That's how she says that word. Like she just looked it up in a dictionary and she wants you to ask her to define the damn word so she can show off how much she knows. She wants to be my girlfriend. Look, I mean to tell you that she's really a nice-looking girl. She is—but she talks too much and she thinks she knows everything and she's beginning to think like a gringa. At least, that's what everyone says. I'm not sure about that. I mean, I'm not too sure what people mean when they say: "You're thinking like a Mexican." Or when they say: "You're thinking all white." See, I'm not so sure about those kinds of rules. Who writes them? Maybe it all gets to me because I think somewhere in between. Guess I do. Well, I live on the border, right? That's what happens when you live in between two countries. I think so. I live in between everybody's rules. Anyway, Alejandra is going around asking everyone to call her "Alex."

"Alex?" I said, "that's a guy's name."

"I know a girl named Charlie," she said, "and she's beautiful."

"Changing your name to Alex won't make you beautiful," I said.

Then she got mad. "Well, you don't exactly look like Antonio Banderas."

She loved Antonio Banderas, was always going on and on

about him as if they were friends or something. I shrugged. Who cared about Antonio Banderas? "Ahh, he's from Spain, anyway. He doesn't know a damn thing about Mexicans. Those people from Spain, they came over here and beat the holy crap out of all the Indians, so they got nothing to be proud of. You know what those Spaniards did—they burned down all the Mayan libraries. And they burned down the Aztec capital. And they pulled all kinds of crap on the Indians on account of the fact that they didn't think those Indians really had a soul. Didn't you know that? It's true. They didn't effen think Indians had a soul. Yup, Antonio Banderas, he's a Spaniard, nothing to do with Mexicans—and he got married to a big gringa." It was a stupid conversation we were having. I mean, that was the problem with Alejandra, she always got me into these conversations that didn't go anywhere. Finally, she told me I was just plain mean. I agreed with her just so she would be quiet. You see, that's the thing, if you agree with a girl, then there's no argument. She's right. You're wrong. And the world is real nice and quiet. Just like it's supposed to be.

The thing about Alejandra is that I kinda liked her. But she really gets to me—and I mean that in a bad way. She likes to repeat everything she reads—and she's always reading. And then she tells me about everything that's in the book. And I always have to tell her, "Look, just lend me the damn book and I'll read it myself," and then she gets mad, and refuses to talk to me until I say I'm sorry, and after that she tells me I have a lot to learn about the way a woman should be treated. I mean, c'mon, I don't think of Alejandra as a woman. Okay, she's pretty. But she's a geek and all the other girls hate her because she thinks she's too good for everybody.

And another thing about Alejandra: She always wants to change her name. This Alex thing she has going, well, it's just the latest name she's gotten into her head. Usually she wants to change her name to the main character of the book she's reading. When she read *Jane Eyre*, she wanted her name to be Jane. When she read *House on Mango Street*, she wanted to change her name to Esperanza, when she read *The Grapes of Wrath*, she wanted to be named Rose of Sharon, and when she read *To Kill a Mockingbird*, she wanted the whole effen world to call her Scout. Not that I didn't like Scout. I liked that book. Scout ruled. A real nice kid. But even if Scout was the best thing since the jalapeño, Alejandra wasn't changing a damn thing by renaming herself. See, Alejandra was just another kid from the barrio whose mom disappeared one day. Maybe her mom got together with my dad.

She's lucky, though. In some ways, I mean. See, Alejandra's dad, he's real young. I mean, he was fifteen when Alejandra was born. And right now Alejandra's sixteen. I mean, do the math, and you see what I'm getting at. And he's a good guy, finished college and everything and now he's running copy stores all over the city—Paper Dreams. He's got a real good thing going. Nice stores and better service than Kinko's and everybody's real proud because he's really done something. I mean, he really has. That's fantastically cool, but Alejandra didn't do any of it. She didn't do crap. So how come she's got so much attitude? What did she do?

And she's always badgering me to go work for her dad at Paper Dreams. She even takes me to the store near the university so I can look it over. "You could work here or at the store of your choice," she says. "And you wouldn't have to have that shitty job at WhataBurger."

You know, I wouldn't be caught dead working for Alejandra's father. I mean, I like the guy. He's a lot nicer than his daughter, if you ask me. I mean, to quote that Steve guy,

Alejandra's father is a very cool cat. But, you know, working for him would be like chaining myself to Alejandra. No thanks. No effen thanks.

And besides, I don't think working at WhataBurger is such a shitty job. And the people I work with are nice to me. I mean, they're always trying to get me to do their homework, but I'm not stupid enough to fall for that. I'm not a *pendejo*. My brother Tito might think so—but I'm not.

And the other thing about Alejandra—apart from the name thing she's got going and the badgering me about working for her father—is the fact that she's always talking about how she wants to move out of the neighborhood. But she says that since they've lived with her grandparents all these years, they're waiting till she graduates from high school. "Then," Alejandra says, "I'm going to go to Stanford and, well, I won't be coming back to *this* neighborhood. By then, my dad will be living in a new house. A house with a view." That Alejandra, she makes me mad as hell. The way she said *this neighborhood* and the way she said *a house with a view*. I mean, what view is she talkin' about? All she's gonna see from that view is a lot of poor Mexicans and a lot of those quintessential strip malls, *quintessential, quintessential, quintessential,* she found that word somewhere as if it were a homeless, mangy cat she decided to adopt—God, she uses that word to death and now I'm sayin' it, I hate that, I really effen hate that, and where does she effen get off lookin' down her nose at the rest of us? A house with a view, my achin' elbow.

I always say that, my achin' elbow, when I get mad. See, when I was a kid, I said *my aching ass* and I got in some serious trouble with my mom. Tía Lisa tried to back me up and told my mom she should get a life, but my mom didn't give in. Nope, not her style. My mom doesn't give in. Not to anyone. Not to memories of my father, not to the next-door neighbor who's always trying to move the property line, and not to Tía Lisa. So, anyway, now I always say my achin' elbow. And I look over at my mom and smile. She shakes her head, but I know she wants to smile too. But she doesn't.

And that Alejandra, when I'm around her, all I want to say is "my achin' elbow" all the effen time. She told me the other day, if I said that one more time she was going to kiss me. I shook my head and told her, "Alejandra, why don't you go hang out with that *vato*, Jorge."

"Jorge Casas?"

"*Ese mero,*" I said.

"I can't stand him."

"*Te quiere.*"

"I don't care if he likes me or not. I hate him."

"Well, if you're ever in the mood for kissing some guy, I'm sure he'd be in the mood."

She just looked at me. "You know something," she said. "Sometimes I really hate you. And if you think Monica Rubio is ever gonna fall for a guy like you, well, my achin' elbow." That's what she said, "My achin' elbow."

She really makes me crazy. And you know what? I really hate it when someone steals your words. It's like, we don't have a damn thing in the world to begin with—and then someone steals your words. I hate that.

Him
(My Brother)

My brother and I, we have a hard time talking. I don't know what it is, but sometimes that happens between brothers. I mean, the thing is that sometimes nothing happens between two brothers. I mean *nothing*. Maybe that's the thing between me and Tito—there's nothing happening between us and so we have nothing to say. I don't know what I'm talking about. I'm just trying to explain something to myself when really I don't have any explanations.

Maybe Tito and I are just trying to run away from each other. Only there's no place to run because we live in the same house. So instead of running away, what we do is run right into each other—like two cars having a head-on collision. Like the other night. He walks into the house about 9:30 at night. My mom was working a late shift for a friend of hers at the hospital—she's sort of the unofficial part-time, fill-in nurse at Thomason. She says the extra money is nice and she really doesn't go in that often so it's a very cool arrangement for her. So, anyway, my mom was working and I was home alone, and good thing, too, because mom would have jumped all over Tito's case for staying out so late. I'm there, lying on the living room couch, and I'm reading a book and he walks in stoned out of his mind and he says, "So, are you fuckin' bored or what?" His eyes were all dilated and his speech was slow and fuzzy.

I look up at him and say, "Nope. I'm just reading."

"You look fucking bored to me."

"You're stoned," I said.

"So fucking what," he says.

"Why are you so mad?"

"Fuck you!" he says.

"I didn't do anything to you."

"Fuck you. Everyone compares me to you. Ram this and Ram that and isn't Ram a good student and that Ram, he sure is gonna make something of himself, not like his brother, and how the fuck do you think that makes me feel?"

"That's not my fault, what they say."

"Tell me you don't fucking smile to yourself."

"I don't. I hate that."

"Sure you fucking do."

"Will you stop using that word?"

"You know what, bro? You're a fucking *pendejo*."

After he said that, he laughed—and then he turned on the television full blast and I walked into my room—which wasn't my room at all because it was *our* room. I walked into *our* room and I kept reading my book and I tried not to think of Tito and his attitude because, really, I didn't know where his attitude came from. I mean, maybe he had a reason. But I'll tell you what, I didn't do anything to that guy, so if he was effen mad at me, well, that was his problem.

So then I hear the television go off. Well, I didn't exactly hear the television go off. What I mean is that all of a sudden the house was nice and quiet, and I hear Tito open the refrigerator and rummage through it, and I figure he's really hungry because he has the munchies because that's what happens after you smoke pot—not that I know firsthand. But I hear all the talk. Yeah, well, people like to talk. So I keep reading and everything's okay. After about twenty minutes, Tito walks into the room and says, "Look, dude, it's time to turn off the lights. I'm tired as hell."

That really made me mad. I mean, the only light that was on was the lamp above my bed. "I'm not finished reading," I said.

"I said turn off the fucking light, dude."

I just looked at him. Then I got up. Then I stood there and said. "You want to come at me? Then come at me. But this light's staying on."

"I can kick your ass in a flash."

"Then go ahead and do it. Get it over with so I can go back to reading." I just looked at him. I knew he could fight. I'd heard about the crap he pulled on other people—and how lots of people were afraid of him. Some people were like that— they made the people around them afraid of them. That sort of thing wasn't interesting to me, but it sure was interesting to Tito. He had this look in his eyes, and I knew he was trying to make me afraid. Maybe I didn't know enough to be afraid. Maybe I just didn't care. This was my space. I had my bed and my light and my book. And I didn't have much else in the whole effen world, so I wasn't gonna let him mess with that. "Go ahead," I said.

And then—just like that—he took a swing at me, and punched me right in the stomach. And, you know, I just doubled over. It was like I was a tire with a flat. A tire that could feel. And I just lay on the floor clutching my book and my stomach felt tight and it hurt like hell. And finally, after about ten minutes, I started breathing okay again. And Tito just stood there staring at me. And when I got up, I lay down on my bed and kept reading.

And I didn't turn off the light.

And he stood there like a statue. Looking at me. Just staring.

I didn't look back at him. I kept my nose in the book, and I concentrated on reading every word.

And then I heard him say. "I fucking hate you."

And I said. "It's a lot of work, to hate your brother."

And then he just walked out of the room.

I kept reading. It helped, to read. It was easier to think about what was going on inside a book than what was going on inside your own house.

An hour or so later I finished the book, and put it down. And then I turned off the light.

I closed my eyes and heard my brother come back into the room. I heard him undress in the dark. I heard him crawl into bed.

And then I heard myself say, "No matter what you do or what you say, I'll never hate you. I'll never, ever hate you."

Tito, he didn't say anything.

And there was only darkness and silence.

Her Again
(Alejandra)

So I'm doing my homework and the phone rings and my mom says, "It's a girl. I think it's Alejandra." And my mom smiles like maybe there's something between me and Alejandra, and she has this smirk on her face. I don't like smirks. And I'm thinking to myself, *Alejandra doesn't qualify as a girl, Mom.* But I don't say it. I just roll my eyes at my mom and say, "She's not my style."

And Mom presses the receiver into her chest and whispers, "She's pretty."

I looked at her, shaking my head. "My achin' elbow."

My mom laughed and handed me the phone. Sometimes, I really like my mom. But she needs to stay out of my life when it comes to girls. My mom has no taste. I mean Alejandra is a real looker. She is. But not in the right kind of way. And really, it's not her looks—it's her attitude. If you just saw a picture of her, you might say to yourself, "She's nice. She's really nice." You might even say "hot." But then you'd change your mind after spending half an hour with her.

So I finally say something to the voice on the other end of the phone. "Hi."

"Hi," she said. "What are you doing?"

I think she wanted me to say something like, "Well, I was just hanging out hoping you'd call." But I didn't say anything like that. "I was doing some homework."

"What?"

"Math."

"Can you add?"

"Yeah, I can add."

"Give me a complicated mathematical formula."

"Ramiro plus Alejandra equals explosion."

"You're being stupid, Ram."

"You need something?"

"Nice guy. Is that how you treat girls?"

"That's how I treat you, Alejandra."

"I've decided I'm going to change my name to Juliana."

"Juliana."

"Yes, Juliana."

"Reading another book?"

"A real good one. And you know what? You're really a jerk."

"Never said I wasn't."

"Steve asked me out."

"Steve who?"

"Steve Gonzalez."

"He's a worse jerk than I am."

"But he's cute."

"That's the criterion?"

"I taught you that word."

"No you didn't."

"Yes I did."

"Okay. You win. You taught me everything I know. Are you happy? And listen, you shouldn't go out with a guy just because he's cute. You know how many mass murderers are cute? All of them. They're all cute."

"Steve isn't a mass murderer."

"Not yet, anyway."

"You're really being a shit."

"No. I just know the guy. He likes to kick dogs. I've seen him do it. That's where it begins. You want to go out with a guy who kicks dogs?"

"Actually, I'd rather go out with you. But you're not asking me. So, you just want me to stay home and wither away?"

"Wither? Don't be so theatrical, Juliana."

"Don't call me Juliana."

"I'm just playing along with your game."

"Fuck you, Ramiro."

"That word doesn't go with you, Alex."

"Alex. That's better."

"Don't use that word."

"Why not?"

"Because everybody else uses it. They wear that word out."

"Maybe I want to be like everybody else."

"What for?"

"I want to be alive."

"You are alive. What's wrong with you?"

"Why don't you ask me out?'

"Because it wouldn't be honest."

"Mister Virtue."

"You want me to feel sorry for you—is that it?"

"No."

"Look. We have this discussion every six months or so. And what do you see in me anyway? I'm not as cute as Steve."

"You're cute in a different way than Steve. And besides, you said cute wasn't a criterion."

"Okay, okay, look, we're friends. We got a good thing going, don't you think, being friends? I mean, we've gone to school together since kindergarten. That's a long time. What's wrong with being friends?"

"Well, when Monica tells you that, when she says, 'Ram, what's wrong with being friends?', how does that make you feel?"

"She's never said that."

"Yeah, well, she says it every time she looks at you."

"You can be really mean."

"How's it feel, Ramiro?"

And with that, she just hung up the phone. Man, you know, I wish I didn't know Alejandra. I really wish I didn't. But I feel kind of stuck to her. I mean—well, hell, I don't know what I mean. But I know how to add, and I'll tell you one thing, Ramiro + Alejandra does in fact = explosion. And it's not the sexual kind either. Just the kind that blows things up.

Then my mom comes into my room and says, "Why don't you like her?"

"Were you listening? I hate that, Mom. I really do."

"I wasn't listening. I didn't have to. I know you. I can see right through you."

I hate when my mom says things like that, because it might be true. And I hate that it might be true. I don't like the idea of it. Not at all. "I don't like her for a girlfriend, and that's it. She makes me crazy."

"You know there was this guy that I used to sort of go out with in high school. He was a good guy—but he was a little too straight for me. He didn't have enough rough edges, and he sort of bugged me. He was like this fly I was always trying to shoo away. I had my eye on this other guy. You know what, I sure didn't know what I was doing." And then she walked out of the room.

That was what passed for advice. My mom liked to say little things like that—then walk out of the room. I knew what she was saying. She was saying that she went for my father instead of that other guy. But, hey, good thing she went for my father or I wouldn't be around. That's what I think, anyway. And my mom's little speech didn't make me want to take at a second look at Alejandra. Nope. I mean, why would I want to get serious about a girl who was always changing her name?

Someday Alejandra is going to find some guy, and he's gonna like her right back. And she's gonna be just fine. They'll be happy as chips and salsa.

Me, I'm gonna be just fine too. Maybe it's okay that Monica isn't too interested in me. I mean, I have enough problems. There's this guy at school, his name's Marcos. And he says girls are just a pain in the ass. It doesn't stop him from asking them out, I'll tell you that. His ex-girlfriend, Angie, says he's just looking for someone to have sex with him.

"Did you?" I asked.

"Hell no," she said, "I'd rather eat peanut butter." I didn't think that was such a funny thing to say—but later I laughed because I remembered that she was severely allergic to peanuts. I mean, peanuts could kill her.

Anyway, I got to feeling a little bit bad about my conversation with Alejandra. I mean, it's not like I was changing my mind about her. It's just that I really wasn't into hurting other people's feelings. You know, I think my mom lives in my head. So I picked up the phone and called her back, and when I heard her voice, I said, "Listen, let's get one thing straight. We're friends. So let's just treat each other right. You do right by me and I'll do right by you. Friends stick together. But they don't kiss and do shit like that. You got that?"

Alejandra didn't say anything for a little while. And then she said, "Okay. So that's the deal."

"Yeah," I said. "That's the deal."

"I can live with that," she said. Then she hung up the phone.

That Alejandra, I'll tell you, she likes to hang the effen phone up on people.

Him
(My brother)

I came home about eight o'clock tonight. Usually, I only work at WhataBurger on Monday nights, Friday afternoons, Saturday mornings, and Sunday afternoons. But tonight I took Celso's shift on account of the fact that his mother was sick. So, when I got home, I found that Tito had stolen all my cash. It wasn't much—$185.00. But, still, that's a lot of money. I put a little away every chance I get, and shit! Now all my cash was gone. And I know exactly what Tito's gonna do with that money. I'm really pissed off at the little SOB. You know, I should have put that money in my bank account with the rest of my college money. But no, I just had to have some cash around like some kind of big shot. Yeah, sure, big shot. So now I'm screwed. You know, I was mostly mad at myself. For being an effen idiot.

Shit, I was so mad I couldn't concentrate on the essay I was supposed to be writing on the Lost Generation. I checked out a few books from the library on Hemingway and some lady named Gertrude Stein, but now I'm just staring at the books. I felt like busting my brother's face. Not that busting people's faces does any good.

Mom had left a note, saying she was doing something with my Tía Lisa—and since she wouldn't be home until 9:00, I decided to cook dinner. I made some tacos. I really like to make tacos. Maybe it's because I like to eat them. And, besides, it's something I know how to make. When Mom came home, she kissed me on the top of my head. She told me about her day, and I listened—though I was only listening halfway because I was still mad at Tito. I just can't listen when I'm mad.

We waited around for Tito to come home. After a while, we

71

just ate. I mean, we were used to eating without him. He gets home whenever he wants. After dinner, my mom got on the computer and started paying her bills. She's really gotten into that lately. Me, I don't trust computers. I write my essays and homework on them. You know, that's it. And the computer has a good speller in its head. That's cool. I went back to writing my essay. But I kept thinking about Tito. I knew he was out there getting loaded on some shit.

It's past midnight and Tito hasn't come yet. My mom's in the living room, pretending to watch television. But I know that she's just worrying. She was talking on the telephone a little while ago. I don't know who she was talking to. Maybe Tía Lisa. If it was Tía Lisa, then she'll probably be coming over in a while—you know, to be with Mom. She's like that.

I hope Tito comes home. I hope he's all right. I hope nothing happens to him. I hope, I hope, I hope. I know he's getting deeper and deeper into all this drug stuff. Yesterday, he stole two of my shirts and a pair of my shoes. I paid for those things with my part-time job at WhataBurger. And today, he steals my money. Okay, I mean I can start keeping all my money in a bank, but am I supposed to put a lock on my closet so he won't steal my clothes? I don't know what the hell I'm supposed to do about my brother.

What a sad kind of house we live in tonight. I hate that sick look of worry on my mom's face. I wonder if all houses have sad nights like these. And so what if they do? Knowing that a lot of other houses are sad doesn't make it any better, does it? It doesn't fix a damn thing.

I'm trying to think of other things. I'm thinking of the Lost Generation—Hemingway who shot himself in the end, and that strange lady Gertrude Stein whose work I don't get and don't like, and F. Scott Fitzgerald who wound up a drunk, and it really makes me sad because I sometimes think my father's out there drunk somewhere, though maybe it's just because I'm always thinking the worst—I can't help myself. And you know what else I'm thinking? I'm thinking about that guy, Jake, who I'm always running into on my corner of the grounds at school and how he's always trying to be nice to me and be my friend, and even though I haven't got anything against him, he's this rich guy, and hell, we don't have anything in common. And really I start thinking that I don't have anything in common with anyone. And why do I think about things I don't want to think about? *And then, there he is again, my father, and he's in my head and he's having a drink with the ghost of Scott Fitzgerald,* shit, I'm thinking about him again. Him. My dad. I think I remember my mother waiting up all night. Waiting for him to come back. Just like she's doing right now. I think I remember that.

My name's Ramiro. They call me Ram. I'm named after my father. I hate being named for a father who disappeared one night and never came back. It's like being named after a ghost.

What a sad house I live in tonight.

Me, Jake
(Back Again)

I have a new theory. Okay, so maybe I grow too many theories in my brain. My biology teacher told me once that my mind was like a petri dish growing all kinds of bacteria. Okay, so maybe he has a point. But my new theory is this: Everybody in the world speaks their own kind of language. And you know what? All we do is translate. No, all we do is mistranslate. That's my new theory. I mean, how else do you explain the fact that nobody understands one another.

Her
(Rosario, Whom I Call Rosie)

I wake up really tired from having all those explosions inside of me. But I'm trying to be cool. I mean, Sally and I are mad at each other, but I'm trying to stay calm. You know the water in the river is so damn relaxed. So I decided I'd be just like that water.

But as I walked into the kitchen to fix myself some breakfast before school, Rosario was sitting there trying to talk to Sally. The discussion wasn't going very well. My mom's Spanish consisted of a lot of hand motions and pointing—all of them having to do with cleaning floors, dusting, and the latest products for cleaning bathrooms.

"I don't understand," Sally kept repeating. And even though I'm mad at her, I decide that maybe I need to, you know, insert myself into the situation. Like I'm a part. Like I belong.

And besides, Rosario was crying. I hated that. I hated to see people cry—especially girls and women. It always makes me feel like I should do something—but I never know what that something is. So, I just sort of watched Rosario cry, and then when she stopped, I asked her, *"¿Que te pasa, Rosie?"* And that's when she blurted out the whole story. It seems her boyfriend, Roman, who was from Michoacan, Mexico, had been picked up by the border patrol. He, of course, didn't have any papers, so they were going to deport him back to Mexico. But she didn't think it was fair because Roman had been living in the United States for more than fifteen years, and all his relatives were dead, and he had nothing back there at all, not family, not land, not a job, nothing. Of course, I think I missed a lot of the details, but I got the big picture. My mother stared at both of us blankly as I asked Rosario some questions, and I found out that she and Roman had been living together for the last ten years and that they had a little girl who was five (I vaguely remembered Rosie being pregnant some years back), and really, she said, they *were* husband and wife—only they'd never bothered to get married. And what she wanted to know was *Couldn't David help them? Wasn't he a lawyer?*

I conveyed Rosie's story to my mom, who seemed to be listening patiently. And I was really trying to forget that I was super destroyed from the night before. And then Rosie and I just looked at my mom as we waited for a response. And then, my mother finally looked me in the eye and said, "Tell her we don't like to get involved in the personal lives of our employees. We have boundaries."

"Boundaries? That's what you want me to tell her?" Sally really does destroy me.

"I don't like that tone, Jacob."

"What tone?" I said. I mean, what is it with adults and that whole tone thing they have going on?

"You know exactly what kind of tone," she said.

"Never mind my tone. Why won't you help them?"

"If Roman is here illegally, well, he knew the risks. He's breaking the law, and I just won't have it. We can't go around harboring criminals."

"Harboring criminals?"

"There's that tone again, Jacob Upthegrove."

There was an explosion inside me. She really did destroy me when she used my last name like that. I just looked at her.

"I know what I'm doing," she said firmly.

Go ahead, I wanted to say, *finish me off. Destroy me to nothingness.*

"Look, Jake, what does Rosario expect us to do? We all have to be accountable for our actions."

God, let's not go there. "Look, if they've been together for ten years, aren't they common-law? Aren't they married? And if they *are* married, doesn't that mean he can stay?" I didn't say anything about her I-just-won't-have-it remark. I mean, I had to focus. I looked at her and waited for an answer.

"I don't know."

"I don't know either. But David would know."

"David doesn't do immigration law."

"He must know someone who does."

"We are not getting involved."

"You won't even ask him?"

"He's very busy with his practice."

"So you won't ask him?"

"Tell her I'm sorry."

All this time Rosie was watching the both of us. I'm not sure how much she understood. But Rosie wasn't stupid, and I'm sure she knew more English than she let on. Look, she'd lived in this country for over twenty years and had become a US citizen. Not that we went to her ceremony when she invited us. I was getting very angry over the kind of people that we were. I was. That's what I was thinking.

Rosie just kept looking at us—at me and my mother. She had that question in her eyes.

"Tell her, Jacob."

I hated Sally at that moment. I swear I did. I looked at Rosie and I swear to the God I didn't even think existed that I wanted to cry. Rosie, she was a nice lady. Real decent. Always treated me like I was something special—even though we both knew I wasn't very special at all. And then I just said it. *"No te quiere ayudar."*

"¿Porque no?" She had a right to ask, I suppose. Why not? Hadn't she worked here for over ten years? I could see the fire

in her eyes. I wondered what the Anger Management Lady would think about that fire.

"*Porque así son. Los dos. Ella y David—así son.*"

She nodded.

Mom wanted to know what I was telling her.

I looked right at Sally. I hated this translator shit. I hated it. "I told her you wouldn't help her. She wanted to know why. I told her because that's just how you and David are."

"You told her that?"

"You don't like the way I'm handling this, Sally, then handle it yourself."

Rosie interrupted our little spat. "*Dile a tu mama que ya no voy a trabajar con ella. Dile que me voy.*" And then she grabbed her purse from the counter where she always left it when she came to work—grabbed her purse, clutched it—and walked out of the house.

I looked at my mom. "In case you didn't get that, she quit."

"Well, she didn't have to do that," she said. "I wasn't firing her. I don't know why she's being so unreasonable."

I'm this woman's son. God. I am so fucking destroyed.

"Mom," I said, "I'm going to give Rosie a ride home on my way to school. I'm sure it'll be a while before the bus comes by again. And then I'm going to find her an immigration lawyer. And I'm going to tell that lawyer that I'm more than happy to pay whatever the fuck he charges."

"Watch your language, Jacob Upthegrove. And you will do no such thing."

"Sally," I said. "Grandma left me quite a bit of money."

"That money's for your college."

"That money doesn't have any restrictions."

"You can't spend it until you're eighteen."

"Which is a week or so away," I said.

"You didn't even earn that money."

You know, I really kept my mouth shut. I really did. You don't want to know the mean things that ran through my mind.

She glared at me. "You'd throw some of that money away on—"

"Stop right there, Sally. Please." I think I looked at her in a very mean and peculiar way. I think I made her afraid of me. I think I wanted to make her afraid of me. I felt all that anger and, for a minute, I just didn't know anything about where all my anger came from. But I closed my eyes and took several breaths. Okay, it was a trick from the Anger Management Lady. When I opened my eyes, all I could think of was that my mother and David were real shits. I just didn't like them. I didn't. And I don't think they liked me, either.

I wasn't sure what I was going to do about all this knowledge. I did know that this was war. And I had never really been to war before, so I didn't exactly know what I was doing. But helping Rosie didn't seem to be such a bad thing to do. And I was going to do it. And I wasn't going to hide it from Sally or David.

As I was walking out the door, I heard Sally say, "If the school calls, then I'm not going to lie for you."

"Don't," I said. "Then I won't have to go to medical school."

I knew the school would call when I didn't show up. And I also knew Sally would cover for me. She was way too in love with appearances. Maybe that's why she hated my T-shirts. She didn't like the way they looked. She didn't like what they communicated to the world.

I caught up with Rosie as she was walking down the hill. She didn't want to get in the car. I smiled at her. *"Yo no soy mi mama." I am not my mother.* That's what I told her. She got in the car. She gave me directions to her house. She lived in an apartment building in South El Paso. When I left her off, she hugged me.

I wanted to cry. I didn't deserve that lady's hugs. I was so fucking destroyed.

Me
(Still Here and Still Mad)

After I left Rosie off, I thought about my mom. I was beginning to understand why I called her Sally sometimes. Maybe I was going to be mad at her for another year. Was that a solution? That woman who gave birth to me, she seriously destroyed me.

I knew it wasn't doing anybody any good by sitting there thinking about Sally, so I decided to do something more productive. Isn't that what the Anger Management Lady was always telling me to do? *Do something productive.* So I decided right then and there to find Rosie an immigration attorney. Not that I had a clue as to how to find one. I sure as hell wasn't going to call David. And then I thought I'd just drive down Montana—you couldn't spit without hitting a lawyer's office on that street. I loved that expression. Sally hated it. She wanted to know where I picked up stuff like that. From living, Sally. That's what I always wanted to tell her.

Just as I was driving up one of the streets to make my way toward Montana Street, I saw a name in front of one of the old buildings, fixed up real nice: ENRIQUE MORENO, ATTORNEY AT LAW." I liked the name and then I remembered seeing his name in the paper. I only knew that the guy was pretty well known and had a good reputation. Not that I remembered any details. I was the kind of guy who skimmed newspapers. I couldn't actually claim that I read them. Anway, I thought, what the hay? So I found a parking spot and walked into his office. Just as I opened the front door, I was confronted by a distinguished fifty-something-year-old man dressed in a suit, who was obviously about to walk out the front door. "Mr. Moreno?" I asked.

"Yes." There was something of a question in his voice.

"My name is Jake."

He nodded. He looked like he was in some kind of hurry—so I thought I'd just get to the point. I offered to shake his hand. He smiled and took it. He had a firm handshake. Warm. I think I liked him. I don't know, he seemed like a decent man—you could just tell.

"Are you in trouble?" he asked.

I must have looked like maybe I *was* in trouble—but to tell you the truth, I had that kind of look.

"I'm not a criminal attorney," he said. He didn't say it in a mean way.

"That's okay," I said, "I'm not a criminal."

He smiled.

I think I laughed. "I just want the name of a good immigration lawyer. I mean, I don't know who to ask."

Mr. Moreno just smiled at me. "Look, young man, I'm on my way to court, but—" He turned to the woman who was sifting through some files. "Olga? Will you give this young man Albert Armendariz's phone number and address?" He turned back toward me. "Just tell him I sent you."

"Yes, sir." I said. "Thank you, sir."

As he walked out the door, all I could think of was that not all attorneys were like David. David would never have stopped to talk to a punk like me as he was running out the door, late for court. Nope, that's not something David would do.

As fate would have it (though I didn't actually believe in fate), one of Mr. Armendariz's appointments had cancelled—and there I was, sitting in the waiting room of his modest office. I don't mean that in a bad way. I mean, if you cared about your clients and you were an immigration lawyer, then maybe you didn't have the money to fix up your office so it looked like something out of a magazine. So, well, he had a modest office.

Mr. Albert Armendariz turned out to be a very nice man with lots of gray hair. Well, he didn't actually have lots of hair, but the hair he had, well, it was gray. He shook my hand and had me step into his office. He had files everywhere on his desk, but he seemed to be organized. Not uptight organized, just organized.

I told him Mr. Enrique Moreno had recommended him highly. He smiled. I think he liked to smile. He was a big man, friendly, fair skinned, and sort of relaxed. I liked that about him, that he was so relaxed and that he just took everything in—sort of thoughtful and analytical. I bet he'd never had to go to an anger management lady.

"You a friend of Enrique's?" he asked.

"Well, no, not exactly. I just, well, I just sort of asked him for some advice. And he, well, he said I should come to see you."

He listened as I laid out the whole Roman-Rosie scenario. I tried to skip over the fact that my mom had declined to help them—even though Rosie had worked in our house for more than ten years. I more or less recounted what Rosie had told me in our kitchen. I tried not to miss anything. And after I finished, I told him I wanted to hire him—to represent Roman and Rosie.

"And he's at the detention center?" Mr. Armendariz asked.

"Yes, sir, at least that's what I understand."

"Do you know his last name?"

"No, sir, but I know Rosie's number. She can tell you all you need to know."

"So what's your interest in this, son?"

"I like Rosie," I said. "She's worked for us for a long time."

"And your parents?"

I looked down at the floor. "I don't think they want to get involved."

"I see," he said. "Do they know you're here?"

"Not exactly."

"Not exactly?"

"Well, no. No, they don't." I kept looking down at the floor. But then I looked up at him and said, "But I'll pay for it. I have money. I'm not poor. And it's my money—not my mom's and not David's. Mine."

Mr. Armendariz just sort of smiled at me. He had this kind of sweet look on his face—but I couldn't help but feel he was being a little condescending. Not in a bad way. But, still. That look destroyed me. But it destroyed me in a good way. You could be destroyed in more ways than one.

"I can pay," I said again.

He nodded. "Look, son, why don't you just give me Rosie's number. I can take it from there."

I nodded. "Do you promise?"

"Yes, son, I promise."

"She doesn't have any money," I said.

"We'll work something out," he said.

"Okay," I said.

"Okay," he said.

I knew what he was trying to say to me. Everything wasn't about money.

He reached over to shake my hand. We smiled at each other and shook each other's hands, and I didn't feel like a kid. I didn't. I almost felt like a man. You know, like an adult. Can you dig that? Unbelievable. I destroy myself sometimes.

I gave him Rosie's phone number. I knew he would call her. I knew he would do all he could. I could just tell. And that was something. That was really something.

As I walked back to my car, I decided to go to school. I was late, but, I mean, I didn't have any place else to go. I called my mom on my cell. "Mom," I said. "I'm on my way to school."

"Good," she said.

"Did they call?"

"Yes, they did."

"What did you tell them?"

"I told them you needed to go to the doctor because you weren't feeling well."

"Good," I said, "I'll tell them I came straight to school after my doctor's visit."

"Won't they ask for some kind of note?"

"If they do, they'll call you."

A part of me wanted to thank her.

But most of me was still really sore at her. But what she said next made me even angrier.

"Jacob, I'm very upset with you," she said. "How dare you take her side."

I didn't say anything.

I just shut off my cell.

Me and Her

(*Her,* My Mom, Who Was in Danger of Being Called Sally on a Permanent Basis)

I sometimes play this game. I run a scene over and over in my mind. The scene is something that's really happened—but in my mind, I change it to the way it should have happened. This was the scene I played over in my mind with Sally as I drove to school. Rosie has just spilled out her story about Roman. I look at Mom and tell her the story—and after I finish telling her what Rosie's said to me, I say: "We have to help them."

And Sally says, "We can't get involved."

"We *have* to get involved."

"We can't."

"It's the right thing to do."

"Jacob, we can't go around helping all the people in the world who have problems."

"We don't have to help all the people in the world. We just have to help Rosie and Roman."

"Where will it stop?"

"We have to help them," I say again.

Sally notices the look I'm wearing on my face, and she says, "Okay. We'll do what we can." She doesn't do it for Rosie. She does it for me. And that's okay. People don't always have to do the right thing for the right reasons—so long as they do the right thing.

I smile to myself as I park my car in the parking lot. I walk into school and think: *Wouldn't it be great if we all lived in our heads all the time?*

But I knew I was full of crap. And I also knew when I got home I wasn't going to mention anything about Rosie. And I knew Sally well enough to know that she would never bring up the subject again. And I knew why, too. She was ashamed of herself. But she couldn't tell herself that—so she just wasn't going to talk about it.

She would go and find a new maid. She would pretend Rosie never existed. And the only time her name would come up was if I uttered it.

I hated the world I lived in sometimes. The world I lived in, it destroyed the holy crap out of me.

That was the thing—the world was designed to destroy people.

Her
(Mrs. Anaya)

I think I'm two people. One part of me just wants to be happy with everything I have and just fit right in to the life that's been handed me—including my father's last name. Embrace it, you know. I mean, you can dig that, can't you? Embrace my name, embrace my life, embrace my Mom, embrace David, embrace all the things they buy for me, embrace my future as Doctor Jacob Upthegrove. Embrace, embrace, embrace. Mrs. Anaya told us in anatomy class that embracing has to be a way of life. A philosophy. "This is the human body. Embrace it. It's all you've got." She's the kind that likes to embrace everything. She even goes so far as to say that we have to embrace pain when it comes our way. Can you dig that? I raised my hand and asked if the prisoners at Abu Ghraib should embrace their pain. She said she didn't appreciate my brand of humor.

"It was an honest question," I said.

"It was a mean question," she said.

"Well, maybe so. But they did some pretty mean things at that prison."

"How do you know?"

"The pictures are everywhere," I said.

"They're obscene," she said.

"I agree," I said. "So should they embrace their pain? Or maybe we should all embrace the obscenity of the whole Abu Ghraib thing. "

"You're going to have to embrace a bad grade in this class if you keep this up, young man."

"Yes, ma'am," I said.

So much for embracing. I wondered what kind of mother she was. I wondered if her kids were always embracing her.

Look, I didn't really mean to diminish her well-intentioned optimism. I didn't. She was a good teacher and a good person. Okay, enough of this lovefest. Look, most of me just wants to shake my head at most things. If you open your eyes and look, there's a lot of things to shake your head at.

"You're an ingrate." That's what Sally says about me. "Nothing makes you happy and nothing is ever good enough." She's not wrong. But the thing is, everything seems so frickin' shallow. I mean it. I don't like country-club crap, and I don't want to live my life like Elaine and David. And I sure as shit don't want to live like my old man, Upthegrove.

Even this whole thing about being a doctor. Hell, I don't want to be a doctor. I'd be the kind of doctor who didn't like my patients. Aren't there enough of those around already? I'm not good with people—something that the Anger Management Lady pointed out to me: "You'd manage your anger better if you got to the root of your problem—you just don't seem to like people very much."

"I'd like them a whole lot better if they were more likable."

"That's not funny," she said.

"I didn't say it to be funny."

And then she said, "Maybe you should just start with yourself. Like yourself first and then go from there."

"Like myself first." I repeated. I mean, can you dig that shit? I mean, my idea of hell would be to spend an entire day in the presence of the Anger Management Lady and Mrs. Anaya. Look, the thing is, maybe I don't like myself all that much. What's so awful about that? But I don't exactly hate myself either. I'd like to think I hold a healthy distrust of myself. I mean, there's a lot to distrust. And what's so great about being in love with yourself? You think that's healthy? I mean, every time I go to a bookstore, I'm accosted by someone who's written another memoir. I mean some people have written more than one memoir. It's like they only have one subject: *themselves*. And look at my old man, Upthegrove, he's a great example. He has a great self-image. And he's also full of shit. Okay, residual anger. *Deal with that residual anger.* That's the Anger Management Lady's voice. It pops into my head all the time, along with the smell of her perfume, which was really awful. She sort of smelled like a rotten tangerine. I told her that once. She said I wasn't making any progress.

"Put it in my report," I said.

"I intend to," she said.

"I think you're angrier than me."

"Your opinion of me is of no import."

"Generally speaking, my opinions on any subject are of no import," I said. "That's why I'm angry."

"It's not wise to diagnose yourself."

She was happy to get rid of me. I'm sure she thought I was going to wind up killing someone. But, me, I'm not afraid of my anger. I've embraced it. Mrs. Anaya would be proud.

After class, Mrs. Anaya told me she wanted to speak with me. "I really think you should rein in your attitude," she said. She looked at me. I knew she was waiting for me to say something.

"What do you think we should do about illegal immigration?"

"What?"

I knew I'd taken her by surprise. This keep-them-off-balance thing is a very good strategy.

"What does this have to do with your attitude?"

"Nothing and everything."

"I don't understand you. Here you are, a young man with

a fine mind and the world at his feet, and all you can do is go around looking for trouble."

"The world at my feet? I don't like that expression. Mostly because it's not true. And if it is true, it shouldn't be true, now should it? Why should the world be at anybody's feet?'

"You really do just like to argue, don't you, young man?"

"Yes," I said. "I suppose I do. But, listen, our maid Rosie lives with a man who's going to be deported even though he's lived and worked in this country for fifteen years and he and Rosie have a five-year-old daughter, and my Mom and stepdad don't give a damn because they don't want to get involved. People like Rosie and Roman are dispensable, I guess—at least to Mom and David. And the prisoners of Abu Ghraib were tortured, not to mention the poor bastards at Guantánamo who may never get a fair trial, and all you can think of is that I have a bad attitude?"

Mrs. Anaya just looked at me.

"You know," I just kept going, "I hate to rain on your parade, lady, but Mary Poppins never showed up at my house—though I sure as hell wish she would. Maybe you can pop by my house and make everything all right by all that embracing you like to talk about all the time—and you know something? If you want to give me a bad grade because you think I have a bad attitude, then all I have to say is that you're not very professional. I got an A on my last exam. And do you know why? Because I got all the answers right. Correct me if I'm wrong, but when I signed up for this course, the title of it was Human Anatomy, not Mrs. Anaya's Philosophy of Embracing."

She just kept looking at me. And finally she said, "That is the first and last time I will ever allow you to lecture me. I don't need you to tell me what *is* and *is not* my job. Is that clear, Jacob Upthegrove?"

That Upthegrove thing was destroying me.

"I would appreciate if you answered, 'Yes, ma'am.'"

"Yes, ma'am."

"And don't ever speak to me in that tone again. Not if you want to remain in this school."

There was that tone thing again. "Yes, ma'am."

She pointed toward the door and I walked out. I spill out my guts, and her only response is to editorialize about my tone. God, she really destroys me.

Her and Him
(Mom and Me. Again.)

So, it was a bad day all in all. When I went home, I just walked straight into my room. I didn't bother with anything to eat. I was tired. I just threw myself on my bed and looked up at the ceiling. Later that evening, my mom walked in and said, "Aren't you hungry?"

I shook my head. I wanted to tell her that I was really more upset about how she'd behaved toward Rosie than how she'd ever behaved toward me. I mean, I knew I was always goading her, so what did I expect? But Rosie?

"You should eat something."

"I'm not hungry."

"I'm sorry I slapped you."

I nodded.

"I *am* sorry, Jake. I am. There's no excuse for hitting."

I nodded.

"But you goaded me."

I nodded.

"You drove me to it, Jake."

"Yeah, that's what I said when I busted Tom's nose."

She nodded. "I'm sorry," she whispered. "But, son, I don't know what's wrong with you. I mean, lately you're utterly impossible."

I nodded.

"Are you going to talk to me?"

"Look, Sally, you walk into my room and you apologize, but your apology doesn't mean crap when all you do is justify your violent actions. I mean, haven't you ever heard of Gandhi? And if I deserved that slap—which I might have, and if I drove you to it, then really there's nothing to apologize for, is there—what you're really looking for is an apology from me. Isn't that right, Sally? So, look, I'm sorry. Though, really, I'm not. I'm trying to be real here, that's all. And that's the one thing in this house that you and David can't stand. You don't like real. Maybe that's what you couldn't stand about Rosie."

"Don't ever bring that issue up again."

Great. Rosie was now reduced to being an issue. "You know what, Mom, you don't want to look at me. You don't. You don't want to see me. In my opinion, you and David are the adults. I'm the kid. And yet it's *my* job to understand *you*. But it's not *your* job to understand *me*. That's how I see it. So, from my perspective, you can see the fundamental unfairness of the situation."

My mother just looked at me. "That was quite a soliloquy," she said. Then she turned around and walked out the door. Then, a second later, she opened the door and said, "Sometimes I think I should slap you more often."

After school the next day, I decided I needed to do some thinking. So I got in my car and went down to the Circle K near Jefferson High School. I really needed a cigarette, and I wanted to get as far away from my neighborhood as I could get. So when I got to the Circle K, I had a plan. I'd just get someone to buy me cigarettes. I mean, I was only a week away from being of legal age, anyway. And, God, I really needed a cigarette. So, I see this guy getting out of his car. The guy, he was Latino, I could tell, he must've been in his early twenties or something like that. And him and his girlfriend couldn't keep their hands off each other—which made me sort of, well, embarrassed, but it sort of made me feel a little lonely. I mean, I didn't have a girlfriend or anything like that—mostly because they always wound up breaking up with me. You know, I don't want to talk about that.

So, anyway, I go up to the guy and I say, "Hey."

He looks at me and says, "Hey."

And then I ask, "You think you could score some cigarettes for me?"

"How old are you?" I didn't know if his question was a good sign or not.

"I'm gonna be eighteen pretty soon."

"Well, dude, it's against the law to buy cigarettes for minors."

"But I'll give you ten bucks," I said.

"It's still against the law."

"Ten bucks is ten bucks," I said.

He looks at me, then he looks at his girlfriend. And I say to myself that maybe this deal will go down, so I wanted to push things along, so I took out a twenty and said, "Look. If you buy me a pack of Marlboro Lights, then you keep the change from this twenty."

He looks at me. "You're not a narc, dude, are you?"

"No way," I said.

He grabbed the twenty and said, "If I wind up in jail, I'm gonna have all of fucking Dizzy Land after your ass, *vato*. You got that?"

I nodded.

So they both go inside the store and I wait. I wasn't worried that the cashier had seen us or anything because we were parked on the side of the building. I just waited there for a while, and finally he comes out and tosses me my pack of cigarettes.

"Thanks, dude," I said.

"Sure, *vato*," he says. And then he says, "And don't get into any trouble. Got that?" And then he just shook his head.

And I don't know why I asked, but I asked, "What's your name?"

He laughed. "Chuy."

I nodded. "Maybe I'll see you around."

He nodded back. "I come here a lot in the afternoons—after work."

I nodded and we both smiled at each other. I don't know what he thought of me, really. But maybe he didn't think I was such a bad guy. I mean, it was just cigarettes, right? I just wanted to have me some smokes. It's not as if I smoked all the time, anyway. It's not as if I was an addict or anything like that.

So I got in the car and headed for the desert. I always had this thing for the desert. It was a great place to think. And so I went way out to this place I knew. I parked the car and just walked. I walked and walked. It wasn't too hot, not really, and the sun was just right, and it was good, you know, to just walk around and be away from Elaine and David and all that stuff at school that they were trying to shove down my throat so that I could get incredibly high test scores so that I could get into one of those schools Elaine wanted me to get into. It took me a while to calm down, but after a few cigarettes I felt much better, and I was happy, you know, just walking around and smoking, with no one to bother me. The thing is, a lot of people really bother me, and when people bother me, well, I have a way of bothering them back. The Anger Management Lady said I had the makings of a misanthrope. "That means, Jacob, that you hate people."

"Yeah, yeah," I said, "I know what it means."

But really, she was wrong about me. I don't hate people, not really; I just expect people to be better than they are. I just have high standards. And maybe because of that, I get a little disappointed. I think I get mad because people disappoint me. I'm not angry, I'm just disappointed. I always wanted to tell the Anger Management Lady that very thing. But you know, I think she'd already made up her mind about me. She'd already decided I was pissed off at the world. Nothing I said or did was going to change her mind about me. That's the thing, I don't argue with people who have their minds made up. Waste of time. A total waste of time.

After a while I got to thinking that maybe Elaine, aka Sally, was right. I mean, she thought I had to do something about myself. And then it hit me that maybe I should drive by St. Patrick's Cathedral. Look, if I was serious about becoming a Catholic, I should go by and check the place out. But then I thought, why do I want to become a Catholic? I mean, I didn't know anything about Catholics. I mean, I knew that priests couldn't get married, I knew that part. And I knew about the Pope and the Vatican in Rome, but that was it. Oh yeah, and I'd read this book about the saints. Very impressive. Really. I'm not being ironic. I mean, this is very serious stuff.

So the thought came to me that maybe before becoming Catholic, I'd try something else. And the more I thought about it, the more I thought maybe I should just give up everything. The thing is, that's how all those saints cleansed themselves. In that book I read, all those saints, they'd all cleanse themselves. It was like they were doing penance. I guess it was like cleaning your room before your friends came over or like taking a bath in the morning so you wouldn't smell bad. It was like that, but the cleaning was on the inside, somewhere in the deepest part of you. If you were going to be serious about God, then you had to be clean in order to get ready. And part of that whole thing was that they gave up all their earthly possessions. I mean, that really blew me away—that they gave up everything. And I mean everything. You take a guy like St. Francis or St. Ignatius of Loyola, I mean these guys were rich. I mean they came from serious money. But they gave it all up—and they didn't mind being poor. As Mrs. Anaya would say: They embraced their poverty.

I got to thinking that maybe I should try something like that. I mean, I really don't know if there's a God. I don't. Who really knows. But the thing is, you've got to make like you know. It's what Elaine called faith. She used to talk to me about faith when I was small—but it never took.

I wondered if I could ever do anything like that—give up all the crap I had. But the more I thought about it, the more I thought it sounded like a good idea. So that was what I decided to do. Why not? I mean, how was I ever going to find out what I needed and what I didn't need? And maybe I'd find faith or God or at least something good.

Yes. I would give everything up. All my earthly possessions. I would give them all away. And I would begin with my car. I figured I should begin with all the big things, and work my way down. I pictured myself telling Elaine. "Let's just give the car to someone who doesn't have one. Rosie, we'll give it to Rosie."

I pictured that look on her face.

She wasn't going to like this.

So, when I got home, Elaine greeted me at the door and said, "I've been thinking."

And I'm thinking to myself, *Oh shit. This can't be good.*

And then she smiled and she almost looked like a little girl and she said, "Look, I've decided it would be nice if you had a party for your eighteenth birthday. Wouldn't that be lovely? And you can invite anybody you like."

The last thing I wanted was a party. I mean, the truth is, I would only want to invite about six or seven people. I mean, how many people does Elaine think I like in this world? How many friends does she think I have? A party? What was a party going to solve? Was a party going to make everything all right between us?

A part of me wanted to ask: "Can I invite Rosie and Roman?" But Elaine looked so happy, and I know she was trying to make up with me. I mean, look, we all have our limitations. And I won't lie. I mean, I love Sally. I do. She's my mom. And I really didn't like this stuff, this thing of being at each other's throats. It wasn't any good for either of us. She was just standing in front of me, looking so happy. So I just smiled back at her and said, "That sounds great, Mom."

She was happy. I mean, I even called her "Mom."

That made Sally real happy.

You know, I didn't know if I was more destroyed when she was mad at me or when she was happy.

Me, Ramiro
(Otra vez, Which Means "Again" If You Don't Speak Spanish)

There are winners and there are losers. Well, big effen deal. I mean, what does that mean exactly? What's a winner and what's a loser? Is Tito a loser? Is that it? And I'm supposed to be a winner? Oh wow, effen wow. I don't think this crap about winners and losers explains a damn thing.

Him
(My Brother)

When I woke up, I had this feeling. You know, *that* feeling, the one where you think that an angry animal crawled inside your body during the night and got lost in there and then got really scared and mad and was trying to scratch its way out. That's the feeling. Bad.

I stared at my brother's bed right across from mine. Tito hadn't come home. I wondered if maybe he hadn't gone to the same place as my father. It was a stupid thing to think.

I got up and sat on his bed, and I noticed something sticking out from under his pillow. When I pulled it out, I saw that it was his spiral notebook. I'd seen him sketching stuff in it sometimes. He liked to sketch things, more out of nervousness than anything else. He just wasn't a calm kind of guy, my little brother. I shouldn't have looked through it. I mean, everybody had their right to privacy—even Mexicans. I know a lot of people think that Mexicans don't care about privacy—but I'm here to tell you that's not true. Whatever Tito wrote in his notebook was none of my effen business. Nope. But there I was flipping through his notebook. And then I found a page that said: WHOEVER SAID THE WORLD WAS A GOOD PLACE TO LIVE IN NEVER LIVED IN MY FUCKING BODY. And he had drawn this big hand flipping the bird off to the whole world.

For a minute, I wondered what it was like to be Tito. And then all the things Tito liked to say ran through my mind: *The world sucks this neighborhood sucks no one thinks I'll ever be fuckin' good enough why can't everyone just leave me alone talk like this don't talk like that.* All the things he ever said became this one long sentence in my mind, and I tried to think if Tito ever said anything good, anything nice, and I couldn't. And I wondered about that. I wondered what it was like to be so effen unhappy and I wondered why. I mean, it wasn't like I was the happiest guy in the world. I wasn't even the happiest guy in the south side of El Paso, but, you know, I thought living was a good idea. And I thought maybe there was some kind of future out there waiting for me. A good future. But, for a guy like Tito, words like "tomorrow" and "future" were just a lot of crap that adults liked to shove down our throats—just lies that got us through the day. Look, I can't say I blame the guy. Adults, in general, were excellent liars.

I don't know why, but I found myself whispering his name over and over: *Tito Tito Tito Tito Brother Brother Brother Brother.* I kept whispering *Tito* and *Brother* over and over and over. Maybe I was sort of praying. Who knows? Sometimes I do things and I don't even know why I'm doing them.

I put my hand on my stomach and took a deep breath, preparing myself for what was coming: a bad day—an *absolutely* bad day. A really bad day. A *really, really* bad day. Absolutely bad. Okay, my English teacher, Mrs. Herrera, says the words "really" and "absolutely" are way overused. Really? Absolutely. Hell, never mind about her. *It was gonna be an absolutely really bad day.* Did you ever tell yourself: *This isn't happening this isn't happening?* Did you ever do that? Well, that's exactly what I was telling myself: *This isn't happening.* And then all that banging around inside me became something else—a sinking feeling in my gut. I could feel that sinking, almost as if I was this rock and I was sitting in the middle of the ocean and I was beginning to sink into the swallowing water. And I knew I would just keep sinking until I completely disappeared. And the thing about it is, well, rocks don't know how to swim. So, in that way, I was like a rock. Can't swim.

Look, I know I'm not making sense. I mean, I'm not a rock.

And what do I know about water? I'm from the effen desert. But, you know, all I'm trying to do is tell you what I felt like. And that's how I felt. Words are inadequate. That's what Mrs. Herrera always says. My question is this: If words are so inadequate, then why the effen heck is Mrs. Herrera teaching English? I mean, it's like trying to drive a car that doesn't have wheels. Who would drive a car without wheels? A lot of people—that's who.

Anyway, thinking about Mrs. Herrera was just a distraction. She was just an excuse to keep me thinking about my mom. My mom. I knew she was worried sick. I mean sick. I mean sick to death. I got up and put on my jeans and a clean T-shirt and brushed my teeth. I kept hoping Tito would walk through the front door—and then everything would be okay. If he would only walk through the door. *Please, please.* Sometimes *please* is a prayer. *Tito* and *Brother* and *Please.* Sometimes prayers are made of those words.

I walked into the kitchen—and there was my mom and Tía Lisa. Both of them talking in whispers.

"He didn't come home," I said. I think I wanted to ask a question, but it didn't come out like that. Stupid. Sometimes, I say such stupid things.

My mom shook her head. "The police were here."

"You called them?"

She nodded. "I don't know what to do." Her lips were trembling. And tears were running down her face.

I had to do something. I had to. So I walked right up to her and kissed her on the cheek. And then she just started crying and I held her. And I hated Tito for doing this to Mom. I hated him. I hated him because he didn't understand anything about love. Not anything. I mean, you'd have to be really effen blind to miss the fact that Mom loved him. God, she did. I mean, if he didn't get that I loved him too, well, that was something else. You know, I wasn't exactly good at communicating stuff like that. I didn't give a border rat's ass if my brother hurt me. I could take it. But Mom? She loved him. God, that woman loved him. And didn't that matter to him? Why didn't it matter? I wanted to let out a whole string of curse words. Believe me, I know some. In English and Spanish—but I didn't say anything. Nope. Not a thing. Didn't say anything. I just held my mom until she stopped crying.

And then my Tía Lisa said, "Just wait till I get ahold of that selfish little—" She stopped herself. She looked right at me. "Who does he hang out with?"

"He doesn't tell me. He likes to keep his life a secret from us."

"It means he's up to no good. That's what that means."

"Well," I said, "we all keep secrets."

My Tía Lisa looked right at me. "Bullshit. Stop defending him." And then she got this look on her face, like she was getting this idea in her head. "What about your friend Lalo?"

"What about him?"

"He's like Tito. He's always up to no good, just like your brother. Call him. Tell him to sniff around. He's got a nose for trouble. I bet he can find something out."

"Maybe."

I think there was something called doubt in my voice.

Tía Lisa didn't give an old shoelace about my doubt. "Call him. Call him right now." She could be pushy, my Tía Lisa. My Tío Lencho said my Tía Lisa was a Mexican Mae West. I didn't know who Mae West was, but I got the idea she was a really pushy lady. And my Tía Lisa, when she decided to get pushy, well, the best thing you could do was just let yourself be pushed.

So, I took the phone into my room and called him. It was

early—not too early. But early. His mom answered the phone.

"Hello," I said, "this is Ram. Could I speak to Lalo?"

His mother liked me. "How are you, *mijito*?" she says real nice. Not that she was really a very nice person. She wasn't. She hung out in bars on Alameda and was always getting arrested, and every time she got good and drunk, she went out into the front yard and yelled at all the neighbors and said ugly things about one of the boys that lived down the street because he was gay and she didn't like *maricones*, and Lalo, who really is a quiet and shy guy, always had to drag her inside, and she would yell at him and berate him and tell him he was a good-for-nothing, brainless idiot, and, well, the poor guy just wanted to die. Drama City. I mean that lady put the d-r-a-m in Drama. Anyway, she went and got Lalo, and then I heard his voice on the phone.

"Hey, Lalo," I said.

"What's up, *ese*?"

"Tito didn't come home last night. We're looking for him. You seen him?"

"Nah, not for a couple a days."

"Who's he hanging with these days?"

"Some guy."

"What's his name, Lalo?"

"Jeremy."

"Jeremy?"

"Jeremy Chávez."

"Don't know 'im."

"Bad news, that guy."

If even Lalo thought he was bad news, that guy must have been a piece of work. It scared me to think that Tito was hanging out with guys like that. "Where does he live?"

"He lives on that street in back of Our Lady of the Light. I forget the name of the street."

"I know the street. You know which house?"

"Yeah."

"You know his phone number?"

"Doesn't have a phone. They're always yanking it out, you know, because his mother doesn't pay the bills, you know, crap like that."

"You want to show me where he lives?"

"We got school."

"We have time before school. It's only seven o'clock."

"Seven o'clock? Dude, why you calling me so early?"

Sometimes that Lalo, I swear. "Look," I said. "Will you show me where Jeremy lives?"

"Yeah, sure. I'll show you."

Them
(Lalo and Tito and Jeremy)

Lalo showed up at my door about fifteen minutes later. I'd taken a quick shower and my hair was still wet when I answered the door—but I'd gelled it up and Tía Lisa said I looked very hip. She likes to say hip. Don't know why. So Lalo gave me a chin up, and I gave him a chin up too. Those chin up things. They're like shaking hands.

And my mom hugs Lalo, and then I think Lalo's gonna start crying because no one ever hugs him. And then my Tía Lisa hugs him—and then he does start crying. And I'm wondering what the hell is going on—except that I know that my mom and Tía Lisa are really upset and then I think I never really know what Lalo's gonna say and how he's gonna act, so I figure everything is kind of normal. I mean, what's normal?

And then my mom said, "I want to go with you—to where Jeremy lives."

And I told my mom, "I don't think that's a good idea. He's probably not there anyway."

And then my Tía Lisa handed me her cell phone and said, "As soon as you find anything out, you call home."

She had this look on her face. So I nodded, took the phone and promised to call her as soon as we hit Jeremy's house. I mean, I didn't think we were gonna find Tito at Jeremy's house. What were the odds? "I promise," I said.

"How long will it take you to walk to Jeremy's house?"

"About ten minutes," Lalo said.

My Tía Lisa looked at me and said, "If you don't call us back in fifteen minutes, I'm going to find you and—" She stopped and shook her head. "I'm going to find you and you're going to be seriously sorry that you didn't call back. You hear me? *¿Me entiendes?*"

I nodded.

I kissed my mom. She likes when I do that. Lalo and I took off—but not before my Mom handed me and Lalo a scrambled egg-and-chorizo burrito. My mom, when she gets nervous, she makes things to eat. When my Uncle Ricardo was sick in the hospital, she stayed up all night and made bizcochos and oatmeal cookies. I mean, the kitchen was flooded with cookies. She made me take some to school and give them out. I wanted to die. But Alejandra helped me out, and we got rid of them in less than an hour. And all day long everybody kept coming up to me and telling me my mom made the best damn cookies in all of Dizzy Land. So it all turned out cool. I mean, look, everyone deals with stress in different ways. Think about it. My mom, she goes straight for the food thing. Me, I head for a book. And Tito, he went for all the crap that was bad for him— like drugs.

So, as we're walking along to Jeremy's house, Lalo asked me if I was going to eat my burrito. I shrugged. "Well, look, I'm not really hungry."

"Good," he said. And he grabbed my burrito, unwrapped it from the foil, and ate it in three bites.

"Shit," I said, "don't they feed you at your house?" And then I thought it was a mean thing to say, because I knew his mom wasn't into cooking and just didn't give an achin' elbow for Lalo.

Lalo laughed. "Hell no, they don't feed me," he said.

I felt bad. Poor guy. Sometimes I should learn just to keep my mouth shut.

"Your mom," he said, "she makes some fuckin' good burritos."

I don't think my mom would've appreciated the F word associated with her burritos. I nodded. "Yeah."

And then he pointed at a house two houses from where we were standing. "That's the house," he said. "That's Jeremy's house."

We walked up to the house. And then both of us stood there. Like idiots.

And then Lalo said, "No cars."

I nodded and repeated, "No cars."

The yard was all weeds and trash and the house looked even trashier than the yard—like nobody even lived there. "Sure this is the house?" I asked.

Lalo nodded. "You know, I don't think his parents are really into the house thing. I mean, Jeremy's dad isn't exactly a fucking gardener."

That Lalo, I mean, what could I say? I kinda wanted to laugh but I still had that I-might-throw-up feeling in my gut. I remembered what Alejandra said about Lalo: "That guy—he's a master of the obvious." Alejandra always said things like that. She and Lalo hated each other. I looked at the house. "And you're sure somebody lives here?"

Lalo just gave me a look, like maybe I just wasn't getting it. "Look, like I said, it's not that nobody lives here—it's that nobody cares."

"Guess not." I looked at Lalo and shrugged. I mean even Lalo's mother made sure her house looked decent. The one thing Lalo's mother could do really well was keep a nice lawn. Her fingernails were always painted real nice and her lawn was always weedless.

So there we were, me and Lalo, standing there in front of a house that was all trashed out. We both just kept looking at the house, and after a while Lalo walked up to the front door and started pounding on it as if he wanted to knock the damn thing down. And then we waited.

Then nothing.

Then Lalo pounded the door again.

"Knock it off," I said. "No one's gonna answer."

Then Lalo pointed his chin toward the front window. "The curtain's open." He walked toward it, then pressed his head into the window. He stood there looking in for a long time, and then he looked at me and said, "You better call your Tía Lisa."

"What?" I said.

"I said you better fucking call your mom and your Tía Lisa."

I didn't like the sound of his voice or the look on his face.

"Look, Ram, you better call your Tía Lisa. And then I think we should call 911."

"What?"

I moved toward the window.

"Don't! Ram!" And then he tried to push me away.

I pushed him back, and I looked at him like he better not mess with me. And then I pressed my face against the window. And then I saw them. Jeremy and my brother. And they were lying there on the living room carpet. They were just lying there. And I thought, *They're dead.*

Him and Her and Her
(Tito and Mom and Tía Lisa)

It only took a few minutes before my mom and Tía Lisa showed up. We all kept banging on the door, hoping to wake them up. I guess that was what we were trying to do. One of the neighbors came out of the house. "No one's ever home," he said. "Can't you tell?" He just kept walking toward his car and drove away.

My Tía Lisa looked at my mother. "I'm going to break that window." Even though she was whispering, her voice sounded like a closed fist about to hit someone.

My mom looked at her, not knowing what to do. She had this look of panic on her face.

"I'll break it," I said. I don't know why I said it. Sometimes *saying* something feels like *doing* something.

"The ambulance will be here soon," my mom said. "They'll know what to do." She tried to make herself calm, but she didn't sound calm, she sounded hollow and distant, and I could see she was trembling. She put her hand on my chest as if she was trying to keep me from breaking the window.

I wanted to tell her that I really wasn't going to do it.

That's when the ambulance showed up. The ambulance and a cop car.

Two cops and two guys from the ambulance moved toward us. Lalo pointed toward the window. They all peeked inside and motioned for us to move away. "I want you good people over there on the sidewalk."

Tía Lisa began shouting at the cop. "That's my nephew in there!" she yelled.

My mother grabbed her arm and pulled her away. I gave my Tía Lisa a look, you know, a look that said *Mom doesn't need this*. One of the policemen was talking to someone on a cell phone—then he did something to the lock on the door and they all rushed in.

I was watching my mom. She went white. I thought she was going to lose it or faint, and all I could think of was that she was like that rock that was sinking into the swallowing water. So I decided just to hold her and then I could feel her sobbing into me.

That's all I remember.

As my brother and Jeremy were being put into the ambulance, a cop came up to us and he starts asking questions: Who are we? What are we doing there? Who called 911?

My Tía Lisa gave the cop a look and gave him all the information he needed—my brother's name, Jeremy's name, his parents' names. "I'm the one who called 911," I said. He looked at me. "He's my brother," I said. "Tito Lopez—the dark one." That's what I said. The policeman wanted to know where the occupants of the house were. Tía Lisa shrugged. "I'm not the cop, you are." Man, my Tía Lisa, she had this thing against cops. Later I found out she'd almost married one and after that, she just figured they were all alike—or something like that. Anyway, the policeman started to say something to my Tía Lisa, then just shook his head. He wrote something down on his pad, shook his head again, and looked at my mother. "Mrs. Lopez?"

My mother nodded.

"Well, they're not dead, but these boys, they've been doing some serious drugs." He might have said heroin—I don't remember. Or maybe he said cocaine. I don't know. He did mention something, but it was as if I couldn't hear. It was weird. I couldn't figure out what was wrong with me, but I felt strange and sick and inanimate. Inanimate. That was one of

Alejandra's favorite words. She said a lot of guys' hearts were inanimate. She loved saying that. Maybe she was right. Maybe my heart had become inanimate. Maybe that was just another way of saying "numb."

We followed the ambulance and the police to Thomason. The hospital wasn't far, not even five minutes. Lalo and I waited in the emergency room. My mom and Tía Lisa went in—then came back out after ten minutes. I don't know, maybe it was longer, maybe it was less. I was a little freaked out. Freaked out—that's not really an expression I use, that's a Tito expression. He loved that expression. He said I was always freaking out about everything. He said I was too stiff. Well, I guess I was stiff compared to Tito. You know, Tito, his problem was that he was too loose. You know, like a loose dog that lives out on the streets. Loose dogs aren't happy. They survive for a while, but they always wind up getting killed.

When my mom and Tía Lisa came out, they didn't say very much. I looked at them and wanted to ask something, but I didn't. They would tell me what I needed to know. Finally, my mom says, "Your brother, he might not make it. And if he does make it, well, he may not—" She stopped and broke down crying.

I was just holding and holding her. And I never wanted to let her go. And I wanted to make everything right, but that wasn't gonna happen. What could I make right? I don't know how long she cried. "I should've done something." She kept saying that in between all her sobs.

After a while, a nurse came in. She knew my mom. Nurses, you know, they all know each other. "Rita, you can come in and sit with him if you want."

She nodded and followed the nurse. She looked back at me and smiled. I don't know why she did that. I smiled back.

I didn't know I was crying. And then I heard a sad moaning. After a while, I realized that the moaning was coming from me. Lalo kept patting my shoulder. Then Tía Lisa put her hand under my chin and held it up and said, "You're a beautiful, beautiful boy." And I could see that she was crying too.

"What are we gonna do?" I said.

"I don't know. We're going to wait. And whatever happens, we're going to love your mother—and we're going to make sure she survives."

I nodded. "What if he dies?"

"He might. And if he lives, he might be damaged. Brain-damaged—and damaged in some other serious ways. You understand that?"

"Yes."

"Well, we'll just have to see."

She was tough and practical, my Tía Lisa. And I wanted to say something—I don't know what. Maybe I just wanted to tell her that I was glad she was there, that I was glad she was my aunt. But I didn't say anything. I found myself squeezing her hand.

"You have to be strong," she said. She was squeezing my hand just like I was squeezing hers.

I nodded. "I can be strong."

I could see the tears coming down her face. "Tito—he thinks he's strong. He thinks boys like you are weak. But he's wrong. You're the strong one. You're the one who's strong enough to make a place for yourself in this mean, mean world. And you'll do it too. But Tito, all he can do is run away. He can't face things. He's like your father. He just can't face things."

I didn't say anything.

The rest of the morning, all I could think of were her

words. *He's like your father. He just can't face things*. I didn't want to believe her. I mean, I think she was right about Tito. But I didn't want to think of my father as the kind of man who couldn't face things. I mean, that's what we're supposed to do in life, face things. Isn't that what we're supposed to do? I didn't want to picture my dad as the kind of guy who just ran away from things. But I knew she was right. I mean, hadn't the guy run away from us? From my mom? From me and Tito?

The thing about my Tía Lisa is that she studied people. She knew how people operated. She was a real expert. She didn't bullshit herself and she didn't bullshit others, either. But it really made me sad, what she'd said about my brother and my father. Sometimes the truth can make you really, really sad.

And then I thought about him, my dad, and I wondered if maybe we shouldn't tell him about Tito.

If he knew, wouldn't he come? Wouldn't he come and see Tito?

Tito was in the ICU. My mom was by his side. I pictured them together most of the day as I paced the ER waiting room, my brother with tubes in him like I'd seen in the movies. I tried to get lost in the dramas going on around me—the woman who kept telling her husband that she knew something was going to go wrong with their baby, the old man who smelled of whiskey and kept muttering cuss words to himself and kept walking outside to smoke cigarettes. The woman holding her little boy in her lap, the little boy looking pale and listless, a strange and dull look in his eyes.

Lalo went to school. My Tía Lisa took him, so she could explain why he was late. She was going tell the principal, Mrs. Casillas, that I would be out the rest of the day. My Tía Lisa, she took of charge of things, knew exactly what had to get taken care of—and then just took care of it. She wasn't the kind to run away from things. Not her.

You know, I suddenly thought about Jeremy Chávez. And I wondered if he was doing all right. So I walked up to the receptionist at the desk and asked about him.

"Are you a relative?" she asked.

"No," I said. "He and my brother, well, see, the ambulance brought them. And I was just wondering."

She smiled at me. She had that mother look on her face, like maybe I reminded her of her son or her nephew or someone she really loved. "I'm sorry, *mi'jo*," she said. "I can't give you any information."

"Well, is his mother here? Can you tell me that?"

She smiled—and shrugged.

"Look, can you just tell his mother I want to talk to her—just so I can ask her how he's doing."

She looked at me.

I just kept looking at her. I think she was afraid I was going to cry. Which, of course, I wasn't.

"Just a minute," she said. She got up from her desk and went into the ER. She came back a minute or two later.

"No one's come to see him," she said. She looked sad.

That made me sad too. I mean, I really hated mothers and fathers who just kind of walked away from their kids. The world was full of parents like that. Their kids were just too much damn trouble. So why'd they have them? I thought of my dad and that got me mad at myself for thinking bad things about him. I mean, I didn't really know him, did I? He might have reasons for staying away. Good reasons. How did I know?

I wandered outside. It was a nice day. October days were always nice, cool and sunny and it almost seemed like it was going to rain. That's how the air smelled. I don't know why, but I walked toward Chico's Tacos even though I wasn't hungry. Maybe I thought it was better to watch the people at Chico's Tacos than to watch the people in the ER waiting room. The people in the ER waiting room seemed like they were about to break. Who wanted to watch that? It was like they were sitting at the edge of the world. They were waiting to fall off. They were waiting for someone to catch them.

But the people at Chico's Tacos—they were happy. They were ordering their favorite foods—and even as they waited in line, they talked and laughed and it almost seemed like they were at a party. That's what I wanted. I wanted to be at a party. Sometimes I wanted to live in a world where there was nothing but parties. I mean, why would that be so bad? Tía Lisa, she knew about parties, she knew about having a good time. But she also knew about the things that needed to get done in order to keep on going. I wondered what kind of things Tía Lisa would write in her notebook if she kept one. I wondered what kind of things my mom would write. I guess we all wrote things in our notebooks. All of us—it's just that we kept our notebooks in our heads. Maybe we all needed to erase some of the things we wrote there. I know I needed to do that. I did.

I thought about my mom. I wondered if she was like the other people in the ER waiting room. Was she sitting at the edge of the world? Was she waiting for someone to catch her? Maybe that's what Tía Lisa meant by being strong. It was our job to catch her, to make sure she didn't fall off the world.

Him
(Jake)

I bought myself an order of Chico's Tacos—then felt bad for being so selfish. I hadn't thought enough to buy something for my mom or Tía Lisa. I walked across the street to the cemetery and found a place to sit among all the graves. I ate my tacos and tried not to think about anything, but really I wasn't sure why I'd bought tacos because I just wasn't in the mood. I wasn't in the mood for anything.

That's when I noticed him sitting there. Not too far away from me. Him. Jake.

He waved.

I waved back.

He lit a cigarette. "Want one?" he asked.

"Nah," I said. "Not now." I didn't want him to know I didn't smoke.

"You don't smoke?"

I knew he was going to ask me that. "I'm just not in the mood." It wasn't a lie, not exactly.

He came up to me and lit his cigarette. I had to admit, he looked like a real expert when it came to the way he handled a cigarette. "No school today?" he asked.

"Not for me," I said. I wasn't about to tell him about my brother. None of his business. "You?" I said.

"Me? Lunch break. I have to be back in about ten minutes." He looked at his watch. "You come here a lot?"

"Not a lot. Sometimes."

"You live around here, don't you?"

"Yeah," I said. *And you don't.* That's what I wanted to say. "Yeah," I said again.

"It's like a park," he said. "I like cemeteries."

I liked them too. I didn't know there were other people in the world who were like me. It was strange to think that Jake might be something like me. I mean, I don't know, it was just strange. And I didn't want him to be like me. I didn't.

"Cemeteries," I said, "they're quiet. The effen world's too noisy."

He smiled. "Yeah."

I didn't know what to say to him, so I just asked him about school. "So are you gonna be a doctor?"

"No. I don't think so. This magnet school thing is Sally's idea."

"Sally?"

"She's my mom. Well, her name's not really Sally, but I call her that sometimes. Makes her mad." He sort of laughed. He had kind of a sad laugh. He looked at me. "What are you gonna do after high school?"

"Live," I said. I didn't say that to be cool. It's just that I was thinking about Tito. And I just thought living was a good idea. And that's what I wanted most right then—to just live.

"But you gotta work." Then he laughed. Jake was weird. He shook his head. "Sorry. That's just what my stepdad always says. 'You gotta work.'"

I nodded. "You have a job?"

"School. That's supposed to be my job."

Only rich people said crap like that. "I work at Whataburger," I said. I don't know why I told him that. Maybe I just needed him to know that some people actually had to work—and not because they wanted to.

"Are they hiring?"

What kind of thing was that to say? I wanted to tell him to screw himself. "Nope," I said.

We sort of nodded at each other. I think I sort of smiled at him—but I don't think it was that nice of a smile. "I gotta go," I said.

He waved.

I waved back.

As I was walking away, I heard him say, "I want you to come to my party."

I shrugged. "Don't know where you live."

"You have e-mail?"

I nodded.

He was waiting for me to give him my e-mail address. People have a certain look when they're waiting for you to give them information. For a minute, I thought about giving him a fake address. What the hell. He could e-mail if he wanted to. I didn't have to answer back. Nope, I didn't. So I went ahead and gave the guy my e-mail address: "Borderchango@elp.tx.com."

He smiled. "*Chango*? Doesn't that mean monkey?"

"Yup," I said.

"I like it," he said. "I'll send you an e-mail."

That's all I needed, a pen pal from the Oh-Wow West Side. I nodded, then walked across the street, waited in line, and ordered two hamburgers at Chico's—one for my mom and one for my Tía Lisa. You wouldn't think a taco joint made good hamburgers, but that wasn't true. Chico's had really good burgers—almost as good as Whataburger's. Almost.

When I was standing there—waiting—I kept thinking about parties. Why did people like them? Why did people throw them? I decided I didn't know a damn thing about parties. Maybe the only party I knew anything about was the long line I was standing in at Chico's Tacos. I mean, everybody was talking to everyone and it didn't seem to matter that they didn't know each other. You know, they just talked about nothing. I guess if you were standing in line with someone at Chico's Tacos, at least you knew you were hanging out with your own kind. Alejandra always lectured me about that all the time. "Sticking with your own kind is so provincial." Alejandra, I swear, she always talked like the last book she read.

You know, she has this dog named Sofie, and that dog is part pit bull and part beagle and part Labrador. She's actually a nice dog, really friendly and smart and really a good-looking dog. She's all white with brown circles around her eyes, and really, she's a very cool dog. And Alejandra, she loves that dog. She saved it from death row at the pound. And she said to me: "If everybody stuck to their own kind then Sofie wouldn't exist. Even a dog knows enough not to be so provincial." That is what passes for logic in Alejandra's world. Sometimes she leaves me speechless.

And you know something else, Alejandra's as provincial as anybody else. If she didn't want to date her own kind, then why the hell was she always trying to get me to be her boyfriend? I mean, why wasn't she out trying to date a guy like Jake? I mean, there was a guy who knew something about parties. He was probably fun. I mean, I'm not really a fun kind of guy.

When my order of hamburgers was up, I took the bag and started walking back to the hospital. I kept trying not to think about Tito. I kept thinking that maybe he would be all right, that he would come back as his old self—not that his old self had been so great. But still, I mean, he would be Tito. He would be my brother. And maybe, after all of this, he would change, and me and him, we could be brothers—real brothers, and we would love each other like brothers were supposed to love each other, you know, like really good friends. And my mom wouldn't be worried about him, and there could be more parties in her life. Maybe I could learn about parties and what they were all about.

I walked real slow.

I didn't want to get back to the hospital. I didn't want to face it.

Maybe there was something in me that was like my father.

Her
(Mom)

When I got back, my Tía Lisa was sitting in the ER waiting room trying to calm down some woman who looked like she was falling apart. The woman's hair was all stringy and oily and she had circles under her eyes and she was all beat up, a fat lip and bruises on her arms, and she was saying she shouldn't have come. "Maybe I'll just go back home," she said.

My Tía Lisa grabbed her by the arm and sat her back down. She saw me and noticed I had a bag in my hand.

"Hamburgers," I said.

She grabbed the bag from me and handed one of the hamburgers to the lady and said, "Here. Eat this. Food is good for you when you're falling apart. Believe me, I know."

She looked at me. The look was almost like a wink.

The lady took the hamburger and stared at it.

"Eat," my Tía Lisa said. She took the other hamburger out of the bag and bit into it. She was hungry. God, she was really hungry. "You know," she said as she gulped down a bite, "it's funny. But Mexicans make the best hamburgers. I swear they do."

The lady stared at the hamburger and took a bite—then another. She nodded. "It's true." And then they both broke out laughing.

And when they stopped, my Tía Lisa looked right at that lady and said, "And after the doctor checks you out, you're going to make out a police report and press charges on that creep you call a husband. You understand me?" My Tía Lisa, she started in on that guy like she was in a cussing contest. I guess she knew the guy. "He's been a *carbón* all his life—and that's all he'll ever be."

The woman nodded. "Okay," she said.

Man, that woman, she had a black eye and had bruises everywhere and she kept holding her ribs.

My Tía Lisa sort of smiled at me. "You know, you can go and see him." She looked toward the door.

I didn't want to. I didn't. But I knew I had to go in sooner or later—so I just nodded. She put her hamburger back in the bag and set it on the seat next to her. She took me by the arm and led me to the window. "I know it's hard," she whispered. "It's not looking good for your brother. You can cry. It's okay." She combed my hair with her fingers. "You have such beautiful hair." She kissed me. "You can cry," she said again. "I did. I mean, what else is there to do but cry. Cry. And then be strong." She talked to the nurse behind the desk. The nurse smiled at me and led me in to see Tito.

I stared at the tube down his throat and at the monitors. Not that it did any good to stare at monitors when you didn't know what the monitors meant. "They resuscitated him," my mother whispered. "He was gone. They brought him back."

I wanted to ask if he was really back.

"They're not sure if—" She smiled at me. "Are you okay?"

"Yes," I whispered. "I'm fine."

"They're bringing in a neurologist—to do some tests."

I nodded. I don't know why, but I reached over and took my brother's hand. I sort of rubbed it—then squeezed it. His hand was so warm. Really warm, and it was big, which surprised me. His hands were bigger than mine. And even though there was all these machines around him and this tube down his throat and an IV and all of that stuff, when I looked at him, I thought he looked perfect. My little brother was handsome. I knew that. I mean, he was much more handsome than me.

And I don't know why, but I just started talking to him. "Look," I said, "I know you and I didn't always, you know, get along. And I wasn't patient enough. But, look, you have to come back. I'm waiting for you. So you just have to come back." I didn't mean to cry, but that's what I was doing and I hated myself because it wasn't helping my mother and I wasn't being strong and I just didn't get what my Tía Lisa had said to me, how I could cry but how I had to be strong. I just didn't get it. And I just couldn't keep myself from talking to him— even though I hardly ever talked to him even though we shared the same room. But I just kept talking. "And you know, I read what you wrote in your notebook. I know I shouldn't have read it, and I'm sorry, but Tito, the world isn't such a bad place, it's not. Just come back and I'll show you it's not such a bad place. I didn't do my job, Tito. I didn't. I'm sorry." And then I couldn't talk anymore because I was crying so much. And then I felt my mom's hand on my back. And she whispered to me, and she said, "He can hear you." That's what she said. "He can hear you."

After a while, I stopped crying. And then my Mom whispered, "It's not your fault." I nodded.

She took my face and held it between her hands. They were so warm, her hands. And her eyes were so soft and I wondered why my dad left her, because I knew right then that she was the kindest woman in the whole world. She just looked at me. "You can't control everything in this world, *amor*, and your brother is one of those things." And then she said, very, very firmly, *"This is not your fault."*

I nodded.

"Say you believe me."

"I believe you." I didn't—but I said it anyway.

She smiled at me and I smiled back.

After a while, I told my mom she should go and walk around or eat something. "I bought you a hamburger, but Tía Lisa gave it to some woman in the waiting room whose husband hit her." I smiled at my mother. "Tía Lisa should have been a social worker." That made my mother laugh, and I was glad that she could still laugh because it meant she wasn't breaking.

As she was walking out, I said, "Can you see if Jeremy's okay?"

She nodded.

I stayed with my brother, just me and him. I don't know how long I was there, but I started telling him about Pip, you know, the guy in *Great Expectations*. I always thought that Tito would have liked that book, so I started telling him the story, about how he lived with his sister who raised him by hand and I explained what that meant and how his sister was a really strict and mean and terrible person but how his brother-in-law Joe was a very kind man. And then I stopped and said, "Men can be kind, you know? They can be."

That's when I noticed my mom was back in the room. I looked up at her and shrugged. "I was just telling him about Pip," I said.

My mother nodded. She looked at me and I thought she was going to start crying—but she didn't. "I've never read that novel," she said.

"I have a copy."

She nodded. "Lend it to me?"

"Sure," I said.

And then she said, "What angel left you at my door?"

I thought it was a really great thing to say. Probably the greatest thing anyone ever said to me. "No angels in Dizzy Land," I said.

We both laughed. It was the second time that day that I'd seen her laugh. That was strange, but it made me happy—even though this whole thing with Tito was making us sad as hell. I wanted to tell her that she needed to laugh more. And me too. I needed to laugh more too.

It would be so effen great if the whole world laughed more—the whole world. I don't mean the kind of laughing that's putting someone down. I mean the kind of laughing that means you've just discovered something really beautiful.

Me, Jake Upthegrove
(I'm Back)

Sally says, "Jake, the world is your oyster. David and I have given you everything you want, and all you do is sit around and think of ways to be sarcastic." See, that's the problem. Sally thinks the world belongs to her and that she can give it to anybody she pleases. Can you dig it? Look, this is the thing: The world doesn't belong to me or Sally or David or to my ersatz father, Upthegrove. The world belongs to everyone. Doesn't it? Well, doesn't it?

Him
(*Him* Keeps Being Me)

The night Sally and I got into a fight, I made a list of all the expressions for anger that I could think of—and then I used each one in a sentence or wrote some kind of commentary. Sally says I'm good at that sort of stuff, you know, editorializing about everything. She's not wrong. But when she says things like that, she makes me feel shallow. Shallow is not a word I want to wear. Sometimes I think that when life is easy for you, it affects the way you think. And the problem with Sally is that she thinks that she's supposed to make life easy for me.

But I don't want life to be easy. I just want life to be interesting.

Sometimes Sally tells me I make life too hard. "It's not supposed to be hard," she says. Look, this is the deal for me: I don't care about hard and I don't care about easy. What I care about is feeling something. Feeling something in my brain. Feeling something in my heart. You know, everyone's always asking, "So what do you want from life, Jacob?" The truth is I don't have an answer to that question. But it's gotta be something more than making money and living in a nice house. Don't get me wrong. I'm not against making money. And I'm not against living in a nice house. I'm just against making that some kind of goal. Screw that goal.

So maybe that's why I sit around and do strange things like make lists about the different kinds of words for anger. Well, hell, it is a strange thing to do. But what's so wrong about writing things down? You can dig that, can't you? When you write things down, it feels like you can stare at the words and they become mirrors—and you can see yourself.

Everyone needs to see themselves.

Everyone. Even me. And that's the good news and that's the bad news. A mirror shows you who you are. And you know something? We don't always want to know who we are. But, as the Anger Management Lady used to like to say: "Deal with it." So this is the list I came up with:

Sore. I was sore at Sally for an entire year. You know, my heart was actually sore. It's a muscle, you know, the heart, a real muscle. And when it gets sore, it doesn't move quite right.

Out of joint. I am permanently out of joint with Upthegrove, my father. And it's not just my nose that's out of joint, it's my whole body.

Pissed off. I am not supposed to say, "I'm really pissed off" around Sally. She says that expression is preadolescent and shows a preoccupation with bodily functions common to children who have just been diaper-trained.

P.O.'d. If I tell Sally I'm P.O.'d, she only makes a face but doesn't lecture me—even though she knows I'm really saying that I'm pissed off.

Angry. "I am really angry" is a dull way to express what's going on inside you when there are explosions going on inside your body. Those explosions, they're like mines set up all over the place, and people come along and trip on them, and they go off. And, well, it's a mess. A bloody mess.

Enraged. I am really enraged by what is happening in the world. Okay, I'm making myself sound really over-the-top altruistic. But the truth is, *I am really enraged* by what is happening in the world that I inherited from the adults around me. Sally calls it an oyster. I call it a disaster. Okay, put the F-word in front of disaster. That's how I see it.

Meltdown. My patience-control mechanisms are having a meltdown (on account of the fact that everything around me is nothing but chaos). You think that because our house is so neat and clean all the time that everything is just fine? Well, the only reason it's been so neat was because of Rosie. And now she's gone.

Disappointed. The most passive-aggressive way of telling someone that you want to kill them but want to maintain your sense of virtuous decorum and self-control is to tell someone that you are "disappointed." Sally loves this expression. Yes, yes, I know I told the Anger Management Lady that I wasn't really angry, that I was disappointed in people. Well, I was just being passive-aggressive, too. See, Sally passed that gene on to me.

Spittin' Mad. I was so mad at Tom that it made me want to spit, which made me spittin' mad, which in turn made me break his nose. Well, we know where this got me.

Burns my Ass. Upthegrove makes me so mad that it burns my ass and when my ass is burnt, I can't even sit down, which makes me even madder because I can't even sit down and smoke a cigarette.

Of course, I could have gone on all night, but I stopped. I mean, I had a list of words that I was going to use in a sentence or comment upon, words like "galled," "boiling mad," "cross," "exploding," "rankled," "peeved," "hacks me off," "furious," "ruffled," "annoyed," "steamed," and "irritated."

You know, I think the Anger Management Lady would have approved of me making a list. The Anger Management Lady was really into lists. I mean, the one thing about lists is that you don't hit anyone while you're doing it. This is good. This is excellent.

Him
(*Him* Is still Me and He's still Here)

I was more than a little bit out of joint. Again. Look, just when I had finally decided to get rid of all my material possessions, I was confronted with a change of plan. I mean, look, I've always felt like I was walking around this world with this really big backpack. I just have way too much stuff. You know, at seventeen, I was all hunched over. And I just wanted to dump everything. You know, walk around without all that weight. Walk straight instead of walking like Cro-Magnon man. Be free. That would be so cool. Very cool.

Everyone has to evolve. I was evolving. Look, let's not get into theories of evolution. Sally thinks "Darwin" is a bad word. She would rather I use the F-word.

See, now that Sally was making all nice to me, well, it threw me. I mean you can dig that, can't you? Sally, I think she stays up at night thinking of new and different ways to destroy me. She sets up little bombs all over the place. I have to be careful where I step.

So just when I decide something, she's there, making me feel like I'm a completely spoiled and selfish human being. Not that I'm not those things—of course I am. But whose fault is that? Sally raised me to think I was the center of the universe (to compensate for Upthegrove, I think). And then when I behave like *I am* the center of the universe, she doesn't like it. Sometimes I feel like I'm driving down the road full speed and there she is—my mother—smiling at me. In the middle of the road. I mean, what am I going to do? Run her over? Sure.

I stayed up most of the night thinking.

I mean, maybe I was just playing around when it came to thinking I was going to give up all my worldly goods. I don't mean I was playing around with my mom or anybody else. I was playing around with myself—and I was trying not to notice. Who was I kidding? Who did I think I was going to turn into—St. Francis? I mean, giving my car away? Giving away everything I had? I mean, my evaluation that I had too many things wasn't wrong. *I did have too many things.* That was absolutely true. And it was also absolutely true that I was indifferent to most of those things. I didn't care—not really—about most of the things I had. I liked the car, the iPod (didn't need two), and my laptop. Clothes, well, I never was much for clothes. I preferred to go barefoot and wore shoes only because Sally made me. I liked my worn-out clothes the best. Old T-shirts, you know, they get softer and softer and they feel good. I loved old T-shirts. And Sally, she was always buying me more clothes and stuffing them in my closet and waiting for me to thank her for the new shirt or the new pair of pants. And my old T-shirts, well, she was always rifling through my drawers and making them all disappear.

She particularly liked confiscating my T-shirts with political messages. My mom, she really objected to me being a political animal. But what happens if you were born with a mind? Why is thinking about shopping better than thinking about the state of the world you live in? Tell me that. She says I'm too young to go around analyzing how the world is run. And one day, when I was going on and on about global warming, she actually said, "It's none of your business, Jacob." She actually said that. Are you getting to the point where you understand where I get all this attitude? Are you getting this? Anyway, one day, I came home wearing a Che Guevara T-shirt. "Where do you get these things?" she asked. "You don't even know what Che Guevara stood for."

Of course, I did. I'd read his biography. Long book. Good

stuff. It was my mom who didn't know. She couldn't even tell you what country he was born in. She wouldn't even be able to tell you why he was killed. But I'm not going there. I'm not. So I looked at Sally and said, "Maybe not. Do you?"

"He was a Communist—that's all I need to know."

"Okay," I said. "Maybe we should move on."

She couldn't have agreed more. "But you still didn't answer my question."

"What question?"

"Where do you buy those offensive T-shirts?"

Offensive? Okay, tell me this. What's more offensive, a Che Guevara T-shirt I bought in an alternative store in South El Paso for twelve bucks and run by a guy who works with the homeless, or a thousand-dollar silk blouse that was made in China my mom bought at a Dallas boutique run by a fashion queen who lives in a gated community? Let's talk offensive. You know, I don't think I was going to get into it with Sally. I just looked at her and said, "We just go to different stores, Mom." That was my answer. I mean, what was the big deal— we were both up to our elbows in capitalism. You know, buying and selling. Admittedly, my T-shirts cost a lot less than her dresses or her shoes—but still, we were operating under the same basic system. I mean, the people who made my T-shirts probably didn't get paid crap for their work. And the people who made my mother's designer dresses didn't get crap for their work, either. So, you see? The same system. I don't know why she couldn't see the bigger picture. She particularly hated my T-shirts that "disparaged the president." Those are her exact words. We, of course, got into an argument. "Let me get this straight," I said. "Your side can disparage my side, but my side can't disparage your side?"

"Your side isn't the president." She actually said that. And, changing her tune, she said, "I didn't know we were on different sides."

"Of course we're on different sides," I said. "Why else are we having this argument?" She confiscated that particular T-shirt anyway.

Not that Sally was winning the T-shirt argument. I mean, I just started keeping my T-shirts in the trunk of the car. When I would leave the house, I just changed into them. You don't always win an argument with words. Sometimes, you win an argument by saying, "Yes, ma'am," and then doing whatever the hell you want to do. The thing is this: I really like winning arguments with words. I like the direct approach. I do. You can dig that, can't you? But, even confrontational people like me have to learn to be circumspect. I love that word, "circumspect." It's a sophisticated, intellectual word for "sneaky." See, the one thing I learned from the Anger Management Lady was that I enjoyed confrontations. At least, that was her theory about me.

But I'd put it another way. See, this is the way I see it. I think all of us have different body temperatures. Look, I know what a doctor will tell you. He'll tell you that all human beings have a body temperature of 98.6 degrees. But that's completely not the case. For example, David and my mom. I mean, their body temperatures are a lot lower than 98.6 degrees, I'll tell you that. I mean, not even global warming has affected the coolness in our household. I don't mean that Mom and David aren't nice people. Crap, I'm the only one who's not nice. But did you ever notice that the word "ice" is part of the word "nice"? You can dig that, can't you? You see where I'm going with this. And me, well, my body temperature is somewhere in the hundreds. See, that's why people think I'm a hothead. You see the connection? But all I'm doing is expressing my body temperature. I, of course, made the mistake of laying out my theory to the Anger Management Lady. She said, on top of everything else, I was going to make a lousy doctor.

"Of course I'll make a lousy doctor," I said. "Most doctors have a body temperature in the low forties."

Anyway, I got away from the subject. Let's see, yes, we were talking about material possessions and clothes. Okay, yeah, well, like I was saying, I was never much of a clothes hound. Guess I didn't get those genes from my mom who has never gone a day in her life without buying something to wear. Can you dig that? What would the economy of El Paso, Texas, do without my mother?

And another thing I got to thinking about: Sally's attitude toward Rosie and Roman. She just didn't give a shit. She didn't. I was at a loss as to what to do about that. But I figured either I was going to spend my whole life trying to change her attitude or I was just going to make sure I overcame my gene pool. Maybe I couldn't do anything about Sally or David. But I could do something about me. God, sometimes I sounded like the Anger Management Lady.

And one more thing I was thinking about that night. A very important thing. I mean, sometimes, when you're thinking about things, you fall on some very important insights. At least, they sound like insights at the time. Look, it was easy for me to get rid of all my material possessions. I mean, what the hell? I didn't pay for any of the shit I had. Not any of it. I didn't pay for my car, didn't pay for my laptop or any of my DVDs or my CDs or, hell, you name it. I didn't pay for anything. Mom and David and Upthegrove paid for all of it. So if I gave it all away, I wasn't really giving away *my* stuff. It was really *their* stuff. So, if I wanted to do without all these things they gave me, then I should just give it back to them. And that's when it hit me. They were buying me. I was theirs. Everything I was and everything I had, was all theirs. And, me too, I was theirs too. They owned me. I hated that thought. Maybe that's why they got so upset with me when I didn't think like them. Maybe they were thinking: You ingrate. I mean, they really destroy me.

But there was one other thing that was mine. My grandmother had left me some money. And it was all mine. Lots of it. I could begin spending once I was eighteen. Elaine and David weren't exactly happy about the whole situation. I guess they figured I'd wind up blowing the entire wad. I'd had about a hundred you-don't-know-anything-about-money lectures since I'd turned sixteen. But the beauty of the whole situation was that they couldn't do a damn thing about my grandmother's will. I could burn the fucking money if I wanted, and Elaine and David wouldn't be able to stop me. I wondered if somehow that money would set me free from Elaine and David. I suspected it wasn't going to be as easy as all that. But, God, I was tired of being owned. God, when that thought entered my head, I just couldn't get rid of it. I found a pack of cigarettes in my drawer and walked into the backyard at two o'clock in the morning and smoked a couple of cigarettes. I hated this new knowledge.

I mean, this is the one thing I never got about that anger management crap. I mean, okay, we can't go around hurting people, hitting them, shooting them, yelling at them. Okay, I get that. But you know, all they ever do is talk about control. No one ever said, "You know, some things *should* make us angry."

See, this is the way I see it. Not all anger is the same. Maybe that's why I made that list. Because there are different kinds of anger. And you know what else—sometimes, anger is a virtue. As long as you're not making someone bleed.

Him
(This Time *Him* Is David)

You know, I have to be honest. I didn't see it coming. I'd like to think I'm the kind of guy who's not easily surprised by the way people behave. I mean, I'm not the type who goes around telling people who've screwed up that they've really disappointed me. As I said, that's a Sally thing, not a Jake thing. Sally loves to say crap like that: "Jacob Upthegrove, you really disappoint me." It's her anger-denial thing. And you know what else, I never want to be as naive as Sally. So, I'm a little cynical—and not without reason. C'mon, the age of innocence is long over.

But, really, this is something *I just didn't see coming*. You know, I feel like I'm back on that freeway and I'm speeding down that road in the middle of the night and I've forgotten to turn on my lights.

It happened the day after Sally told me she wanted to throw me a birthday party, the day after I'd stayed up half the night thinking about my life and the screwed-up world I live in; the night I stayed up making a list of words for anger; the night I decided I wouldn't be making any grand statements about my life by giving up all my worldly goods—the ones I hadn't earned or paid for.

So, it was a Friday afternoon, and I'd forgotten to tell Sally and David that I had the afternoon off—teacher in-service or something like that. Look, I don't pay attention. They say we have the afternoon off, well, we have the afternoon off. Who am I to question authority?

So, there was a group of people that had decided to go hiking up at McKelligon Canyon. And you know, I love the desert and I didn't mind the group too much—a little nerdy, most of them, but nice. You know, the kind of people that try a little too hard, but you know, they were okay. So they invited me to come along. And I say, "Why not?"

So I drive up to McKelligon Canyon to hook up with them, and I park my car where the group's at. I mean, they weren't hard to spot. But as I'm getting out of my car, up ahead in one of the parking spots next to one of those picnic tables, what do I see? I see David's car. David's car, I think. Well, maybe not. But I look closer and I see that *it is* David's car. And he was sitting there on one of those benches making out with some woman. And I thought, *Shit, am I seeing things? David, with another woman?* Don't get me wrong, David's not ugly, not by a long shot. And he keeps in shape, goes to the gym, all that rot. But he's not my idea of an object of desire. And the last thing I think of when I think of David is this horny guy with his tongue down some woman's throat. I mean, what self-respecting woman would let David come on to her like that? I mean, no offense against Sally—but, well, I've always questioned her taste in men.

So, anyway, I keep watching them, and when they come up for air, he smiles at her and they're talking real sweet-like, and now I know for sure that it is David.

A part of me is smiling and another part of me is saying, *Shit, shit, shit, what is Sally supposed to do?* And then I think, *Hell, Sally doesn't even know.* But now I know. So the real question was: *Shit! What am I supposed to do with this new information?* And then it hits me, I should walk right up to that no-good, poor excuse for a stepfather and (apparently) even worse excuse for a husband—I should walk right up to him and do exactly what I did to that Tom guy in ninth grade. I see myself punching David right in the kisser. I see his nose bleeding and me daring him to try something. Anything. But you know, this violence thing, I really have thought about it a lot—and hitting people really isn't a solution, and even though part of me was really way out of joint and mad as hell, well, another part of me was confused as hell.

I sat down on a rock and lit a cigarette. I waved at the group who was sitting around one of those permanent rock-and-cement tables. They all waved back. And then I thought, *Well, what happens next?*

I could have lived without this information.

Too late.

Now I knew.

I finished my cigarette—then joined the group. "Let's climb," I said.

So, we hiked. People talked to me and I was completely numb. I don't remember anything anyone said to me. I think I smiled a lot. I must've smiled a lot—because, afterward, everyone kept telling me that they had no idea I was so quiet and nice. Can you dig that? They destroyed me. I mean, really, there's nothing quiet or nice about me.

When I was driving home, I had to pull over on a side street.

I was trembling, and as I lit a cigarette, I noticed I was crying. Why was I crying? I never liked David. Not really. Why was I crying? You know, I never did like this business of crying. It makes me feel like I'm still a little boy carrying around a stuffed bear named Ned.

Me
(Sometimes I'm Just Me)

When I got home, Sally was waiting for me. "Have you been smoking?"

"Yes," I said.

"You're not old enough to smoke." She didn't say it like she was really mad—just, you know, well, this is the thing—she didn't want to get into an argument with me. But she was just letting me know she was on to me. Fair enough.

"I'll be old enough to smoke on my birthday. I'll be eighteen."

She nodded. "I know how old you'll be. I was there." She smiled. "Cigarettes cause cancer."

"Cars cause globing warming."

She gave me a look. "I don't want you smoking. I'm serious." Her voice was soft. She didn't want to fight.

"It's probably just a phase," I said.

I must have looked sad or something. I must have. Because she didn't argue with me or put me down, she just laughed. And then she kissed me. I let her hold me. I thought of David and that woman groping each other in a public park. I could feel my heart pounding.

"Are you okay, Jake?" She looked at me.

"I think I'm catching something," I said. I knew she'd be able to tell that I'd been crying.

She nodded. She felt my forehead. "You feel warm."

I nodded. "I'll take an aspirin." And then, because I felt bad about David and that woman, I wanted to make her feel good, which was stupid because she didn't know, and I said, "I really *would* like a party."

That made Mom smile. And I was glad I'd said the right thing for once. I mean, I really don't worry about saying the right thing very often—but sometimes I do.

"Make a list," she said. "Make it as big or as small as you like."

"Big," I said. That made her really smile. She was really going to put her whole self into throwing me this party.

Why not? Why the hell not.

She gave me an aspirin and I went to bed. She was so happy. That smile of hers when I said, "Big." That smile. It really destroyed me.

I just wanted to sleep forever. I didn't want to think about anything. I kept seeing Rosie's pleading face in my dream.

I woke up around ten o'clock or so. It's weird, when you fall asleep in the late afternoon and then wake up—you don't know where you are. After I cleared my head, I remembered about David and that woman, and I had this feeling in my gut. I decided that I was just going to lie there for the rest of my life which was really no solution to anything. But, if you just lie in your room, at least you're not out on the street hitting anybody. On the other hand, lying around in your room is really nothing more than running away from your problems. A very Upthegrove solution. My father's son, after all. My old man would have probably approved. But, the thing is, you can't make yourself disappear and you can't make other people disappear either—that's called murder. That's called violence. That's called "life" in the pen. The Anger Management Lady *would not* approve.

So, I dragged my depressed ass out of bed and found myself wandering into the kitchen, rummaging through the refrigerator. Not that I was hungry.

I looked up and saw that David was smiling at me. "Feeling better?"

I shook my head.

"Well, you're probably catching something," he said.

"Yeah," I said. "And Mom?"

"Oh, she had a meeting."

Sally loved meetings. I nodded—then looked right at David. "Did you have a good day?" It sounded weird. I mean, I never asked him stuff like that.

He smiled. "Yeah, I had a good day."

"Worked hard all afternoon?"

He nodded.

"Important case?"

"Yes," he said, "very important."

"Good," I said.

We kept nodding at each other—and I wondered why we were such strangers. *My fault*, that's what I thought. But another part of me thought: *Shit! Why is this my fault? He's Fifty. I'm seventeen. He's having an affair and I'm having a glass of calcium-fortified orange juice.*

And then he said something that really destroyed me. "I have to work late tonight. Will you tell your mother? Tell her she can reach me on the cell."

"Why not at your office?'

He looked at me a little strangely. Yes, there was definitely a look. "The office? My cell? Same difference."

I nodded. "Yeah, same difference."

After David left, I had the urge to follow him. In fact, I got this idea into my head that I'd drive to his office just to see if his car was there. And then I tried to remember the other car, that woman's car, what kind of car? It was red, sporty, maybe a Mustang. Yeah, I think it was a red Mustang. So maybe I'd drive to David's office to see if he really was working—and to see if that red Mustang was parked right alongside his at his office. But then I thought, What am I? A private eye? And what did I want? Sordid details? Did I want to become like those pathetic adults on that show *Cheaters* who humiliated themselves and their lying-good-for-nothing-two-timing spouses on national television? I mean, I already knew. David was cheating on my mother. I saw it. I didn't really need to know any more. I didn't.

Shit. The question was still there, in the pit of my stomach: What was I going to do with this knowledge? Shit, shit, shit, shit, shit.

I left Mom a note that David was working late. I told her I still wasn't feeling well and that I'd gone to bed. Maybe I would be safe in my bedroom. When I was a little kid, I used to think that I was safe in my bedroom. When I was alone. Safe. Alone. I don't know exactly where I got that idea. Maybe it was because I spent most of my years as a boy alone.

You know, I started thinking. When I was a kid, Upthegrove was gone, and for a long time my mother seemed like she was real sad. At night, she used to put me to bed early and tell me to go to sleep like a good boy. I had a bear named Ned and she used to put him in my arms, and me and Ned, we would just hang out. Only Ned wasn't much company and I wasn't good at all that make-believe bullshit. I don't know why. I just wasn't good at it.

One night, I didn't want to be alone and I decided I wanted to talk to my Mom—but when I stood at her door, she was sitting there, howling like a brokenhearted dog. I mean it. I must have been about six or so. I mean, she was howling. It scared me.

So I just walked back into my bedroom. I mean, I thought, well, I might not be feeling so great but I knew I was feeling better than my mother. So, I just took Ned in my hands and told him it was just as well he wasn't a human being. Bears named Ned didn't get married, didn't have kids, and didn't get divorced.

But right after that, my mom met David. And she was gone most nights. I had a sitter. Her name was Lila. I liked her okay. She dressed in black—I liked that. She had a tattoo. I liked that, too. My mom didn't like it, but she lived two doors down and she was the daughter of one of her closest friends—so it was all okay. I really liked her. She was cynical but she was kinda sweet, too. And she was really, really nice to me. And I really liked her name. Lila. It was a cool name. She used to read to me even though I was way too old to be read to. But it wasn't kid stuff. It was stuff she was reading for school. Short stories by famous writers, things like that. And I really liked them. Yeah, Lila was really great. One day, after she read me a story, we got to talking about it. And then it happened. I told her I loved her. I didn't even know I was going to say that.

She looked at me and smiled. "I love you, too," she said.

"Do you mean that?"

"Of course I do."

You know, I think she did mean it.

But not much after that, she stopped coming over. Later, I found out she got pregnant. I don't know what happened to her. She got sent away or something. You know, it really destroys me how some people make other people disappear just because they do something that makes them look bad. And then right after that, my mother comes into my room one night and tells me, "David and I are going to be married." She looked really happy and I got the feeling that I was supposed to be really happy too. Only thing was that David was never much interested in me. Maybe my mother noticed. Maybe she didn't. Even Ned was more interested in me than David—and Ned was an inanimate object.

Shit, I hated all this remembering. You can dig that, can't you? I mean, sometimes remembering can really destroy you.

Mom said David was going to save our lives. That's exactly what she said. Sure. And here he was having an affair with some airhead who worked in his office—not that I knew that she worked for him.

Look, this is really going to destroy my mom. She may not like that expression, but that's the only expression worth using here. And that's the sorry truth.

Me, Ramiro
(Getting Sadder. Every Day, Getting Sadder)

There are pieces of the world that are yours. And pieces of the world that will never be yours. And the sad thing is that nobody ever tells you the truth.

Her
(Alejandra)

When I walked back into the ER waiting room, there she was. Alejandra. Talking to my Tía Lisa. As if she belonged there. You know, like my mother's oleander, the one she'd planted outside our front door. That oleander, after a while, it just belonged there. The oleander. Alejandra.

She waved.

I waved back. "I heard about Tito," she said. Lalo. Who else would she have heard it from. That Lalo, I swear, just couldn't keep his mouth shut. As if telling people things would make anyone like him. And, anyway, Alejandra hated Tito. And Tito, hell, he hated her back.

I nodded.

"So how's he doing?"

I shrugged. I felt a little uncomfortable. And mad, too. Mad that she was there. I mean, I'd been crying. And you could tell. And crying in front of your mom was one thing—but standing in front of Alejandra with the signs of leftover tears, well, that was another thing. "They're doing some tests," I said.

Tía Lisa nodded at me. "Look, why don't you get out of here for a while. The neurologist won't get here for another hour or so. Maybe longer. You know how they are." She shrugged. "There's really nothing for you to do here, so why don't you just get out of here. Breathe some air."

"There isn't any air in Dizzy Land," I said.

"Let's take a ride," Alejandra said.

I knew the script. Sure I did. "Sure," I said. I mean, even a wolf is smart enough to know when he's caught in a trap.

Tía Lisa gave me a kiss. "Oh," she said, and then she fished for something in her purse. "I got this for you."

I stared at it as she put it in my hand. I'd always wanted a cell phone. I didn't know what to say. I just kept staring at it.

"You know, it's a good thing to keep in touch. So I thought I might as well get you one."

"But—"

"I got a family plan."

I smiled at her. "What about ugly overages?"

"You watch too much TV, you know that?" She laughed. But the truth was that I hardly watched any television at all. Television bored the hell out of me. She handed me a little book with instructions and she gave me the number to my new cell phone. She gave it to me in front of Alejandra, who never forgot anything. Alejandra was smiling.

I just kept nodding. And then I looked at Tía Lisa. "You know a cell phone can be like a leash."

"Exactly," she said. And then she laughed.

You know she was such a cool cat, my Tía Lisa. The coolest cat I'd ever met. Really. I mean, I think everyone should have an aunt like her. Everyone in the world.

"So how was school?" I didn't know why I asked that. I didn't really care. I mean, who cared about school. Look, even the obnoxious overachievers who cared about school didn't really care. All they cared about was what all this was going to get them. Money. Jobs. You know, like a hamburger with the works. Look, sorry, I work at Whataburger.

Alejandra just shrugged. "I got an A on my essay about Hemingway."

"I thought you said Hemingway was a misogynist."

"That's what my essay was about."

"That's cool."

"You don't think that's cool at all."

"Yes, I do."

"You think it's stupid that I'm a feminist."

"Look," I said, "that feminist stuff, that was really sixties. Retro City."

"Well, look, feminism didn't take. I'm the new wave."

New wave. Sure. Leave it to Alejandra to try and rescue feminism. "Okay," I said.

She shot me a look. "I hate Hemingway and I hate boys."

"Sure you do."

Then she shot me another look. "Some guy asked me out."

I smiled. No, it wasn't a smile—it was a grin. My Tía Lisa had explained the difference. She said a smile was friendly. She said a grin was the same thing as making fun of someone and trying to pretend it was just a smile. And then she said, "Women don't grin. Only men do that."

"You're grinning," Alejandra said.

How do they know these things? "Guess I am." Why deny it? "So who asked you out?"

"Bernie."

"Burn the worm?"

"Yeah. Burn the worm."

"Well, everyone says he looks like Andy Garcia."

"Yeah. So?"

"So I guess you said no."

"That's exactly what I said."

I grinned.

"Stop that," she said.

"Okay," I said.

I grinned again.

She just ignored me. We drove around a while. She put on a CD of the Beatles. She liked that old group. Her dad's favorite band. She was singing along. She actually had a nice voice. She could sing. I never knew that about her. The thing about Alejandra was that she was actually pretty complicated. She was really conserv-o. You know, CONSERV-O. And then she could be this very hip girl. And then she'd be this very straight and traditional girl, and then she could be this radical thinker (but definitely not radical when it came to boys). So she's singing and I was thinking that she was born too late. The sixties would've really suited her. Really. Absolutely. You know, there they are again, those two unnecessary, overused words. Finally, I decided to step out of my head and say something. "Where are we going?"

"Scenic Drive." Then she just kept singing.

I'd been to Scenic Drive before. You could park and look out at the whole city. And you could see Juárez and downtown—and I mean, *you really could see everything from there.*

We didn't really talk very much as we drove. I kept thinking about Tito and I wondered if he was ever going to wake up. Maybe we'd lost him. *We had lost him.* But maybe we'd lost him a long time ago.

He was always gone.

He. Was. Always. Gone.

Not present. Not around. Angry. Moody. Lonely. Lost. Private. It was as if he just didn't want us to know him. It was as if he never liked the world. From the minute he was born, he just didn't like the idea of being alive. I think that's why he hated me. I remembered. I don't know why I was remembering this one thing. This one day, I was humming. I don't know what I was humming and I didn't even know that I was doing it. And he was really pissed off. "So what the fuck is there to hum about?" There was fire in his eyes.

I just looked at him.

"What are you thinking about?"

"Him," I said.

Alejandra nodded. She knew who "him" was.

When we got to the lookout point, I realized I hadn't even paid any attention to the scenery. I mean, it really was a great place and I hardly ever got to go up there, and I'd sort of missed the whole drive up the mountain because I just couldn't step out of my head.

We both got out of the car and looked out. I was glad she'd brought me there. It was a nice thing to do. Alejandra, she could be so nice. Really nice. Okay, she *was* really nice. It was just this thing about trying to make me her boyfriend that made me really effen nuts. I mean, what did she see in me, anyway? I wasn't the world's most handsome guy. I knew that. Okay, I'm not ugly, but I'm a little on the skinny side, and, well, who knows what she saw in me.

"Are you okay?"

I nodded. "Yeah."

"You worried about Tito?"

"What if he doesn't make it?"

She didn't say anything. And then she just shook her head. "Look, Ram, worrying about it doesn't solve anything."

"Yeah, sure. You're the world's biggest worrier."

"No, I'm not."

"Yes, you are. You worry about the clothes you wear. You worry about your hair. You worry about your father because he works too much. You worry about whether or not your grandmother's been taking her insulin. You worry about whether or not your tires have enough air or too much air. Alejandra, you worry. That's what you do. So just don't tell me not to worry."

She nodded. "Okay."

It was the first argument with Alejandra I'd ever won—but

I wasn't exactly savoring the moment. We found a place to sit in the little park they had there. Both of us just stared out at the cities of El Paso and Juárez. We sat there for a long time. And it was nice not to say anything, just to sit there. We don't always need words. Too many words, that's the problem. Words beat the crap out of us every day. I don't care if the words are in English or in Spanish or in Swahili. Words. They're like bullets. *They are bullets.* Yeah, I really liked that Alejandra and I were without words—even if it was just for a little while. We sat, we breathed, we watched the sun going down. I thought, *Such a sad and strange day.* I wondered if anything was ever going to be the same again. The world changes. That's what the world did, it changed. But when it changed and moved around, it dropped some people off, left them behind. Tito was one of those. You know, left behind.

The world kept spinning.

I was dizzy from all that spinning.

When the cell phone rang, it scared me. I flinched. You know, like when you're startled. Like when you think someone's going to hit you. It's not your mind that does that, it's your body. Sure. Like I know so much. The cell phone kept ringing. You know, I just wasn't used to carrying one around.

I was almost afraid to answer it.

Maybe Tito had died. That's exactly what I thought. *He's dead. Tito is dead.* I answered the phone, took a breath, listened, heard my mother's voice. "Are you okay?"

"Yeah. I'm with Alejandra. We're on Scenic Drive."

"That's good."

"Is Tito okay?"

"No change," she said. Her voice was flat. "The neurologist just left. They're running some tests."

"What kind of tests?"

She was quiet for a minute. Running words through her mind. Making sure she'd say the right thing. "They want to see how much brain activity Tito has."

I didn't say anything. I knew what that meant. I mean, Mom was a nurse. I'd heard her talk about these things. Most of my life, I'd heard about all this. It was never good. "How's Jeremy?" I don't know why it was important for me to know how he was doing. Maybe he was like a mirror. A mirror for Tito. If Jeremy lived—then Tito would live.

My mom didn't say anything. Not a word. Sometimes, you didn't want words. Sometimes, you had to have them. Had to. Words.

"Mom?"

"He didn't make it, Rammy." My mom's voice was so soft.

"Oh," I said. I wondered if his mother had gone to see him before he died. I wondered if he had a father who cared. And I suddenly wanted to ask my mother if maybe we shouldn't try to get a hold of my dad. I mean, shouldn't he know? Shouldn't he care? Damn it, shouldn't he?

Alejandra had dinner with us that night. My Tía Lisa cooked. She was a good cook. An excellent cook. Not as good as my mother, but her sopa de fideo was fantastic. We tried to be normal—not that we were ever really that normal. Who's normal? What's the norm? That was a math question. Families weren't math. So, there we were eating, being the kind of family that we were. We talked about stuff. Alejandra had my Tía Lisa laughing about all the boys at school. Even my mom was laughing. I was glad she was there.

I knew my mom would be going back to the hospital that night. She was taking some vacation time from work. I mean, we never really took a vacation anyway. And she said she wanted me back at school. I said no. "You're across the street," she said. "If I need you, I'll call."

It got late. Alejandra said she had to go. But she helped pick the plates off the table. You know, her grandmother raised her right. I mean, in some ways she was very spoiled. In other ways, she wasn't spoiled at all.

I walked Alejandra to the car. I got that hint from my mom. You know, I got one of those looks. So I walked her out. "Thanks," I said. "You're really decent."

She smiled at me. "That's a pretty good compliment. Coming from you, I mean."

"Yeah, well, it's true. You're really decent."

"But am I pretty?"

She always went fishing, that Alejandra.

"You've always been pretty. And you've always known that. I don't know why you need me to tell you that."

She laughed. "Figure it out."

I grinned.

She noticed—but see, I didn't say anything. Then she said, "He wasn't always a druggie."

At first I didn't know who she was talking about—and then I figured it out. She was talking about Jeremy.

"You knew Jeremy?"

"Yeah. I've known him since he was a little kid. His mother used to drop him off at my house. And we'd play for hours. He was a real sweet boy. He really was. I used to boss him around and all he ever did was smile."

She stopped talking, and I could see she was crying.

"And someone beat that sweetness out of him." And then she got this real tough look on her face. "I hate his parents. I do, Ram. I hate them. How come they get to live? Jeremy's dead—and those good-for-nothing lowlifes, well, they just get to go on living."

And then she just broke down and sobbed.

I pulled her close to me.

I just let her cry on my shoulder.

I didn't say anything. I just held her and let her cry. I hated to see her like that. I couldn't stand it. She cried and cried for a long time. "He was so sweet, Ram. You should have seen him when he was four. The sweetest boy in the world."

Her
(Mom)

My mom came into my room. Quietly. It was late. Not that I was asleep. I was just lying there thinking. I'd stopped staring into the pages of the book I was reading. I was staring—not reading. The words were invisible. I had the book on my chest when my mother walked in. She sat on Tito's bed. I knew she wanted to talk—but I was afraid of what she might say.

"They did all the tests?" I don't know why I asked. I already knew they had.

She nodded. "We'll get the results tomorrow."

I wanted to ask her what she thought. But no, I didn't. I just lay there in bed, a useless book lying on my chest. Just lay there and watched her.

"He was shooting up heroin," she said. "I didn't even know kids did that anymore." She looked at me. "Did you know?"

I shook my head. "No. Guess I'm not really with it. You know, Mom, I'm kind of a loner. I mean, Alejandra's always nagging me to join the human race."

My mom smiled. "I know."

"I'm sorry," I said.

"Don't be sorry. You're the kind of kid who knows himself. That's pretty rare."

I thought it was a funny thing to say. I didn't know myself at all. I didn't have an effen clue. I didn't.

I pointed to Tito's pillow. "Maybe you should read his notebook."

"Maybe I should," she whispered. Her voice was so soft now. Like she was afraid of words—because she'd learned how hard they could be. She'd probably learned that from my father. I was learning too. She reached under the pillow and pulled out the spiral notebook. She placed it on her lap and she kept sliding her hand across the surface of it. Almost like she was trying to unwrinkle everything in her life and make it smooth.

Then she hugged the notebook.

Then she just broke down and sobbed.

I watched her. That's what I did.

And then I found myself whispering, "I'll never hurt you like that, Mom. I promise." I said the wrong thing. I made her cry even more. I was always saying the wrong thing.

Me
(Ramiro. Also Known as Ram)

The next morning, I woke up early.

The house was really quiet.

Everything felt so funny. Funny as in weird. Not even the floor felt real. It was as if I was walking around in a new world. But not a good new world—a bad new world. I found a note on the kitchen table.

> Ramiro,
> I'm at the hospital. I couldn't sleep, so I just decided to go back and sit with your brother. I want you to go to school, okay? Just keep your cell phone on (put it on vibrate so they don't take it away from you). Tell your teachers you might get a phone call because your brother's very sick. Anyway, I don't know that anything eventful will happen today. I'll be in touch. Try and make it a normal day. Can you do that?
> I don't know what I'd without you.
> You're an angel.
> Mom

I don't know exactly what Mom meant by me being an angel. If she meant that I didn't get into any trouble, I don't see how that was much of a virtue. I mean, maybe I lacked imagination. Look, maybe I was just this dull and boring person. Being dull and boring didn't make me an angel. I hope to God angels were more interesting than a guy like me.

I walked over to the computer and checked my e-mails. We only had one computer. We shared it. We kept it on a little table in the kitchen. It was a family Christmas gift. It had even made Tito happy. I was surprised the guy hadn't hocked it.

But there it still was. It was Tito who was gone.

I checked my e-mails. Not that I got lots of messages. Sometimes Lalo sent me crazy notes. He didn't have a computer at home, but his older brother who was married had one and he stayed with him a lot, and when he was there, he'd send me crazy crap that didn't make much sense. It was just a game. Sometimes I got e-mails from school friends—mostly wanting to know stuff about assignments. Everybody knew I always paid attention. I mean, paying attention cut down on study time. That's the way I saw it. I was practical. See what I mean about dull and boring.

And, of course, Alejandra, she e-mailed me about two or three times a day. When I opened my e-mails, there was a note from Jake: *Ram, you're invited to my party. Don't forget.* It had an attachment with directions to his house which began at Thomas Jefferson High School and ended at his front door at the top of Thunderbird Drive. And then he'd added: *Bring a friend.* How the hell did he know I had any friends?

I had another e-mail too. From Alejandra. Of course. She'd sent me a note. Guess she'd stayed up late, because I noticed she'd sent the note after midnight. *I hope Tito lives. I'm sorry I was so mean to him.* It was a very nice and sweet thing to say. I liked her a lot for writing that to me. But, you know, Alejandra, she just never knew when to quit. *I talked to my dad. And he says you can come work for him at one of his stores. You know, working at Paper Dreams is better than flipping burgers at Whataburger.* That really made me mad. We'd talked about this thing a hundred times. And I told her straight and plain: *I'm not effen gonna go work for your father.*

I made some toast, drank down some orange juice, then hit the shower. I grabbed my backpack and went off to school. I had to turn back when I realized I'd left my cell behind. I wasn't used to carrying one around.

I don't know why, but I found myself standing in front of Jeremy's house. I almost wanted to make a sign: EFFEN DRUGS KILLED JEREMY CHAVEZ YESTERDAY. HE USED TO BE THE SWEETEST BOY IN THE WORLD. I imagined myself making that sign and pounding it into the yard—sort of like a political yard sign. My lips were trembling and I knew I was gonna start crying and I hated that.

I took a breath.

Okay, I said, *let's try and make this a normal day.*

When I got to the front of the school, I looked across the street toward Thomason Hospital. People were going in and out. How many people would die today? How many people would go home? An ambulance drove up. I didn't even hear the siren. That was strange, that I didn't hear it. I just saw it.

I kept picturing my mother holding Tito's hand. I kept picturing her trying to convince my brother to come back to us.

Maybe he didn't want to come back.

Maybe it was too late.

I was crying. I knew I was crying. Damn it to hell, I had to stop that. I had to stop. What was wrong with me?

I felt someone tugging at my arm. I didn't even have to look. I knew it was Alejandra. "It's okay to cry," she said.

"No, it's not," I said. "I'm just feeling sorry for myself."

At least she didn't try to argue with me.

She walked with me. And then we were standing right in front of my homeroom class. "You're going to be late," I said.

She nodded. "Just because you're sad doesn't mean you're feeling sorry for yourself," she whispered. She squeezed my hand and walked away.

That Alejandra. She always had to have the last word.

Him
(Jake)

I called my mom during lunch. She didn't say anything. All she said was that after school I should just come by the hospital. "No hurry," she said. "Just come by." I didn't like the sound of her voice. I really didn't. I almost asked her if Tito had said anything. Was he talking? But he wasn't. I knew that. It was that thing, that big thing called hope. It was taking my body over, that word. It was. I was beginning to get real cozy with that word. I was hoping that my brother would come back. I was hoping that life was a game of hide and seek. And that Tito was just hiding. And I was calling out that everyone could come home free. Hope. I was lost in that word. And my mom? She was lost in that word too.

After school, I headed for the Circle K down the street. I just wanted to get some air. And then I'd haul my skinny ass back to the hospital. I called my mom on the cell phone. It was weird, to have a cell phone, even though most people thought having one was normal. She answered her phone.

"Hi," she said.

"I'm walking to the Circle K," I said. "I'm going to buy a Coke." I always watched my *gonna*s when I talked to my mom. Watched my cursing and my *gonna*s. It was strictly *going to* when I talked to Mom. She didn't say it, but I knew why she wanted me to be careful with the way I used words. Words. Again. She didn't want people to think I was a stupid, uneducated Mexican. Because that's what people thought. She didn't want people to think that of me. We never talked about it. But I knew. "Yeah," I said, "I'm going to buy a Coke and maybe a snack. Do you want something, Mom?"

"No," she said.

"I'll be there in a little while."

"Okay," she said. She sounded really far away.

"Are you there in the room with him?" I asked.

"Yes."

"Has he—" and then, I don't know, I just stopped, didn't even know what I was going to ask.

"He's the same," she said.

I wanted to tell her that everything was okay, but everything wasn't okay, so why did I want to tell her that. And then I wanted to make a stupid joke. *Well, he never said much anyway.* I don't know what's wrong with me sometimes. I mean, why would I even think of saying such a stupid thing to my mother who was lost in a word called hope and who was sitting in a hospital room with my brother who was on life support and who was probably already brain-dead. God, I'd said it to myself. I'd said it. My brother was probably dead.

"I love you, Mom." That's what I said. Even though I thought stupid things and said stupid things, I sometimes wound up saying the right things. I said the right things often enough to make people think I was actually smarter than I was.

"You *are* an angel," my mom whispered.

I shut off my cell and kept walking toward the Circle K. And I started to think of my father and I wondered if maybe he wasn't dead. I mean, he might've been dead. And, hell, to me he might as well be dead. Really, I mean it. I was getting mad. I didn't like myself very much when I got mad. I got mean. I didn't want to be mean. And then, for the first time in my life, I wondered what I would say to my father if I actually ran into him. And then I started having a conversation with him in my head. I'm looking at him and I'm saying, "Hi, Dad."

And he looks at me and smiles and says, "I've missed you."

"All my life? Have you missed me all my life?"

And he says, "All your life."

And then I say, "Are you back to stay?"

And right there, in the middle of my completely fictitious conversation with my father, Jake pulls his car over and says, "You wanna ride?" It was all so natural and ordinary as if the guy was a natural and ordinary part of my life. Like a cactus in the desert. You know, ordinary. I thought of my mother's oleander. Belong. Everyday. Yeah, sure.

I looked at him and shrugged and said, "Sure." And I point my chin down the road and say, "I'm goin' to the Circle K." And I just get in his car, like he's my friend and everything is natural and ordinary—yeah, sure. I don't know exactly why I did that. Got in his car. Really, I don't. I mean, he wasn't my friend. Not really. I knew his name and I knew he lived on the west side of town and that he was probably a rich guy. Well, the son of a rich guy, which amounts to the same thing. I mean, his address and the map to his house on the e-mail just about told me everything I needed to know. And for sure, he was richer than me, and probably he was also the good kind of gringo, which made me smile when I thought that because he probably thought that I was the good kind of Mexican. And, you know, things are really screwed up in this world of ours.

So, anyway, what did I know about Jake? Not much. I mean, I knew a little bit more about him than I knew about my father. And wasn't that effen sad. And what the hell did he know about me? He knew my name. Ramiro. He even knew enough to call me Ram. So there it all was. We were complete strangers and I had no idea why we were pretending to be friends and I had no idea why he had stopped to pick me up and why I had gotten into his car as if he was an every day part of my life like my mother's oleander. But there I was, sitting in his car. He offered me a smoke like he was used to offering me a smoke.

I take the cigarette—though I wanted to tell him I didn't smoke. I mean, I was not a *vato* and I was not a dude. I was not interesting. I was not cool. Mr. Angel. Not that I hadn't smoked before. But, well, *I didn't smoke.* So, he lit his cigarette as he drove, then handed me his lighter. And I lit up, real natural like it was something I did every day, and the thing tasted like an old cat had just crapped in my mouth, but, you know, I knew how to pretend. I mean, that's all I did at school. So I just pretended that I was really into the cigarette. How hard was that? I mean, what was I gonna do? I mean, I didn't want to appear to be as uncool as I actually was in front of a gringo from the Oh-Wow West Side. Look, I'm fine with being a square—when I'm by myself. Around other people, well, things change. I could just see my Tía Lisa making fun of me. "Don't be so square, Rammy." A very serious, uncool guy. That would be me.

And then Jake said, "There's this guy. His name is Chuy." He said "Chuy" real smooth—like he was a Mexican, like he said the name all the time, but *I* knew and *he* knew that he didn't hang out with guys named Chuy. "See," he says, "Chuy waits for me sometimes, and he buys me cigarettes. I buy, he flies. Know what I'm saying, dude?"

Dude. Not a word I liked. I nodded. "Yup." I didn't want to talk too much. He had a nice car. Leather seats. I felt like I was in an effen commercial and I thought one of those old-time singers like Bette Midler or Carly Simon or Carole King or one of those singers my mom liked so much was about to break into one of those effen old songs. And then he just pushed a button and a CD came on and I recognized the voice.

"You like Bob Dylan?" Jake was sort of singing along.

"Yeah," I said. I mean, I didn't love Bob Dylan or anything like that. But Alejandra's dad loved Bob Dylan. And that meant Alejandra loved Bob Dylan too. This meant he had always been forced on me. Let's face it, the guy could *not* sing. Okay, he had something. Something very unsquare about that guy. Steve would have called him a very cool cat. I mean he was definitely a cat. "He's cool," I said. And then I blew some smoke out through my nose and it really did feel like an old cat had crapped in my mouth.

Jake parked on the side of the Circle K and there was this guy waiting for him. Jake walked out of his car and handed the guy some money and we waited a little while and the guy came out and handed Jake a pack of cigarettes. And then I saw the guy had his own pack of cigarettes and I figured that was the deal. Jake got Chuy to buy him cigarettes because he wasn't old enough and then he paid for Chuy's cigarettes too. Everybody won out.

I kinda smiled at Chuy and he greeted me with his chin and I greeted him with mine. And then he smiled and said, "Hey, aren't you Ram?"

"Yeah," I said, "I'm Ram."

"I know your Tía Lisa. She's a very cool lady."

I nodded. Chuy opened up his pack of cigarettes and walked away. I wondered if that guy had ever asked my Tía Lisa out on a date. I figured they were about the same age. He probably had. I figured my Tía Lisa let him down gently. "You don't have to get ugly when you say no." She was always saying stuff like that.

I walked into the store and bought myself a Coke and Jake was right behind me. And then I thought to buy me a stick of cinnamon gum so I wouldn't smell like cigarettes when I walked into the hospital. Jake bought a Dr Pepper and some mints, you know, those really strong ones that came in a tin. I never liked those. Too expensive, anyway. I mean, you bought stuff like that and you wouldn't have enough left to go to college. Well, okay, you get my point.

As we walked back to the car, I asked Jake to drop me off at the hospital. "My brother's real sick," I said.

He nodded. I mean, he looked like he was real sorry to hear it. And he didn't ask any questions, which I really appreciated. Look, the guy had some class. The right kind of class. As he pulled out of the parking lot, he asked me if I was going to his party. "It's tonight," he said.

And then I remembered it was Friday and that I had to go to work, and I thought, shit, shit, shit, and I didn't tell them at work that I couldn't go in. Shit. But I didn't say anything to Jake about any of that. "If I don't have to work," I said, "and if my brother, well, you know." There were a lot of ifs in my sentence.

I think Jake got the ifs. "Hope you can make it." He just nodded.

He left me off in front of the hospital.

He waved. I waved back. He wasn't so hard to be around. That didn't mean I wanted to go to his party.

Her and Him
(Mom and Tito)

My mom looked up at me when I walked into the small room in ICU. They'd moved Tito into a more private room. It was nicer. Well, it was hard to think of it as nice. Just more private. Private was good. Especially when there was so much sadness. Who the hell wanted to be sad in public?

She was reading a book. My mom. Out loud. To Tito.

She looked like a painting. A beautiful painting. The most beautiful painting I'd ever seen. My mom. Reading.

"I'm reading him the story." She showed me the book. *Great Expectations.*

"He's never read it."

"I like it," she said. "Maybe your brother likes it too."

"Bet he does," I said.

We were whispering. She put the book down on the bed and it lay there right next to Tito.

"The neurologist says he doesn't have any brain activity."

"Oh," I said. I knew what that meant. "None?"

"I read the results myself."

"Oh."

"We might take him off the respirator." She stopped. I didn't want her to keep talking—but I knew she had to say this. Maybe not to me—but I think she needed to hear herself say this. So I just listened. "When we take him off the respirator, he'll die."

I wanted to say, *Mom, he's already dead.* It was such a mean thing to think. So I just kept my mouth shut. That's not a bad thing, to keep your mouth shut. My mom kept staring at Tito. And there were tears running down her face. And I just didn't know what do to. Keeping your mouth shut doesn't exactly qualify as doing something.

"I have to talk to your uncles. And to Lisa."

I nodded. Really, that's all she could say right now. She just couldn't talk. She was all out of words. Like a river without water.

Everything inside me wanted to ask, "And don't you have to talk to Dad?" But I knew those words would be like a slap. So I just swallowed them. We were both quiet and wordless for a long time. I just stood there next to her, both of us staring at Tito. And then, after a while, she said. "Lisa called your work. She told them you wouldn't be going in this weekend. She didn't want you to get fired."

I shrugged. I mean, getting fired from flipping burgers wasn't the end of the effen world. "Lisa's great," I said. I thought about Chuy, Jake's cigarette guy, and how he'd said she was a very cool lady. I hoped she'd find someone nice. I hoped she'd marry a guy who'd never leave her.

I reached for the book. "Why don't you go home, Mom? I'll read to him for a while."

She smiled at me. She didn't want to leave. She wanted to stay there forever, I think. It would just be us three—her and Tito and me. A family. And we would belong to each other forever. But I could see in her face. I could see she understood what I wanted. I wanted to be alone with Tito. Just for a while. I think she understood that. "Okay," she said, "I marked the page."

"Go home and rest," I said. "I'll call Alejandra when I've read enough. She'll take me home."

My mom, she was so tired.

I liked the quiet after she left. I've always liked the quiet. When I was a little boy I used to wake up and listen to the quiet. The quiet would make me smile.

I read to Tito for over an hour. And I kept hoping that the

book would bring thoughts back into his brain. God, I was beginning to hate this hope inside me. Sometimes, hope kept you from seeing the truth. Sometimes hope made you keep holding on to something that you should let go of.

Her
(Alejandra. Again and Again)

Alejandra came to pick me up. I don't know what time it was. Maybe it was around 5:30. She wanted to see Tito. The nurse let her come in even though she wasn't technically allowed in—only family. I mean, I guess Alejandra was family. I'd known her since I was four. Not that I knew why Alejandra wanted to see him. But she'd told me she *had* to see him. The word "no" did not exist in Alejandra land.

She sat down and took Tito's hand. I was amazed by that. She wasn't afraid and she didn't tremble. She just sat down and took his hand. And then she just talked to him. "I'm sorry I was such a bitch. I should've been nicer. I'm really sorry. I mean it." And then she reached over and kissed him on the forehead. She looked up at me. "They say that hearing is the last thing to go."

"Yeah?"

"Yeah," she said. "Ask your mom, she'll tell you."

That was when I realized that Alejandra was turning into a woman. Not a girl anymore. A woman. And I felt like a real idiot, because I didn't feel like I was anywhere near becoming a man.

When we were driving back to my house, I didn't know what to say, what to talk about. I didn't want to talk about Tito. And—I don't know why—I blurted out the fact that tonight was Jake's party. I. Am. An. Effen. Idiot.

"Are you going?"

"Tito's dying."

"He's not dying tonight," she said. Like she was a real expert. You know, Alejandra thought she was an expert on everything. That's why people didn't like her.

"Mom probably won't let me go, anyway."

"Well, that's a lie. You think she wants you just moping around the house?"

"I don't want to leave her by herself."

"I bet your Tía Lisa and all your uncles are coming over tonight."

I knew she was right. "You think it's right that I should go partying?"

"Maybe it would be good for you. You know, think about something else. Just for a few hours."

"What about if I just don't want to go?"

"You'll never change."

"What's that supposed to mean?"

She parked her car right in front of my house. It was almost dark. My Tía Lisa's car was in the driveway. Alejandra was shooting me a look.

"Look," I said, "this is the thing—I don't like going places where I don't belong."

"He invited you."

"Invited me? That doesn't mean I belong."

"Why are you mad?"

"I'm not mad."

"That was a nice thing, you know? And what does your mom say when someone does something nice for you?"

Sometimes Alejandra sounded like an old lady. "I get it. I see where this is going."

"Didn't she teach you to say thank you?"

"She taught me to say *gracias*."

"*Gracias*, thank you, same thing."

"No. *Gracias* is better than thank you."

"Whatever. And, Ram, where the hell do you think you belong, anyway? A garbage can?"

"Let me ask you a question—when you walk into Chico's Tacos, how does that make you feel?"

"Chico's Tacos? It doesn't make me feel like anything. I just walk in and order my tacos."

"And when you walk into Whataburger?"

"I order a hamburger. No onions, in case I meet someone. And don't think I don't see you rolling your eyes."

"Yeah, I'm rolling my eyes. But listen, how does it make you feel?"

"It doesn't make me feel like anything."

"And when you're buying something at the Dollar Store on Alameda?"

"Which one?"

"Pick one. Doesn't matter."

"There's a lot of them."

"And I bet you've been to every one."

"So?"

"So how does it make you feel?"

"It doesn't make me feel like anything. It feels normal, you know, like something, well, like something normal."

"Exactly. That's what I'm talking about. You see, when you walk into Chico's Tacos, it feels normal, and when you walk into Whataburger, it feels normal, and when you walk into the Dollar Store, it feels normal. It feels just right. Because you belong. But if you walk into the Dome Restaurant or Café Central, it would feel like maybe you shouldn't be there."

"How the hell do you know that, Ram? You've never even been to any of those places."

"Like I said, I don't go where I don't belong."

"Well, Jake invited you to his party and I think we should go."

"We?"

"The invitation says: 'you and a friend.'"

"How do you know what the invitation says?"

"They all say that. They all say bring a friend. Am I right?"

I hated that I was a bad liar. I wanted to lie to her in the worst way. "So what? So what if he said I could bring a friend? So what, Alejandra?" I was getting mad. I was. "You think I want to take you? Is that it?"

"I bet you want to take *la suelta*."

"Monica's not loose and you know it. How come girls are like that—when they don't like a girl, they start saying stuff about them like they put out and stuff like that? That's not cool."

"Okay, okay, just don't lecture me, Ram. Look, I'm a better friend than she is."

"Maybe I'll take Lalo."

"Lalo? He's embarrassing."

"Not to me."

"Look, Lalo won't go."

"How do you know?"

"He's not into gringos. And he's like you. He won't go where he thinks he doesn't belong."

"That's because he's smart."

"That's because he's an idiot. Smart people know they belong everywhere."

"Yeah, sure."

"I belong anywhere I go," she said. "So I guess you'll have to take me."

"Lalo will go if I ask him."

"Look, Ram, you're asking me. That's who you're asking."

"I'm not going, Alejandra."

"Alex."

"What effen ever."

"Look, Ram, it was nice of Jake to invite us."

"You know what? I don't like going to parties when I'm the only Mexican invited."

"You're not a Mexican. Your mother was born in this country. Even your grandmother was born in this country. You're as American as anybody else."

"You know what I mean."

"Yeah. Sure." She rolled her eyes. "Fine. Look, have you ever been to a party where you're the only Mexican invited? Have you?"

"Nope. And I'm not going to start."

"You know what?" She looked at her watch. "It's 6:15. I'm going home to get ready, pick something nice to wear, and then I'm going to pick you up at eight o'clock sharp. And you know what else? If you take me—you won't be the only Mexican there. And will you stop with this Mexican thing?"

"Yeah, yeah," I said, "We're just as American as they are."

"It's true."

"Sure it's true. Me and Jake Upthegrove, we're the same."

I was really making her mad. She shot me a look. "Eight o'clock, Ram."

"No."

"You're going. I'm going. We're both going."

"You're not my girlfriend."

"Who said I wanted to be?"

I rolled my eyes. "My achin' elbow." All of Dizzy Land knew she wanted to be my girlfriend.

She shot me another look.

"Stop that," I said.

"Stop what?"

"Stop with those looks. And we're not going." But I knew there was no use fighting Alejandra. She'd made her mind up about the party. She was going to hound me to death until I

177

just effen gave in. Then I looked at her and smiled. "So who are you going to go as?"

"What's that supposed to mean? It's not a costume party."

"I mean are you going as Scout or as Esperanza or as Rose of Sharon? Or are you going as Lady Macbeth?" I knew she was reading *Macbeth* in English class because she kept e-mailing passages from the play and then she would write in big letters: isn't that fantastic!!!!!!!!!!!!!

Alejandra looked at me for a long time. I mean, I swear her eyes were on fire. "Sometimes I just want to slap you," she said. "I really do." But she wasn't mad enough to change her mind about going to Jake's party. No such luck. "I'll pick you up at eight," she said again.

"Stop repeating that," I said. "I heard you the first time. And how can you drive? You don't even know where the party is."

"That's your job—to give me directions."

Leave it to Alejandra to make me feel like an errand boy. "Okay," I said. "But only if my mom lets me go. I mean, I shouldn't even be going. Tito's in the hospital and if something happens—"

Alejandra interrupted me. She was always interrupting me. That was her job in the world. "I'm up on the situation," she said. "Look, we both have cells. Your mother will call."

"I don't feel like a party."

"You never do."

"I'm sad about Tito."

"Of course you are."

"And you know, Alejandra, that piece of the world isn't ours."

"What piece of the world?"

"The piece of the world where Jake lives."

That made Alejandra really mad. I don't know why she wanted to hang out with me. I always just made her mad. Mostly on purpose. But not always. Sometimes I was just being me. And there was nothing wrong with that. "My achin' elbow," she said. "The world belongs to those who take it."

"Yeah, well, make that into an effen bumper sticker."

"It's true, Ram."

"Look, the world's already been divvied up—and guess what? We got Dizzy Land."

She shook her head. "The world belongs to everyone, Ram."

"When you run for president, I'll vote for you."

"Damn right you will."

Alejandra was a true believer. Essentially she believed all that crap that everybody had a good shot at getting somewhere in the world. I didn't believe that. Not for a second. But I felt mean trying to set her straight. "Okay," I said, "the world belongs to everyone."

"Why do you say things you don't believe?"

"Look, you want to go to Jake's party? We'll go. And then afterward, you can tell me who the world belongs to."

Shit! So I'd stepped into her trap. Caught. I was going to a party I didn't want to go to. I knew my mom would let me go. She and Tía Lisa and some of my uncles were all coming over tonight. I knew that. And they were going to discuss what to do about Tito. About how they might take him off life support. Maybe they would talk about trying to get a hold of my dad. And I also knew that maybe they felt it would be better if I wasn't in on the discussion. *That's not how I effen felt. I mean, why shouldn't I be in on the discussion? Especially if it had to do with my dad.* But I know things about adults. And they weren't about to ask me how I felt. It was a club. And I knew I didn't belong in that club. Not yet. And my Tía Lisa would smooth things over by saying something like, "It's good for you to get out of the house. Maybe someone will give you lessons on how to start being a *vato*." You see, she'd turn it all into a joke, and I would be forced to play along. Shit! And I would laugh. Ha! Ha! Effen ha!

And I would go to the party.

With Alejandra.

Hell, hell, hell, hell, hell. Well, at least Alejandra would be happy. She was so effen excited about this party that her panties were practically melting. I didn't make that expression up. Nope. Lalo made that up. He liked to say that about girls. So, I stole that expression from him. From Lalo, who had even less than I did. Well, I guess everybody steals words from everybody else. All the time. All least they can't throw you in jail for that.

Shit.

I was going to Jake's party.

With Alejandra.

And if she told me to call her Alex just for the benefit of a bunch of gringos I didn't know, well she could effen forget about it.

Jake
(Like a Bad Penny—I Keep Coming Back)

Okay, I have another theory. I guess you could say the petri dish grew more mold. Okay, my new theory is this: People have parties because they're sad. They think a party will make them happy. That's my new theory. Okay, I've had better theories. I can't always be deep. I can be as shallow as the next guy. I'm entitled. I mean, maybe I'm becoming like Upthegrove.

Me
(In the Middle of the Night)

I woke up in the middle of the night. Just couldn't sleep. I kept thinking of that scene in the kitchen with me and David. I thought of how it should've turned out. I pictured myself drinking from a glass of orange juice. I pictured David walking into the kitchen and asking me, "Feeling better?"

"Nope," I say.

"Well, you're probably just coming down with something."

"You know what I'm coming down with, asshole, I'm coming down with detectivitis."

"Detectivitis?" he says. He's amused. I walk into his office and pour myself a drink. He follows me, and I give him a scotch. I hand him his drink as he looks at me. Dumbfounded.

I take a drink from my bourbon on the rocks. "Detectivitis," I repeat. And then I light a cigarette. "See, there's this guy. He's an attorney. He's fifty years old or so. And he's married. And he's supposed to be working on some big case, only the big case turns out to be a twentysomething woman who drives a red Mustang. And, you know—" I stop and stare at the stupid look on David's face.

He doesn't say anything.

"Detectivitis," I say again.

"It's not what it looks like," he says.

"Tongue down throat is tongue down throat."

"You have a dirty mind, young man."

"Not half as dirty as what you're doing with Ms. Red Mustang." And then I look at him—and I know he's getting a little scared.

"What are you going to tell your mother?"

"I'm not going to tell my mother anything. You're going to tell her." And then I walk out of the room.

I like the scene. But you know something, it all sucks. No matter how you want to look at it, it all sucks.

What am I supposed to do here?

I didn't want to think about this. I didn't. And then I start thinking about Rosie and Roman. And I don't want to think about them, either, and anyway, how was Sally going to throw a party without Rosie? Who was going to clean the house? Sally needed directions on how to turn on the vacuum cleaner.

I started worrying about everything.

So I got up from my bed, sat at my computer, and started making a list of people I wanted to invite to my birthday party. I put everyone I'd ever met on that damn list. I mean everyone. But when I got to a hundred, I decided I wasn't being very selective. So I cut the list down to my top fifty. Of course, I thought that maybe they could all bring someone if they wanted—so we were back up to a hundred. I was pretty happy with my list. There were some very cool people on the list. And there were more than a handful of shits.

About half of the people on the list were kids I'd gone to middle school with. About ten of them were kids I played soccer with. The rest were from my high school. And I put this guy, Ram Lopez, on the list. I liked him. He was a very cool guy, I could tell. He was real. Everything about him was real. Not that I knew him all that well. Probably, he wouldn't come to my party. But maybe he would.

After I finished my list, I just stared at it. I knew my mom, aka Sally, aka Elaine, would be very happy with this list. She was going to have a great time.

Shit. I could hear my heart beating.

I wondered about hearts. I mean, was it just this fantastic machine that pumped blood?

You know the one thing doctors can't tell you? They can't tell you why people feel. They don't know that.

My heart. There weren't good things going through it. I hated Upthegrove. And I hated David. I hated guys period. We all sucked. Every single damn one of us.

Her
(Katie Scopes)

On Saturday morning I got up early—even though I'd hardly slept at all. I took a shower, then printed out my list and handed it to my mom as she was having a cup of coffee and reading the morning newspaper. "Here's the list," I said.

She looked it over and nodded. "It's a nice list," she said. It was such a Sally thing to say. I knew she didn't like some of the people on the list, but she was being true to her word. It was my party and she was letting me invite anyone I wanted. "I see Katie Scopes is on the list." She couldn't help herself. She hated Katie Scopes. She'd caught us in my bedroom once. We were sort of lying on my bed groping each other. Well, not sort of. Look, groping is groping and we were experimenting and to tell you the truth the experiment was a huge success. It felt good to grope. Until my mom barged in. She glared at us. Mostly she glared at Katie.

I can still see that glare Sally was giving Katie Scopes. Listen, the thing about women—they always blame the girl. It's the girl's fault. The guys are all assholes, but it's still the girl's fault. I wonder if parents go around telling their girls that "the world is your oyster." You know, if I was a girl, I'd be a rabid feminist. And you know what? I wouldn't give a BMW what a guy thought of me. I'm serious. You can dig that, can't you? I mean, guys, they really destroy me.

I remember that after Katie left, my mom and I got into an argument. "I don't want her in this house," she said.

"There's always her house," I said, "and then there's the old reliable backseat of my car." Of course, I didn't have a car back then, but I thought I'd throw that in.

"You don't have a car," my mother said. "And if you keep

groping that girl, you'll never have a car."

Katie never came over again. But not because she was banned from coming over. She didn't know she was banned. I never told her. She told me the next day that she wanted to die she was so embarrassed. See, the thing about Katie was that she was really a good girl. She really was. Something happened to her when she was a kid that really screwed her up and she was always trying to forget, but she was really just a hurt kid. Anyone could see that. Except her parents. And my mom. You know, adults can't see. What's wrong with them? You know, it's like Mr. Moore, our English teacher, whom I really hate. That guy, he loves books. He's a snob—but he really loves books. But the thing is, he doesn't love us. In fact, he seems like he's out to prove that we're all idiots. So what gives?

Well, I was inviting Katie Scopes and that was that. I looked at my mom as she kept scrutinizing the list. "You'll be nice to her, won't you, Mom?" See, I called her Mom. Not Sally. Not Elaine. Mom.

She nodded. "Yes, Jacob, I'll be nice to her. Just don't take her into your bedroom."

I gave her a look. "She's got a boyfriend."

"Only one?"

"Stop it, Sally."

We both laughed. Sometimes, that's just the way we got along.

She looked at the list again. "Who's Ram Lopez?"

"He's a guy who goes to Jefferson High School. We've sort of gotten to know each other. Nice guy."

She nodded. She was suspicious of him, I could tell. I mean, half of the people on my list couldn't be trusted to tell the truth to a lie detector machine—even though they knew they were going to get caught. And was she suspicious *of them*?

'Course not. But a guy with a name like Ram Lopez—well, her ears went up like a dog guarding a warehouse.

"How many people are you having over?" I asked. I knew she and David were planning on having people over. Of course they were.

"Oh, just a few."

"Have as many as you want," I said. I was feeling very generous. "You guys stay inside, and we'll take the backyard. Deal?"

She smiled. "Deal. But I don't want any smoking out there."

"Well, it's my birthday, and I think I just might smoke my fool head off."

She shook her head.

"I'll be of age."

"Well, you'll be older, but you won't be wiser."

"I have time," I said.

"No drugs," she said.

I didn't do drugs. Who needed drugs? I had Sally and David.

I went into my room and called Katie Scopes. I knew she'd probably be asleep, but I felt like talking to someone and I also wanted to give her the heads-up about my party. I was really surprised when I heard her voice on the other end of the phone. I mean, I always figured her to be the kind of girl who slept until noon. I was just going to leave her a message. But there was her voice. Like magic. I really liked her voice. It wasn't too girly. You know, there was something real about the way she talked.

"I thought you'd still be asleep."

"Jake."

"Yup."

"Hey! I miss you."

She said it, just like that. Without even thinking how it would sound. Very cool. "I miss you, too," I said. "How's Frog Lips?"

"Don't be mean. I really like him. And his name's Mark."

"Do you grope each other?"

She laughed. "None of your business."

"Bet you do."

"Bet you wish you were Mark."

"Not on your life. And just to prove it, I want you to drag him along to my party."

"Party? Jacob! You're having a party!"

Katie loved parties. "Yup. Turning eighteen. Friday at eight. My house."

And then Katie got real quiet. And then she said, "Does your mom know you're inviting me?"

"Yup."

"And it's okay?"

"Yup."

"She won't look at me like, you know, like I'm a real whore."

"Nope."

"You sure."

"Positive. Sally won't bother you."

"Still doing that off-and-on-Sally thing, huh?" All of a sudden, I felt something in my throat. Like I just couldn't get any words out. And I just got real quiet.

I didn't know I was going to say what I said next. "Listen," I said, "you wanna go grab a cup of coffee?"

She was real quiet. And that little piece of quiet, I knew I really needed someone to talk to. And Katie knew it too. I mean, isn't that why I'd called her? I mean, I could have just e-mailed her. But I wanted to hear her voice. Because she had a good head and good heart, and even if she had issues with getting high all the time, she was a very fine person. She was. And I trusted her. I hadn't even put all that into words or thoughts until right then, in that little piece of quiet.

"Pick me up in forty-five minutes," she said, "I'm all smelly. I haven't showered yet." She hung up the phone. That was the thing about girls—if they weren't your girlfriends they were real honest—and told you everything—even personal stuff like "I'm all smelly. I haven't showered yet."

When I picked her up, she looked different. She wasn't wearing black, for one thing. And she didn't look all drugged out. She was really pretty and she seemed calm and she reminded me of the sky. Just the kind of sky we had that morning. Clear and blue and perfectly at peace with itself. How had she done that? God, looking at her destroyed me. "Hi," she said. And then she kissed me right on the cheek. And she smelled clean and new and, I don't know, I mean, I think I just wanted to sit down and cry. Right there. Can you dig that? Shit.

We went to this very cool coffee shop where they have lots of art on the walls, and I kept wanting to tell her that I felt like I was going to explode. I mean, have you ever seen a firecracker after it's exploded? I mean, *it is so destroyed.*

We were just sitting there, making small talk—you know, how was school, was I really gonna be a doctor and what colleges was I applying to and she was for sure wanting to go to Oberlin because she played the oboe and they had this fantastic music program and all of a sudden, Katie looks at me and says, "You're crying."

"I am?" I didn't even know it.

She reached over and wiped my tears with her fingers and she said, "Baby, don't cry."

And that made me really want to cry even more, and you know something, I'm not the crying type, so I knew this thing with Rosie and this thing with David and Ms. Red Mustang was really destroying me. And I didn't really want to have a fucking party, but Sally did, and I felt bad for her because, hell, she was my mother, and David had played her like an old piano, and I was so fucking destroyed. I mean, I'll admit this, not one of those people I was inviting was really a friend. Not really. I knew them. They knew me. But this friend thing, I wasn't good at it. I didn't have any. Who was I kidding. So, there I was, sitting in front of Katie Scopes. Crying.

"Tell me," she said.

"Okay," I said.

"Do you remember Rosie?"

"Sure," she said.

"She quit." And then I told her the whole damn story. All of it. And I didn't even know how angry I was about the whole thing until I was telling her the whole story and I could feel my whole body shaking. And I knew I was yelling when I said, "It's just not right, Katie. It's not right. And it's not decent."

Katie was really calm. I mean, she was better at listening than she was at groping—which is why I'd probably always liked her. "No," she said, "it's not right." Then she smiled and said. "I like that word, decent. That's you, Jake. Decent."

It was a really sweet thing to say. I gave her a smile right back. But I wasn't going to let myself be distracted from my misery. "But the life I have—it gets better."

She took a sip of coffee. And, all of a sudden she looked so, well, she looked like a woman. Not a girl. A woman. "Better?"

"Yup." And then I just knew I was gonna blurt it out. Might

as well put it all out there. I mean, look, I hated having that knowledge locked inside me. It was like having a bomb that kept going *tick-tick-tick* inside you. I mean, the thing with having a bomb inside you was that you just didn't really know when it was just going to fucking explode. "David's having an affair."

She sort of smiled. "David, as in your stepfather?"

"The very one."

Katie seemed to take the news in stride. I mean, it didn't seem to shock her in the least. In fact, she sort of smiled. "Who'd want him?"

That made me laugh. It was nice, that she made me laugh. "She drives a red Mustang," I said. "And I suspect she works in his office."

Katie nodded. "Well, David's not a bad-looking man—in that kind of fatherly way. But, he's not very interesting. I mean the guy is pretty dull."

Katie knew. I mean, he and her father were friends. She'd been around him.

"So what am I going to do?"

"About what?"

"About him and Ms. Red Mustang."

"And you're sure?"

"I saw them making out."

"Making out?'

"You know, they were groping. I saw them."

"Where?"

"At McKelligon Canyon. They had their tongues down each other's throats."

"Yuck."

"Yeah, well, yuck or no fucking yuck, what am I supposed to do with this information? Am I supposed to just pretend I don't know? Is that the deal? Tell me. What am I supposed to do? What about Sally?" I think I was almost yelling. I was pulling my hair. I do that, when I get really upset, I pull my hair.

Katie started going through her purse. "I have something to calm you down."

I shook my head. "No thanks."

She shrugged. "Well, at least take a breath."

"You sound like the Anger Management Lady."

"Well, breathing works." She laughed. "I mean it doesn't work as good as Ambien."

"Where do you get that stuff?"

"You don't want to know. Are you still going to be a doctor?"

"You mean, am I going to grow up to be one of your drug sources?"

"Exactly."

We both laughed.

"Look," she said, "the real question is this: Is it better for your mom to know or not? I mean, she might know already."

"You think so?"

"Yeah. She might know. And maybe she's just decided to ignore it. I mean, he's not going to leave her or anything."

"What if it were you?"

"If it were me?" She had really nice eyes. Hazel. Today they looked green against the lavender T-shirt she was wearing. "If it were me, I'd grab him by his private parts and squeeze. Then I'd throw his ass out the door and lock it."

That sounded about right to me. "So I should tell her, then. I mean, she has a right to know."

"I don't know. Your mom, she's not, well, she probably sees things differently. I mean, she might hate you. For telling her."

"Great. He has the affair, and I'm the fall guy. I love this world. I mean, it really destroys me." I polished off my coffee. "So you're telling me I shouldn't tell her."

"That's not what I'm saying. I'm saying you need to think about it."

"I don't like this. What would you do—if you were me?"

"Well, I can't say."

"What do you mean, you can't say?"

"Look, the thing about people like you and me, Jake, is that, well, we're very rash. Very impulsive."

"What's so bad about that?"

"Nothing. I like us fine just the way we are. But other people aren't like us. And this thing between David and Ms. Mustang, well, it's not just about you, Jacob. It's about your mother and her marriage, and—"

"Well, apparently, her marriage isn't a very good one."

"But it's *her* marriage, Jake, *not yours.*"

Sometimes that Katie was too analytical for her own good. "In other words, I should just keep my fucking mouth shut."

"No. I didn't say that. You're not listening. I said you really need to think about it."

I was tired of thinking about it. "But shouldn't she know?"

"Yes. That's my answer. *But it's my answer, Jacob.*" God, she was calling me Jacob. Where was that coming from? "What's your mother's answer?"

"My mother doesn't want to see anything. She's like a kitten. She doesn't want to open her eyes and see the world she lives in. You know what she said about global warming? She said—and this is a quote here, Katie—she said, 'Some people just hate it that the oil companies are doing so well. Why can't we just be happy for them?' That's what she said. Can you dig that shit, Katie?"

Katie laughed. "Don't turn her into a caricature."

"She does that all by herself." That was true enough. "Look, doesn't she have to grow up sometime? Don't you think so?"

"Is that what this is about? Is it about your project of trying to make your mother grow up?"

I glared at Katie. I really did. "Are you going to be a psychologist or something?"

"Actually, I really want to be an analyst. But, my grades tell me I'm headed toward becoming the head cashier at Wal-Mart."

She made me laugh. She did that on purpose. I was getting mad. "You know what this is about, Katie? It's about guys getting away with all the bullshit they get away with. It's about people like my mother who enable them. There's a word. Enable. That's an Anger-Management-Lady word. She said that at every one of our sessions. *I am not here to enable your anger*. Yeah, sure."

Katie reached over and took my hand and squeezed it. "You still mad at Upthegrove?"

"I'm going to be mad at him forever."

"Good for you."

"Are you mocking me, Katie."

"'Course not." She sort of smiled at me. Maybe she was mocking me. Not that it mattered.

"You know something?" I said. "I don't think I like being a guy."

That Katie. She reached over and kissed me on the cheek. "You're the sweetest guy I've ever met."

Man, she really destroyed me. I mean, if I was the sweetest guy she'd ever met, she had to get out more.

When I got home, Sally was on the phone with some caterer. She looked up at me from where she was sitting with a pad at the kitchen counter. "We're going Italian," she said. "Small pizzas and three different kinds of pasta, and a foccacia to die for."

I smiled.

She went back to the phone.

Foccacia? What about Rosie's chiles rellenos? What about her pastel de tres leches? A party without Rosie around and I still didn't know what the hell I was supposed to do about the David and Ms. Red Mustang thing. I guess I was just going to keep thinking about it.

Great. I got to live in my head some more. You know, Jake land is not always a great place to live. It's not even a great place to visit. I guess, as far as Sally was concerned, the real question was: Is Jake land a great place to have a party?

Her and Him
(Sally and Me. *We Really Are Strangers*)

All weekend long, the house was all about "the party." I took a look at Sally's list. She and David had invited about twenty people. I mean, they were going to have their own party. Why not? I mean, I didn't care. I really didn't. And, because she just couldn't cope with all she had to do, she hired a new house-keeper. Her name was Carmen. She was younger than Rosie.

"This is Carmen," my mother said, introducing her.

"*¿Que tal?*" I said. I shook her hand and smiled. I didn't want to like her. But, look, this had nothing to do with Carmen. I wanted to look straight into Sally's eyes and say, "And this time I refuse to be the fucking translator." But I didn't say it. I just smiled. And then another thought occurred to me. I would tell Carmen to be careful of my mother. Sooner or later, she would turn on her. But I channeled the Anger Management Lady. I took a breath and just kept smiling.

As I made my way to my room, Sally followed me, reading the list of her guests off. Like I cared.

But then I asked her how come they didn't invite the Kerns. I mean, the Kerns lived right next door. "Well," Sally said, "they don't really fit into our crowd." I knew what that meant. It meant they had bad politics. I mean, it meant they had my politics.

"But I like them," I said. "And they're nice."

"Well, yes," Sally said, "They're nice. But, you know, they wouldn't have a good time."

"I get it," I said.

"You get what?" Sally asked.

"Never mind," I said. And then David walked into the room and they looked at each other and they started in on the good old-fashioned no-alcohol lecture. Not that it mattered. Look, the thing about adults is that they're not really in charge. I mean, they're in charge of the world, they really are (which is too fucking bad), but what they're not in charge of is us. Their children. They're not. They don't get it. See, the thing is, if they had a clue, they'd know that the lovely young men and women who wanted to drink at my party were going to drink. This was the deal. They would have their own stash out in their cars. Every twenty minutes, they'd make a beeline for their cars, take a swig of whatever they brought, and come back to the party laughing their fool heads off. I knew the drill. We all knew the drill. I mean, I was planning on having my own stash too. I mean, I was going to ask my friend, Chuy, to get me a bottle of Jack. And if not Chuy, hell, I'd find someone.

I'd hide the bottle in the backyard, and spike my Coke, and, hey, party! Not that I was planning on overdoing it. I mean, I wasn't that much of a drinker. I mean, I wasn't a drinker at all. I'd had a few beers. I'd had a scotch once when Sally and David were out of town. Scotch didn't do it for me. I'd never touch it again. Besides, that was Upthegrove's drink. I'm not planning on following in his footsteps.

And speaking of Upthegrove, Sally told me she'd spoken to him. "We talked last night," she said, two days before my party.

"So, how is he?" I asked.

"He's going through a divorce, poor thing." Poor thing? I just didn't get this poor-thing business. I really didn't. How does being a jerk with too much money qualify as being a poor thing.

"Another one?"

"Don't take that tone with your father," she said. God, she really did destroy me. She did. And then she smiled. "He asked about you."

"So that's supposed to make me happy?"

"He asked about you," she said again. As if, by repeating this statement, I was supposed to jump up in the air with glee like a basketball player who'd made the winning shot at the buzzer.

"Did he remember my name?"

"Jacob—"

"Sally, don't use that tone," I said. "If he's so interested in my well-being, he could give me a call. He could write me a letter. He could e-mail me, for Christ's sake."

"Do not use Christ."

"You're right. I shouldn't do that. I don't even believe." I swore I wasn't going to fight with her about anything. On account of the David-and-Ms.-Red-Mustang thing that she didn't know about. But the gloves were off when it came to Upthegrove. And, anyway, screw channeling the Anger Management Lady. Screw it. "Look," I said, "I don't want to talk about that guy. He's a loser. And just because he inseminated you with his seed doesn't make him a father."

"Jacob, I refuse to let you talk to me that way."

"No hitting," I said.

I could see that look on her face.

"I'm sorry," I said. I wasn't sorry—and there I was saying it. I was stooping pretty low here. "I'm glad Upthegrove asked about me."

Sally smiled. "He said he's sending you some money for your birthday." Now, there was a real gift. He was sending me something he had too much of. Wow. Can you dig that crap? That guy, he destroys the shit out of me.

"Money," I said. "Wow."

"You know," she said, smiling. "He just might come to your birthday party."

Okay. I was going to put a stop to this bullshit. It was *my* party. A party I was having to make Sally happy because I felt bad because her dull husband had decided to make his life more interesting by having an affair. Look, enough of this martyr stuff I was pulling. Maybe Sally thought it was a great idea to invite my father to my birthday party, but it wasn't going to happen. No way. Sometimes, I wasn't having any of this destroyed business. I mean, sometimes, it was me who was going to do a little destroying. Sometimes, it was their turn to say, "Jake, I am so destroyed by what you've just said to me." I looked at Sally and decided to let her rip. "Uninvite him."

"What?"

"I said uninvite him. You asked him to come, didn't you?"

"I thought it would be—"

I stopped her. I didn't want to know what she thought about this issue. I really didn't. "If you don't uninvite that poor excuse for a Homo sapien, then I will tell you one thing: I will cancel the party."

"What?"

"I said I'll cancel the party."

She was stunned. I could see she was starting to cry. "I did it for you," she said.

"Really?" That sounded so mean, but I'm telling you, the gloves were off. The swords were drawn. "Just once," I said, "why don't you ask me what I want for my birthday?"

"What?" She was wiping her tears.

"I'm going to be eighteen years old and Upthegrove has never once made an attempt to communicate with me."

"Well, you see, your father—"

"Stop making excuses for him. Can you do that? That's what I want for my birthday. I want you stop making excuses for him." Crap. I knew that shit was going to hit the fan if I ever told her David was having an affair. Here she was, defending Upthegrove to my face. And she didn't give a damn what I felt. She didn't. I was invisible. Well, damn it to hell, I wasn't going to go along with the ghost role Sally thought I should be playing.

"You're a very self-centered young man." That's what she said as she blew her nose on a napkin.

"Let's see," I said. "All of this is my fault, is that it?"

"You could be more forgiving."

"Okay," I said. "What should Upthegrove be?"

"What?"

This whole damn thing was really getting to me. "I don't drive on one-way streets, Sally." Shit. I'd called her Sally. "If I should be more forgiving, what should Upthegrove be?"

"I don't know what you're talking about."

"Yes, you do." You know, this whole conversation was going absolutely nowhere. "Sally," I said, "If you don't uninvite him, then I'm canceling my party."

"But he'll be devastated."

"Or maybe destroyed," I said.

"I can't believe you came from me."

"I probably came from hell," I said. And then I just looked at her. Crap. I was the son of a woman who literally could not tell you the difference between a shoelace and a snake. I was a shoelace (not a huge accomplishment). Upthegrove was a snake (no editorial needed). I just kept looking at her. "I'm your son," I whispered. I was crying. Why was I crying? I hated tears. They were so unironic. "The fact that you invited him. That devastated me, too. I matter less. It's good to know."

I walked out of the room.

I knew she would uninvite him. I knew she would think less of me because I'd made her do it. Like always, she would think it was me who was being a spoilsport. She'd come up with a brilliant idea as part of my birthday present. And me, the ingrate, I'd ruined everything. Again. I saw the whole thing clearly now. I was an obstacle. I was a speed bump and she was in a hurry to get to her destination. Where was she going, anyway?

You know, I just didn't get it. Why would she invite Upthegrove to my birthday party when she knew he never called me? And she didn't have that many good things to say about him, anyway. But they talked sometimes. Why did they talk? Look, the point is that none of this had anything to do with me. Their son. The Birthday Boy.

Yeah, she would uninvite him to a party that was more hers than mine. She would play the martyr. She would run to David and tell him how mean I was. Then, they would continue the charade of this little family of ours and continue with the plans for the birthday. To David and Sally, Rosie and Carmen were interchangeable. The show must go on. How did I wind up with a part in this play? I didn't even audition.

Happy birthday Jacob Upthegrove.

Sally and me. We weren't working.

I started thinking: Why the hell was I protecting her from David's affair? And then it dawned on me. Two epiphanies in one day. I wasn't protecting her—*I was protecting myself.*

If I brought her the news, the messenger would be shot. Katie Scopes was absolutely right.

Sally. She destroyed me. Again and again and again. She really destroyed me.

You know what else? I destroyed myself. I was just a big coward. Maybe I was just like Upthegrove. Maybe I deserved to be stuck with his name.

You know, the Anger Management Lady, she said I needed serious therapy. She was completely wrong. I didn't need therapy—I needed a new set of parents.

Him
(Ramiro)

That day, I just headed to the cemetery at lunch. See, there's this cemetery right across the street from Chico's Tacos. I always thought that was interesting. I mean, Alameda is an interesting street. "Bad zoning," David said, one time when he had to pick me up from school. "I like all the piñata stores farther up the street," I told him.

"You go in those places?" He said it like I was crossing the border to another country—a country where no one with any sense would ever travel to.

I nodded.

"Anyone in there speak English?"

"What's your point, David?"

The conversation stopped. "Bad zoning," he said again. Hell, I liked the cemetery. It had this very sweet but weird elk that greeted you as you entered. I mean, what was a statue of an elk doing at the entrance to a cemetery. It was like he was lost. Only he didn't look lost. He looked perfectly happy.

So I was just sitting there at the cemetery, smoking a cigarette. That was what I was having for lunch. I wasn't hungry. Sally had my head spinning. That's what she always told me, "Jacob, you make my head spin." Okay, so I wasn't easy to figure out. But neither was she. I mean, where was the logic behind this woman's actions? And, as I'm sitting there arguing with myself, I see Ramiro hanging out. And I thought it was very cool that he came here to think, and I thought I wasn't wrong for thinking he must be a very cool and different sort of person. His own man. You can dig that, right? But as I studied him a little more, I thought he looked really sad. And that made me feel bad. I mean, look, people had problems. Me and

Sally and David, hell, those weren't problems, those were dramas. I mean, Rosie had problems. Serious problems.

I waved at Ramiro.

He waved back.

You know, I tried to make conversation. I'm not really a shy person. But talking to people isn't always easy. And this guy, Ram, he didn't really feel like talking. I offered him a cigarette. He didn't take it. He said he wasn't in the mood. Anybody else would've just said "sure" or "no thanks" or "I don't smoke"—you know, common things like that. But Ram, he said, "I'm not in the mood." I thought that was a very cool thing to say. And he liked cemeteries—just like me. It was true what Ram said, "the effen world's too noisy." That was true. I mean, what was wrong with a little quiet. I liked quiet. I mean, the world was like a radio station that was tuned in to all the music in the world—except that you couldn't really hear any of the songs anymore because all the songs were playing full blast—and all of them shouting at you at the same time. I mean, everything was lost and it was just a big loud scramble.

You know, as I was talking to Ram, I asked him if he lived around here. It was dumb. I mean, of course he did. It was me who didn't belong. Not him. I mean, I was on his turf. And I think he didn't like my question. But then he tried to, you know, talk to me. He knows I'm only there because I'm part of the magnet school thing—so he's polite enough to ask me if I'm going to be a doctor. So, I just told him it was Sally's idea. But when I asked him what he wanted to do after high school, he said a very cool thing. I mean, very cool. He said, "Live." And he didn't say it to be a wiseass. He didn't. And he wasn't mocking me. Believe me, I'm the king of mock. I know mock when I hear it. Only, you know, I just didn't leave it alone. I can't ever leave anything alone. So instead of just nodding—

like I should have, well, I said, "But you gotta work." And immediately I knew I sounded just like David and I wanted to kick myself. I mean, the guy knew more about work than I did. What the hell did I know about work? Look, Sally told me once that "work" was just another word for someone like me. Well, she should know. That's all work was for her, too. A word.

So, I'm sitting there, getting deeper and deeper and I'm wondering why this guy just doesn't bop me one. And then I just keep going, asking him if he had a job and then I tell him that school was my job and he was probably thinking that only rich people said shit like that. And, of course, he would be right. And when he told me he worked at Whataburger, I asked if they were hiring.

Instead of telling me to go to hell, which he probably should have, he just said, "Nope."

I really hoped the guy would go to my party. I mean, he's real. And real isn't just another word. Not to me. You know, his e-mail handle was Borderchango. Very cool. Border monkey. I mean, that really *is* cool.

You know, I don't know what Ramiro makes of me. I don't.

So when I got home, I wrote Ramiro an e-mail. I gave him directions to my house. Look, I don't even know if the guy has wheels. Still, I hoped he would come. I mean, it would be very cool to make a new friend. Look, I could use one.

And on Friday afternoon, as I'm driving away from school, I see Ramiro, and I offer him a ride. He shrugs, gets in the car, and we drive to the Circle K. You know, and it seemed like we were friends. Well, it seemed like it. I left him off at the hospital. He told me his brother was sick. And I think it's a very serious thing. I got the feeling he was really sad. But he wasn't saying anything to me about it. I mean, the guy doesn't really know me. So, I reminded him about my party. He smiled.

I think he was just being nice. He's probably the kind of guy whose mother raised him to be polite. Sally, she raised me to be polite too. It just didn't take.

You know, after I left Ramiro off at the hospital, I wanted to go back. I wanted to ask him about what was happening with him. Maybe I was just tired of my own bullshit. You know, I was always in my head. Jake land. Shit. It was as if I always wrapped myself in my own thoughts. It was like no one could rip that blanket away from me.

I drove pretty slowly all the way home. When I was at a stoplight, there was this guy asking for money. I called him over. "You want to buy me some liquor?" I asked.

"It'll cost you," he said.

The guy was really ratty-looking. I mean, these guys don't exactly have good hygiene. But I didn't give a shit. "Get in," I said.

"But what about my corner?" he says.

These guys. They're as bad as property owners—always afraid someone's going to intrude on their turf. "I'll bring you right back," I said.

So, I just buy the guy off. I mean, this was business. He buys me a bottle of Jack Daniels, and I buy him one too. And I throw in a twenty. He's happy. I'm happy, and when I drop him off at the corner, no one's taken it away from him. He smiles at me and says, "Anytime I can help you out, just let me know."

I don't know who was more pathetic—him or me.

I drove home. I wasn't looking forward to this. Sally would be happy. God, she would be so happy about all of this.

When I walked in the door, the caterers had just arrived. David was directing them to the patio. "Where's Mom?" I asked.

"Oh, so you're calling her Mom again?" David smiled.

"Yeah," I said. "Today." I smiled back.

"So," he said, "what would you like for your birthday?"

"A party's enough," I said.

"No, no, please, anything you want. I mean it."

He was smiling at me. Being real sincere.

I wanted to look at him and say, "I want you to tell Mom you're having an affair." I wanted to see the sick look on his face. But that's not what I said. "Anything?" I said.

He nodded.

I mean, the guy thought I was going to ask for another expensive toy. I mean, that would be easy, right? He could afford anything. He and Upthegrove went to the same guy school.

"I want you to help Rosie," I said.

He just sort of looked at me.

"You know, I don't know anything about immigration law."

I just smiled. "It's okay," I said. "I've hired someone."

He looked at me. "Does your mother know?"

"It's not really her concern. She's made that clear enough."

"Why are you doing this?"

This is what I wanted to say: "I don't know. Why are you having an affair?" That's not what I said. This is what I said: "Because I like Rosie. Is that a good enough reason?"

"Be careful who you take up with."

That's what he said. *Yeah, buddy, you wanna tell me about the lady in the red Mustang?*

"You can pick your friends," I said, "but you sure as hell can't pick your mom. Or who she marries."

He didn't say anything. He just changed the subject. "I need to show the caterers where to set up."

I nodded. Was I having a good time yet?

Just then, my mother stepped into the kitchen. She'd spent the whole day making herself look good. And she *did* look good. "Hi, Mom," I said.

"Hi, sweetie," she said. And then she hugged me.

I wondered what Ramiro's mom was like. I bet she wasn't like mine at all. I bet she was more real. Ah, what the hell did I know about real?

THREE

Me, Ramiro
(Who Am I, Anyway?)

Alejandra is the only person I know who knows who she is.
My dad? Hell, he probably doesn't even exist anymore. And
Tito? He doesn't exist anymore either. And my mom, she's in
a sad place and I don't know if I can follow her there.

And me? Hell, I don't think I even want to know who I am.
What would be the point?

Me?

I kept changing shirts.

I kept studying how the shirts looked on me.

I kept wondering if my dad had liked going to parties. When he was my age, he must've gone to parties. Maybe that's where he met my mom, at a party. I don't know why I was thinking about that guy again—but I think it had something to do with Tito. Exactly. That was exactly why I was thinking about him. Him. My Dad. The guy with the black eyes and the aging hair and the fire written all over his face. You know, maybe he was the kind of guy who didn't worry about little things like what shirt to wear. Maybe he didn't worry about anything. Didn't worry about my mom. Didn't worry about me. Didn't worry about Tito. Just effen didn't worry.

Maybe, because he'd been born handsome, he didn't have to worry. About anything. Certainly not about the shirts he wore. Couldn't be bothered. And probably all the girls wanted to touch him—no matter what shirt he was wearing. But girls weren't exactly reaching out to grab me. That's for effen sure. Hell, what did it matter what shirt I wore.

You know, it suddenly came to me that I'd never actually been to a party. All those birthday parties when I was a kid—they didn't count. Nope, didn't count. I kept trying to think back. When had I ever gone to a party? Then I remembered that I'd gone to Alejandra's *quinceañera* when she turned fifteen. She'd even asked me to be her escort and I was dying because I knew I had to say yes. But then I was saved when her grandmother insisted that her cousin be her escort. Alejandra wasn't too happy about that. It was her one chance to get me out on a date—a really public one. And her grandmother got in the way. What could you do about grandmothers except agree with them?

And actually, it turned out to be a nice party. A really nice party. And I'd had a good time and I'd danced and everything. But, you know, *quinceañeras* were family things, so there were as many adults there as there were kids our age. Kids. I hated to call ourselves kids. But, I mean, what were we? The way I was thinking, I didn't think of myself as a kid, but I definitely didn't see myself as a man. So what the hell am I? I'm a tadpole who's about to turn into a frog any second now. So what happens after that? Wait around and get kissed? Sure, why not?

So, I had exactly one party on my résumé. One. Well, at least I hadn't lost track. So what was I going to do at Jake's party? I didn't know anyone except Alejandra—so I was probably going to spend the whole time with her. Well, maybe that wasn't so bad. Look, she'd been very cool to me and my mom about Tito. And she was a real friend. She'd never turned her back on me. Not ever.

I heard my mom knock on my door. "Alejandra's here," she said. She walked into my room. *My* room now. Tito was gone. I'd always wanted my own room. But not like this. When you get what you want the wrong way, well, you don't want it anymore.

I looked at my mom. "How do I look?" I shrugged. I was wearing a white shirt and jeans. I'd ironed the shirt myself.

"You look fine," she said. "Very handsome."

I wasn't very handsome. I was okay. I wasn't ugly. But "very handsome" was pushing it. Look, she was my mom. "I don't really want to go."

"It might be fun. You could use some fun."

I nodded. "Tito's not going to make it, is he?"

She didn't look like she was going to cry. Maybe she'd cried enough. All my uncles and aunts were in the kitchen and the living room, and I knew they were having discussions. I was glad that they were there—and that she wasn't alone. I mean, I wasn't much help. I knew that. "It doesn't look good, Rammy."

I really didn't like to be called Rammy. But my mom, she'd earned the right to call me anything she wanted. "You can tell me," I said.

"Go to Jake's party. Have a good time."

"What about Dad?" I hadn't meant to ask that—I really hadn't. It just came out. I looked away from her.

"What about him?"

"Shouldn't he know?"

She nodded. She was trying to decide what to tell me. There were so many things she kept inside. So many things she didn't tell me. Silence. That old addiction. Yeah. I never knew if she was protecting herself or protecting me or—look, I just didn't know. But I hated it. I effen did. Finally, she decided. I could tell. I could read her sometimes. "I've been trying to reach him," she said.

"You have?" I tried not to sound too eager. But I was. Almost like a kid who saw candy flying out of a piñata. I just wanted to dive into all effen good stuff falling to the ground.

She nodded.

"And?"

"I'm still trying."

I nodded. When you don't know what to say, well, you can always nod. I'm good at that. Nodding. Practice makes perfect.

"Look," she said, "you think your father has a right to help me decide about Tito. I know you do. I can see it."

She was right. It hurt her, I think. I mean, the man had never done an effen thing for us. And Mom wasn't the kind of person who believed in rights without responsibilities. I mean,

I'd heard that lecture a hundred times, that's for effen sure. And I didn't even disagree with that whole philosophy. But the thing is, maybe this was my chance. My chance to see him. To meet him. To look at his face. Just once. To look into his eyes. God, just to look into his eyes.

I nodded.

"I'm trying my best to reach him, Ram. I am." Right then, I *did* think she was going to cry.

I just hugged her. "It's okay," I said. "Maybe he wouldn't come anyway."

She hugged me back. And then she combed my hair with her fingers. "You look just like him," she said. I know it killed her to say that. "So beautiful."

You know, my mom, she really was a very fantastic lady. I smiled at her. "I'll have a good time tonight," I said. "I'll even be nice to Alejandra. But I'm not going to kiss her." I said that to make her laugh. And it worked.

She laughed. I watched.

Watching her laugh was better than watching her cry.

By the time I walked out into the living room, where all my uncles and aunts were eating and drinking coffee and beer, Alejandra had already managed to make herself part of the family. You can't turn your back on girls like Alejandra. They plant themselves everywhere they go. And then they just start to grow.

"She's beautiful," my Tía Lupe said. And then she looked at me. "And we're all so proud of Mike." Mike was her father. Alejandra was soaking it all up. My Tía Lisa looked at me and winked. She hugged me. "Be nice to her," she whispered. And then she pinched me. And even though I didn't really want to go to Jake's party, I couldn't wait to get the hell out of that house. Uncles and aunts. Do they go to school to learn how to embarrass the hell out of their nephews and nieces? There must be a school. Or some kind of training manual. It even had a title: *The Mexican-American Manual for Uncles and Aunts or How to Give Your Nephews and Nieces an Inferiority Complex.* They all read a chapter every night before they went to bed.

The air outside was cool. It felt good. Good. And there wasn't any smell coming from the sewage treatment plant. So Dizzy Land wasn't Dizzy Land tonight.

Alejandra and I didn't say anything to each other as we walked toward her car. I opened the door for her. "That was nice," she said.

"Yeah," I said. "Well, I'm nice."

"Like your family," she said. "They're nice. You're lucky."

I nodded.

"I mean," she said, as she started up the car, "look at poor Lalo. His mother's a walking nightmare. And Jeremy's parents were even worse."

"Yeah, well, I got a dad who's missing in action."

"And I have a mom who left and never looked back. I don't worry about it anymore."

"Is that true?"

"Almost true." And then she laughed.

"Almost true?"

"Almost true is as close as we get sometimes. But, look, Ram, I got to keep the best parent. And so did you. So what do we get by feeling sorry for ourselves? Look at Tito. All he ever did was feel sorry for himself." She pulled out onto the street.

She was right. About getting to keep the best parent. About Tito feeling sorry for himself.

She glanced at me as she drove. "You got the directions?"

I nodded.

As we drove down the freeway, she was singing along with the radio. It was an old song. She really did have a nice voice.

"We're going to be the only Mexicans there."

"Knock it off. What is it with you?"

"We're different."

"Yeah, well, we're not that different."

I shrugged.

"They're really not more evolved than we are. They're not."

That made me laugh. "Well, they sure as hell think so."

"Look," she said, "there are so many Mexicans in El Paso that nobody even notices us."

"Sure," I said.

"Forget about it," she said. "We might even have a good time. You might meet a girl."

"My achin' elbow."

She laughed. "I might meet a guy."

I laughed too.

I got this feeling. I don't know. Maybe it was because of Tito. Maybe it was because of my mom. But I had this feeling.

Maybe everything would be different after tonight. Better different. I just tried to relax. I listened to Alejandra sing as she drove. I was lost. In her voice. And I just didn't effen care. If I was going to be lost, I might as well be lost listening to Alejandra sing as she drove.

Us and Them
(Me and Alejandra and Jake's Friends)

It was a really nice house. Okay, nice was too small a word for that house.

It certainly was the most expensive-looking house I'd ever walked into.

The party was already going and I was glad we weren't there any earlier. I mean, I would've only felt stupid and out of place if we'd have gotten there early. I hated that. But, this way, me and Alejandra, we could almost be invisible. Mrs. Upthegrove—who wasn't Mrs. Upthegrove, but Mrs. Ballard—greeted us at the door. She was a little plastic—but very nice. "I'm Mrs. Ballard," she said, "Jake's mother." She sure wore a lot of makeup. Not like Mom. Mom hardly wore any.

Alejandra shook her hand. She knew exactly what to do. She smiled and introduced herself.

"And aren't you lovely?" Mrs. Ballard said. Lovely. My achin' elbow. Then she turned to me. "I'm Ramiro," I said. "Ramiro Lopez. My friends call me Ram."

She smiled. "I'm so glad you could come." Look, she was trying. I mean, she had good manners and she was greeting everyone at the door. And I don't know if she really was glad that we were there—but what did it matter? Look, it must've been pretty tough to stand in your own doorway and greet a bunch of high school kids who are generally out to lunch on their manners. So I decided to cut her some slack. You know, the thing is, I can be hard on people.

She led us through the kitchen which led to the patio. A very cool patio. A very cool patio full of people. I mean, there were people everywhere, talking and laughing and the music wasn't too loud which was good because, you know, I really wasn't into loud. You know, Mr. Uncool Cat. That's me. And there were even more people standing around and dancing out on the lawn. It was sort of like a movie. People in the movies always lived in houses like this. See, people in the movies didn't live in houses like mine, that's for effen sure. Hollywood screenwriters didn't know shit about how we lived in Dizzy Land. See, people in the movies either lived in houses like this one or they lived in houses that were all graffitied and full of rats. See, my house was just, well, kind of ordinary. No rats. No graffiti. But no patios like this one.

One of the caterers (who looked like he might be from Dizzy Land) handed me and Alejandra a Coke. We sort of nodded at each other, and he was probably wondering what the effen hell was I doing here.

I looked around. And, I mean, this was a big party. I mean, there must have been a hundred people. And there was a DJ spinning tunes, a Chicano guy who had a real deep voice, and the tunes he was spinning were okay. Not great. But okay. I mean, I'm not like this music rat. I'm not that cool. I'm not a cat. I'm not a dude. I'm not a *vato*. I'm just Ram. Uncool. Okay. Okay.

Alejandra and I wandered out into the backyard.

We were drinking from our Cokes. Real cold. Good. I liked Cokes.

"Shit," I said.

She smiled. Then she pointed with her chin toward the back of the yard. "See the view," she said.

I could see all the lights of the city.

"That's what I want," she said.

"What for?" I said.

"Because it's so beautiful." She whispered it. Whispers. They were serious.

"If you ever get that, will you forget?"

She knew what I was talking about.

"I won't ever forget. Not ever." She laughed. "I'm a girl who was born and raised in Dizzy Land." She said it like it was some kind of award she'd won. That made me happy.

And then some guy walks right up to her and says, "Hey." He was tall. Some kind of jock, by the way he looked. He seemed like he was all about himself. You know the type. Someone gave him the world as a gift. It's like he woke up every day—then walked around waiting for someone to unwrap the gift. Just for him. Not cool. Not a cool cat, not at all.

"Hi," Alejandra said. Kind of shy, but okay. She was never too shy. Just okay shy.

"What's your name?"

I swear she was going to say Alex. But she didn't. "Alejandra," she said.

He nodded. "Cool," he said. I already didn't like him.

She looked at me. "And this is my friend, Ram."

We shook hands.

"Ram," he said. "Hey. I'm Abe."

"Hey," I said.

"So, you wanna dance?"

Alejandra looked at me. I shrugged. It was like a "go ahead" kind of shrug. And, well, me and Alejandra, we knew how to communicate.

"Sure," she said.

I watched them as they disappeared into the crowd that was dancing on the lawn. I sort of stood there and walked toward the back of the yard. I looked out at all the lights. And then I hear Jake's voice. "I see you made it."

I turned around. "Yeah, I made it."

He looked happy. He did. Happy looked good on him. I'd never seen that on his face before.

"I brought a friend."

"Yeah, I saw you come in. She's—" he stopped. "She's a real looker."

"Yeah. She is."

"She your girlfriend?"

"Nah. I've known her all my life. She's, well, she's like my best friend. But definitely not my girlfriend." He got even happier when he heard what I said.

"I'm glad you came."

"Big party," I said.

"I don't really know most of the people here."

"You don't?"

"Well, I used to know them. You know, went to school with them when I was in middle school, played soccer with a lot of them, you know, stuff like that? Anyway, I'm glad you came."

I sort of shrugged. I'm good at that. "You gotta nice view."

He nodded. "The thing about a view is that it lies to you. It tells you everything is beautiful. It's a fuckin' lie."

"Guess you're right. You know," I said, "lies can be really beautiful. You know, we can fall in love with lies." I was thinking of my father. Maybe that's all he was. A lie.

"Yup. I know about falling in love with lies." Then he laughed. "And you know, views, well, that's what views are all about."

He took out a pack of cigarettes. "Want a smoke?"

"Sure," I said. "What the hell."

So there I was with Jake, standing around and smoking. Not that I liked the cigarette. It made me feel dizzy. Well, hell, I was from Dizzy Land. That's where I lived. And Jake? Well, he lived here. Here. In a house with a view. Well, maybe it was a lie—but it sure looked good to me.

After a while the silence between us just got to me. I mean, usually, it was Jake who was the talker. I just always talked back. "Great party," I said. Maybe I'd said that already.

"Think so?"

I don't know why, but I laughed.

"Why are you laughing?"

I shrugged. "Sorry," I said. "To tell you the truth, I wouldn't know a great party from a shitty one."

That's when Jake started laughing too. "Yeah," he said, "me neither."

"Would you like something in that Coke?" he asked.

"I don't know," I said. Uncool. I was embarrassed. Look, I wasn't gonna get all shitfaced with my brother dying in a hospital. My mom didn't need that.

But right then, I heard Alejandra's voice. "He doesn't really drink," she said. As if she had been a part of the conversation all along.

Jake just stared at her. It was sort of dark in the backyard, but there was plenty of light coming from different places. And we could all see each other. And I could see that Jake was really into staring at Alejandra.

"Do you drink?" he asked. All of a sudden, I started to feel like maybe I was in the way.

"Sure," she said.

"Like hell," I said.

She laughed. "Well, what's a drink?" She looked at me. "You're driving."

I just gave her a look. "Cool," I said. But I didn't say it all that nice. I looked at Jake. "We get along like this."

He smiled.

Then Alejandra looked at him. "You're not a jerk like your friend, are you?"

He laughed. "Who knows? Which friend?"

"Abe."

"Yeah, well, Abe's very special." He laughed again. "I'm Jake."

"I'm Alejandra. Nice party."

"Yeah," he said.

"Great view."

"They're just lights," he said. Then they just sort of nodded at each other. And I knew what I was seeing. I mean, they were really going for each other. Right there. Right in front of me. And a part of me really just wanted to smile. I mean, maybe Alejandra would stop bugging me now. On the other hand, what did she know about this guy, Jake? What the hell did she know about him? I decided I had to watch the two of them. I mean, if they were going to drink, I was gonna be on both of them like a piece of gum that got stuck to your shoe on a hot day.

"So why's Abe a jerk?" I think Jake knew the answer to the question already. But, you know, getting to know people, it's a game.

Alejandra pointed at the guy who was leaning into some girl at the edge of the lawn. "Look at him," she said. "He tried to kiss me."

"That's what guys do."

"Not without my permission."

Jake smiled. "So what did you do?"

"I told him I was a black belt in karate. And that he shouldn't try it. He just laughed. And then he moved in. I grabbed his hand and spun him around. You know, I could have had him on the ground." She sort of shrugged.

"Is that true? Are you a black belt?"

Jake was so effen impressed. Hell, I'd been going to Alejandra's karate stuff since we were in first grade. Look, her dad spoiled her, gave her lessons for everything she wanted—and she always needed an audience. I was good for that. Her dad would always pick me up. You know, that black belt stuff, hell, it was old news. I mean, it was old as chicken soup. But Jake, he was just eating it all up. And, well, she *was* a black belt. And, you know, I wouldn't mess with her if she was really pissed. I wouldn't. I'd seen her in action. It was funny; she was perfect when she was doing her moves. Perfect. I always wondered why a girl who was so brainy and nice-looking and could do so many things, how a girl like that could be so damn insecure—especially when it came to boys. I decided right then and there that it had to have something to do with her mom. Moms who left—they were just like dads who walked away and never looked back. They left scars. I knew about all that.

Jake and Alejandra just kept talking to each other for a long time and I just kinda listened.

"You know what I think?" Alejandra said. "I think your friend, Abe, thinks I'm easy just because I'm Mexican."

Jake sort of shrugged. "That's probably true. Except—" He stopped and laughed. "The truth is that Abe thinks all girls are easy. He thinks they all want to sleep with him. That's the way he is."

"I'd rather sleep on a mattress full of cockroaches. And he's your friend?"

"Not really."

"Then why's he here?" I'll tell you one thing, Alejandra didn't let go of things. Here she was at Jake's party, challenging his guest list. Man, sometimes, well, hell, that's just how she was. Nothing anyone could do about it.

Jake smiled at her. I mean, the guy couldn't stop smiling. I thought he was just gonna lean into her and kiss her. "You know, I invited everybody."

"Why would you want to do that?"

"Look, the truth is, this is really more Sally's party than it is mine."

"Sally?"

"That would be my mom."

"You shouldn't call her by her first name. She's not your friend, she's your mother." I'm telling you, that Alejandra, she'd lecture anybody. Not that Jake seemed to mind.

"Well, Sally's not her real name. I just call her that. It makes her mad."

"Why do you want to make her mad?"

"Because she makes *me* mad, that's why. It's my way of returning the favor." Right then, Jake took a really deep drag from his cigarette. "My mom and I don't get along all that well sometimes, you know? It's complicated."

"Things always are." Alejandra didn't sound superior when she said it. She really didn't. All of a sudden, her voice got real soft. I guess she'd noticed the look on Jake's face. Like, well, *like things really were complicated.*

Jake moved a couple of feet away and reached down and pulled out a bottle of Jack Daniels from under a bush. He brought the bottle over to us and sort of smiled. It wasn't a happy, crazy-kind-of-guy smile. It was a quiet smile. Quiet and, well, real. You know, I guess I just figured Jake hung out by himself because he wanted to smoke and because he thought he was a little bit superior. I always figured him as the kind of guy who just had to be the smartest effen guy in the room. But, you know, the guy was sad.

He handed his can of Coke to Alejandra. "Hold this," he

said. So there Alejandra was, holding two cans of Coke, hers and Jake's. Jake poured some Jack into his can. Plenty, that's for sure. Then he looked at Alejandra. "Want some?"

"Sure," she said. Then he poured some Jack into her can of Coke. Plenty, that's for sure. They both kind of looked at me.

"Don't look at me like that," I said. I gave Alejandra a smirk. "I'm driving."

I don't know why exactly, but we all just started laughing. All of us. I wonder if we were all laughing for the same reason. Maybe we were all laughing for different reasons. Anyway, we just sort of hung out for a while. Then Jake says, "I'm glad you came. I'm having fun." And then he smiled. And all that sadness went away again. Then he put the bottle back under the bush.

"So," he says, "are you into politics?"

Alejandra laughed.

"What's so funny?"

"Well, that's a real conversation-starter."

"It is for me."

Alejandra got a kick out of that. I could tell.

"Well," he said, "*Are* you into politics?"

"I guess."

"You guess?" He looked at me. "What about you, Ram?"

"Me?" I said. I didn't really know what he meant about being into politics. I guess I had my own ideas. Ideas I got from my mom. But not just from her, but also from walking around and taking in all the shit that was happening in the world. "Well, I'm against all those loan sharks that rip poor people off with those high interest rates. It's effen obscene. I'm really against that. And I think people should make a living wage. So, maybe that makes me political."

Jake smiled. "Cool." He looked at Alejandra's T-shirt. "So are you an environmentalist?"

"Yes," she said. "It's not cool not to love the earth." That Alejandra, I had to hand it to her. She knew how to answer a question. And then she shrugged. "And I bet neither one of you believes in gender politics."

God, I could tell she'd just read something. She was always all about the last book she read or the last article. And since she'd gotten into the Internet, she'd only gotten worse.

"Gender politics?" I said.

She smiled. "Exactly. Men think they're superior. They've constructed a whole world around that philosophy."

She said the word "constructed." She'd definitely read an article.

Jake laughed.

"You're making fun of me." She gave him a look. It was like she'd known him all his life. Those are exactly the kinds of looks I'd been getting from her since I was five.

"No, I'm not. It's just that I don't think men are so superior. My father, Upthegrove, is nothing but an adolescent who disappeared into Florida. He's a slacker with money. Those are the worst kind. And my stepdad, hell, I won't even get into that one. And guys like Abe who thinks girls are continents he can colonize just because he wants to. He thinks he's fucking Christopher Columbus and every girl he meets is the New World. Shit. Men aren't superior. They're idiots. And just think, someday I'm going to be one of those idiots. I can hardly wait."

That really made Alejandra laugh.

But just then, our little party within a party got interrupted by this very cool-looking girl. "Hi," she said, "I'm Katie." She had really black hair. I mean, you could tell she dyed it. But it looked nice. And she had a really nice face. Soft. Kind. Very nice.

She was looking right at me. "I'm Ram," I said.

"Ram," she said. "That's nice."

And then Jake interrupted us and asked her, "Where's Mark?"

"Mark?" she says with this really funny look on her face. "He left."

"He left?"

"Yeah, he just came for a while. He's got this family dinner going on, and he, well, he had to make for the road."

Jake didn't seem too sorry to be losing that particular guest. Maybe he liked her. "This is Alejandra," he said. He even pronounced her name right. The guy must've taken Spanish or something. Or maybe not. You know, in El Paso, Spanish was just in the air.

Katie and Alejandra smiled at each other. And then Katie looks right at her and asks, "Is Ram your boyfriend?"

Alejandra smiled real big and said, "No." That's all she said. No. But it was a pretty definitive no. All these years of trying to get me to be her boyfriend and already she'd dumped me for Jake. Not that I minded.

Katie smiled. She looked at me and said, "So, you wanna dance?"

I wasn't turning her down. No way. "Sure," I said.

And there I was, on Jake's lawn, dancing with a girl named Katie. You know, I don't know how long we danced—but it was a while, that's for sure. And, well, I could have danced with Katie all night. Not talking or anything. Just dancing. Not that I was a good dancer. Not that she cared. That was good, that she didn't care. She leaned toward me and whispered. "You have really nice eyes."

I sort of shrugged.

"You're shy, aren't you?"

I shrugged again. So we just kept dancing.

Finally, we got interrupted. Some guy walks up to us and asks Katie, "What the fuck do you think you're doing?"

"I'm dancing." She looked at him and said, "I thought you had to be at a family thing."

"Yeah, well, I got out of it. I'm gone fifteen minutes and you're dancing with another guy."

She rolled her eyes. She smiled at me. "Look, Ram, I have to straighten something out." She took the guy by the arm, and they disappeared through the gate. I felt like an idiot. Well, that's what I get. I mean, what did I expect? Did I really think she was gonna let me kiss her or something? Look, I came to a party and I danced. For me, dancing constituted a complete change. I went from being uncool to being Mr. Excitement. Yeah. Sure.

I walked to the back of the yard. Jake and Alejandra were still there. Only they were standing real close to each other. That made me smile. I mean, maybe now Alejandra and I could be friends in peace. Still, I wasn't sure I trusted Jake. And I wasn't sure Alejandra should be trusting him either.

Just as I walked back toward them, we all hear this voice, "Jacob? Jacob? Where are you?"

Jake shrugged. "That's Sally. I'm being paged." He handed his spiked Coke to Alejandra, popped an Altoid, and sort of rolled his eyes. "I'll be back."

He disappeared, moving past the crowd that was dancing on the lawn, toward his mother's voice.

I looked at Alejandra. "You're going to get drunk."

"No, I'm not. How was your dance?"

"Her boyfriend showed up."

She smiled. "You shouldn't trust a girl like that."

"Well, at least I danced."

She smiled. "Yeah."

I laughed. "I see the way you're looking at Jake."

"Yeah?"

"Yeah. Don't get drunk."

"Look, I'm not an idiot. I'm not going to get drunk."

"I'm watching you, Alejandra."

"Finally," she laughed. "You're finally watching me."

"That's not what I meant."

"I know what you meant."

"You like him, don't you?"

"I do like him. There's something very sweet about him. And he's handsome."

"You even think I'm handsome. What do you know?"

Alejandra took a drink from her spiked Coke. "This is good," she said. "I like it." Then she just looked at me. "You *are* handsome, you idiot. You know what your problem is—you have an inferiority complex. You're always thinking less of yourself. Why are you always beating up on yourself?"

"What are you, a shrink?"

"I'm just telling you what I think, Ram."

"Yeah, well, you're always telling me what you think."

We were quiet for a little while. We just sort of watched people dance. People who were our age. People we didn't know. I don't know what Alejandra was seeing when she was watching all those people. Maybe she just saw something normal. But that's not what I saw. I saw people who thought they owned the world. Shit. I didn't know where I got these feelings. I didn't. But that's just how I felt.

Alejandra kept sipping on her drink.

"Are you getting drunk?" I asked.

"A little," she said. "Not much. But a little."

"You should slow down."

"Don't worry. I'm not going to have another." She laughed. "I like the way this feels," she said. Then she looked at me. "You blame yourself, don't you?"

"What are you talking about?'

"You blame yourself because your father left. And you blame yourself for what's happened to Tito. You have to stop doing that."

"You're drunk."

"A little bit. But not really." And then she looked at me. "You'll be disappointed—if you ever meet him."

I knew she was talking about my father. "Maybe I won't be."

"You will be. Believe me."

That's when I knew that she'd met her mother. When? I wondered when. So I thought, what the hell, I'll just ask. "When did you meet her?"

"Last year."

"What was she like?"

"Numb. She was pretty and she was numb and, you know something? I didn't like her. I don't think she felt anything when she saw me. I thought I had all these things to say to her, but I didn't. Why should I tell her anything? What right did she have to know anything about me? And when I asked her why she left me, all she said was she didn't really remember. I waited for her to say something more. Something profound. But she didn't. She didn't remember. 'I was way too young.' That's all she said. She didn't say things like *aren't you pretty* or anything like that. She didn't ask me anything. Nothing. You know, I'm glad she left me with my father. I'm glad." Alejandra wasn't crying. She sure as hell wasn't feeling sorry for herself. "Let him go," she said. "Missing parents can become an addiction. And you know what addictions do? They fucking kill you."

"Hey, hey," I said. "Watch that mouth."

"Yeah, okay," she said. "But look, let your father go. He's poison. He's killing you."

But I couldn't let him go. I couldn't. I couldn't let go of Tito and I couldn't let go of my dad. All I knew was that they lived in my head. But mostly they lived in my heart. And that was the worst. Look, it didn't matter whether they loved me or not. Because I loved them—even if I didn't want to. And I didn't know how to stop.

Then, all of a sudden, there wasn't any more music and Jacob's mother was telling everybody they should leave. I mean she was yelling at everyone—and she looked like a crazed woman. I'm telling you that the woman was really hysterical. And I didn't really know what was happening, but the whole party turned into real chaos.

I just looked at Alejandra and she looked at me.

I don't know why, but we just smiled at each other.

I took the keys away from her. "Let's go," I said.

"What about Jake?"

Me, Jake
(Without Sally and Without Upthegrove)

Tell me again that I don't have any reason to be angry. Tell me again that it's me who's all screwed up. Go ahead. Believe me, I can take it.

Me and Them

(*Them* = My Guests)

I actually thought the party was going really well. Well means excellent. It didn't start out so great with that little encounter I had with David. Still, the encounter was meaningful. Maybe not comfortable or comforting—but certainly a cut above most of our other encounters which were, well, forgettable. Anyway, I decided to put David on hold. C'mon, it was my party. I wanted to get into it. David. On hold.

I started to get a little worried for a little while. Not that I'm much of a worrier. Sally pretty much has that category all to herself. But, look, what if no one came? And why should they? I mean, at one time or another they had all visited Jake land, and a lot of them had come out of that place a little bruised. Look, I hurt Tom with my fists. But most people, I just hurt them with the things I said. Yup, Jake land wasn't always the friendliest town on the map.

And the other thing is that I'm not a joiner. I'm not a belong-to kind of guy. I go my own way. Always have. Some people, well, they always think they're missing out on something—just hate to be left out. Me, I always figure whatever happens can go ahead and happen without me. If I wasn't me, I wouldn't be going to my birthday party either. Why would anyone else come? Shit. I should have invited the Anger Management Lady. She was a good citizen. She would have come. If only to check out the results of her great work.

I paced. I smoked. I worried. And then, people started showing up. I popped an Altoid and smiled, and, well, we had a party. See, the thing is that most people are nicer than me. That's why they were here. And Sally, she was happy. She greeted everyone at the door like she was Lady Bird Johnson.

Okay, that's a very retro Texas thing to think. You know, Sally, she has a picture of her and Lady Bird Johnson in her home office. Not that she needed an office and not that she belonged to her political party, but hey, a Texas celebrity was a Texas celebrity.

One of the first guests was Tim, Tom's younger brother. He was dating Sheila. Sheila was my last girlfriend. We didn't have anything in common except that we both wanted to have sex. And then we discovered that we really didn't want to have sex with each other. Long story. She didn't like my sense of irony. She didn't like my style. And she didn't like my feet. My feet? What was that? But we were still friends. E-mail friends, mostly that's what we were. Anyway, Tim comes up to me and says: "Happy Birthday."

"Thanks," I said. I didn't bother to tell him that my real birthday wasn't until Monday. He wouldn't have cared. I barely cared myself.

"You know," he said, "Tom still hates you."

"Good for him," I said. Look, I did break the guy's nose, after all. Ancient history. But I knew about grudges.

"He says he might kill you someday."

"Tell him not to bother. I'm already dead."

Tim laughed. "Already dead. You kill me."

Kill me? Who was he, Holden Caulfield? "I'm serious," I said.

He just kept laughing. And when he stopped, he said, "You know what? He deserved it."

I just looked at him.

"I mean it. He's just a bully. He's always been a bully. And he'll always be one. You know what? Bullies have no sense of humor."

He was right. "I'm sorry about all that," I said. I'm not really sure what I was being sorry about. It just popped into my mouth. Sometimes, that's the way it is. Things pop into your mouth, then what you say assaults other people's ears.

"You know," he said, real serious, "sometimes I want to break his nose a second time. I hate him."

I felt bad for the poor guy. It couldn't feel that good walking through life hating your own brother. Look, he hated him enough to go around telling people. That's sad. We're talking sad here. "Well, if it makes you feel any better, I hate him too."

That made him laugh. So, see, the party was off to a good start. I was even having a halfway meaningful conversation. And meaningful in a better way than my conversation with David.

And Katie Scopes showed up with her new boyfriend (and a stash of drugs, no doubt). My mother greeted her at the door and actually hugged her. "You've gotten so lovely," she said. There was no sarcasm in Sally's voice. No surprise there. Sally only did sarcasm with me—otherwise, she played it straight. Shallow but straight.

Katie smiled. She managed to kiss my mother's cheek. I know that took a lot. People like Katie and people like Sally just didn't fit. Different countries. I mean, these people did not like to cross into each other's borders—legally or illegally. They just didn't give certain people visas to enter. She shook David's hand and I knew she was slyly studying him. They exchanged those weird, uncomfortable greetings. Well, look, everyone was trying to be civilized. When Katie hugged me, she whispered in my ear. "Ms. Red Mustang has very bad taste in men." That made me laugh.

I gotta say, Katie looked great. You know, it was good, that we'd wound up friends. You know, I started to think that this party thing was going to turn into a very fine thing. And

Katie's boyfriend? Well, I guess you could say he was good-looking in a very scruffy kind of way. His name was Mark. And Mark, well, he had some deficiencies when it came to expressing himself verbally. "Dude," he said, "another fuckin' year."

"Yeah," I said. "Another fuckin' year." This guy didn't need any of Katie's drugs to sound like Cro-Magnon man. No, sir, his family's gene pool pretty much called into question Darwin's theory of evolution. But, I mean, a lot of the guys I grew up with were like that. So there we were, Mark and me. Nodding at each other.

I finally got tired of nodding. My neck was beginning to hurt. I grabbed a Coke and handed it to him.

He sort of looked at the can.

"It's a Coke," I said.

"Dude," he said. Then he took a swig from the can and decided it just wasn't interesting enough for him. He took off to look for Katie. You know, she had the drugs. I got it. Look, some couples weren't hard to read. They were like a bad book. Listen, bad books, you know exactly where they were going. That's why you threw them against the wall or donated them to the neighbor's garage sale.

But it was all great. Excellent. I was having a pretty good time. I was digging the whole scene. The thing is, if you want, you can be invisible at your own party. That's alright. In the sixties they used to say "far out." I was thinking to myself that maybe I'd go on a campaign and bring the term back into usage. I mean why let such a cool expression go extinct? Didn't we save the spotted owl?

So, I was walking around the patio and the backyard talking to people. And lots of girls kissed me on the cheek and said really nice stuff to me. And guys, well, they were less articulate. Look, my gender has a lot to answer for. Katie Scopes, she keeps reminding me of that fact. But the thing is, Katie Scopes only goes out with the most unevolved guys on the planet. What's that about?

So, as I walked around, the members of my own gender ran into me and kept saying things like "Dude!" and giving me high fives and, well, you know, it was all sort of cool—and you could either embrace the whole scene or be ironic. Either way, it was fun.

The first girl I ever kissed, she was there. Her name was Danielle. I hadn't seen her for a long time. She grabbed my arm and led me to the edge of my backyard. "You've gotten so beautiful," she said.

I didn't exactly know what to say to that. I sort of laughed and said, "You're only saying that because you're going out with Sam." I hated Sam. I won't go into that.

"What's that supposed to mean?"

"Look," I said, "I look pretty beautiful compared to Sam."

She shook her head and laughed. "Still can't take a compliment, huh?"

I lit a cigarette.

She took it away from me. She took a hit and just held on to it. I got it. She'd colonized the damn thing. So I lit another. "Didn't know you smoked."

"Sometimes. I steal them from my mother."

"How is she?" I liked her mother.

"She compares everyone I date to you."

"I think that's funny."

"Why?"

"Look, most mothers don't want me near their daughters."

"My mother doesn't care about appearances. She liked your T-shirts. And she said you were the only smart boy I ever dated."

That was probably true. It also wasn't much to brag about. Danielle was like Katie. She wasn't into smart. I was definitely noting a trend here. Danielle must have been perfectly happy. Sam was a bodybuilder. Look, at least the guy could talk. Okay, no compound sentences came out of his lips, but he could handle adjectives and adverbs. I laughed. "She's the only mother in the universe that likes my T-shirts. Sally likes to steal them and throw them away."

"Still calling her Sally?"

"Well, we've progressed. Now I call her Sally to her face."

"How does that go down?"

"How do you think?"

"She tries."

"Yeah. Me too. Everyone tries."

"I miss you," she said.

That surprised me. I was a real shit to her. I was. I wasn't exactly the easiest guy to be around. I didn't have to ask for exit interviews. I knew the score.

"Aren't you going to ask me why?"

"Okay," I said. "Why?"

"Because you're beautiful, that's why. And you're the only boy who's ever kissed me who didn't know how beautiful he was."

"I don't get it," I said.

"Someday, you just might," she said. She finished her cigarette. Which was really *my* cigarette. And then she shrugged. "I think I'll go and dance with Sam."

I smiled at her. I was glad I'd invited her. Still, it was strange what she said, that I was beautiful. Maybe irony was the new beautiful. You know, like El Paso was the new Austin.

And then, as I was standing around, John came up to me. John. John who'd been sent up to a boot camp. Discipline problems, they said. And pot problems. And, well, problems all the way around. I stood in solidarity with him. And you know, he looked pretty good. A little beaten down. But okay. And as he was talking to me, I noticed Ram walk onto the patio. Ram and the most beautiful girl I'd ever seen. I mean, she was a serious beauty. An interesting beauty. The kind of beauty that lasted. I was destroyed. I was. She was wearing a T-shirt that said THINK GREEN. God, I was destroyed, destroyed, destroyed. I mean I was seriously destroyed. I mean, there were all these things going through my head and John was talking to me and telling me how he was trying real hard to turn his fucking life around, and I just gave myself a really good lecture and made myself listen to him. Look, Ram and the girl he walked in with, they weren't going anywhere. So I stood there, lit a cigarette, and listened to John.

And, look, I won't get into it, but as I listened to John, I was seriously impressed. I made a note to start hanging around with him some more. I mean, he had a mind. And it even seemed like he had a heart. You know what he said? He said, "Jake, I'm tired. I'm really tired. You know, all I've really done since I was ten is play hide-and-seek. Not gonna do that anymore." I just stood there and looked at him. He looked like some kind of saint. I'm serious here. I mean, the look on his face. The guy was giving sincerity a good name. And then this guy shows up, and he's standing real close to John and then John says, "This is Gregory." I'd never met Gregory. He was tall and dark and had a really deep voice. But I noticed something. They were, well, you know, I think they were boyfriends. Not that it bothered me. That was cool. And maybe that was John's problem, that was the whole hide-and-seek thing. But maybe now, as Mrs. Anaya would say, maybe now he was ready to embrace. I wondered what Mrs. Anaya would say about embracing homosexuality. I made a mental note to ask her. Then maybe she really would throw me out of her class.

And then I started to get the fact that now that Gregory had arrived on the scene, John wouldn't mind it so much if I moved on and talked to someone else. It may have been my birthday party, but, well, I wasn't Gregory. I could tell that they just wanted to move to some corner of the yard and be alone. I could dig it. Look, I could see the alternative romance novel written all over John's face. He was looking at Gregory and his eyes were saying *you really destroy me*. And then I saw that girl, that girl who walked in with Ram. *And she was dancing with Abe.* Change the "b" to "p" and you know just what kind of guy he was. That really fucking destroyed me, that she was dancing and talking to Abe.

Shit, I just moved toward the backyard to look for Ram. If I stuck with Ram, I'd get to that girl. God, she really was destroying me—and I didn't even know her. Right then and there, I decided I believed in God. And I even had a prayer for him. "God, please let Ram and that girl be friends. Just friends. Please, God."

I'm sure that God, if he existed, had a very ironic look on his face. Who could blame Him?

Her
(Alejandra)

Ram looked a little out of place. He was at the very end of the backyard, keeping to himself. But he didn't seem like he was having a miserable time or sitting around feeling sorry for himself. He was just watching. Taking things in. I figured that's the way he was.

I walked up to him and we just talked. He was easy to be around. And we got into a conversation, and he didn't seem to be as reluctant as the other times I ran into him. Maybe the guy was just shy. Or maybe he just didn't trust me. But, you know, he'd come to my party, so I figured he didn't hate me. That was the thing, I always figured most people didn't like me. As the Anger Management Lady would say, "You don't help yourself out, Jacob."

So, anyway, we talked and I was having a real good time. And then that girl, Alejandra, joins us *and it turns out that she and Ram are just friends*. And, well, happy birthday, Jake! And then, you know, I offered to spike their Cokes. Ram didn't take me up on the offer, but he was very cool about it. You know, that guy, he's totally unaffected by peer pressure. I mean it. The guy knows who he is. But, Alejandra, she's game, and unlike Katie Scopes, she didn't seem like the type to be really into mood-altering substances. And then who should show up just then? Katie Scopes in the flesh. And immediately she starts giving Ram the eye. You know, that Katie, she was really something. Her unevolved boyfriend Mark leaves the party and she makes a straight line for the newest kid on the block. She liked Ram, I could tell. You know, Ram was a helluva lot nicer guy than Mark. And he sure as hell was smarter. Maybe Katie would figure that out.

Anyway, it was really nice of Katie to take Ram out to dance. It was like a birthday gift. That meant Alejandra was all alone. With me. I thought that was very cool. I mean, I was so fucking destroyed. I didn't even know what to say to her.

"You like the Silva Magnet School?"

"It's okay." That's exactly what I said. How's that for articulate?

"Do you want to be a doctor?"

"No."

"Why?"

"I just don't."

"Then why are you taking up someone else's space?"

I had never thought of it that way. I could see immediately that Alejandra was a practical girl, spoke her mind. Not a bad trait. An excellent trait.

"I did it to please my parents." That was so lame. Especially because I spent so much energy trying *not* to please them.

She smiled. "I don't take you for being a pleaser." She studied me. "Still, they're your parents."

"Well, really just my mom."

"That wasn't your dad standing beside her at the door."

"You mean the guy saying nothing."

"Yeah, that one."

"He's my stepdad. Only I don't think of him as a stepdad. I think of him as my mother's husband."

"You don't like him."

"No."

I was telling her things about myself. I kept trying to tell myself to knock off all that sincerity. I mean, my irony must've been tired or something. You know, taking fifteen or something.

"Why don't you like him?"

"Because a dead armadillo is more interesting than him. Because he's only interested in his job. And because he's having an affair." Shit! I didn't know I was going to say that. I destroyed myself. I did. Shit.

"What?" she said.

"He's having an affair."

"How do you know?"

"I saw them."

"Are you sure it was them?"

"Absolutely."

"Where?"

"Are you planning on being an attorney?" Ah, I was feeling more myself.

"As a matter of fact, that's one of the things I'm thinking about."

"You'll be brilliant."

She laughed.

"Can I kiss you?" I can't believe I asked her that. I was really destroying myself by all the things I was saying.

She took a sip from her spiked Coke. "No."

"Why not?"

"I don't know you."

I took a big swig from *my* spiked Coke. "Well, if you kissed me you'd know me better."

"Nice try." She smiled at me. "Maybe if you asked me out."

"What about tomorrow?"

"It's a date." She took another drink from her Coke.

"Serious?"

"Serious. Give me your cell phone."

I swear I was shaking. I reached into my pants pocket and pulled out my cell. I handed it to her.

She opened it—then punched in her number. "There," she

said—then handed me back my cell. Cool. She knew how to handle herself, I'll tell you that. Man. Wow.

"So," she said, "does your mother know?"

"About our date?"

"About your stepfather's affair, you idiot."

She called me an idiot. But it was sweet, the way she said it. "No," I said, "she doesn't know."

"You haven't told her?"

"No."

"What? Why not? She's your mother."

"I only just found out."

"How many days?"

"A few."

"What are you waiting for?"

"Why are you so sure of yourself?"

"Do you love your mother?"

"Most days."

"Most days?"

"We have a problematic relationship."

She was just looking at me. I wasn't sure I liked that look.

"What's that look?"

"You should tell her."

"She'll hate me if I do."

"She might. You know, sometimes you just have to do the right thing. You're not responsible for the way your mother reacts." You know, I was beginning to think that Alejandra was related to the Anger Management Lady.

"Maybe not. But what's the right thing?"

"Don't play dumb. Dumb doesn't work on a guy like you."

She was de-stroy-ing me. I walked over to where I kept my bottle of booze. I poured a little more of it into my Coke. I took a big drink. I put the bottle back in its hiding place. "I don't know what to do," I whispered.

She took my hand and squeezed it. It was so warm and sure and beautiful, that touch. I wanted to cry. And I didn't even know why.

I looked at Alejandra.

She looked back at me.

Then she said, "Are you one of those guys that just wants to lay a Mexican girl?"

"What?"

"They're a dime a dozen."

"No," I said. "I'm not one of those guys."

She didn't say anything.

"Do you believe me?" I wanted her to believe me. It had been so long since I'd wanted anything from someone. *Please, believe me.*

"Yes," she said. Her voice was so soft. And she was looking directly into my eyes. "I believe you."

I wanted to stay that way forever. Just Alejandra. Standing next to me. Saying *I believe you.*

And then we both saw Ram walking toward us.

And then, I heard my mom calling me. Shit. She wanted me to go perform for her friends, to shake their hands. I felt like a fucking monkey. Sally, I wanted to yell, just back off. I'm having a good time here.

I shrugged and walked toward Sally's voice like a robot. But I turned around. I looked at Ram and he just sort of shrugged. And then I looked at Alejandra. Her eyes said: *Go. Go and take care of business.* She was like that. Already I knew something important about her. She took care of business. She was so unlike Upthegrove. So unlike Sally. I was so destroyed.

Alejandra. Alejandra. Alejandra.

Him and Her
(Sally and David)

I found my mom standing at the French doors that led into the patio. She'd had a drink or two. Not that she was drunk. But she was so, well, happy. Give Sally two glasses of wine and she wins the happy award. She kissed me. "Come and greet the guests," she said.

I smiled. What else was I supposed to do?

She led me around the living room, introducing me to all of her friends. I didn't pay any attention to their names. I shook their hands. They all kept repeating *happy birthday*. I answered back *thank you. Thank you, thank you, thank you.* And right in the middle of the whole embarrassing ordeal (embarrassing for me, not for them—I mean, these people weren't embarrassed about anything), the doorbell rang. I couldn't wait to get away from the whole scene. "I'll get it," I said. I headed for the door before Sally could object.

I opened the door, and there she was: Ms. Red Mustang. I think everything inside me just came to a complete stop. Complete. I finally took a breath. Unbelievable. There she was up close and in the flesh. Something inside me panicked. But then I got calm. All of a sudden a part of me was smiling my ass off. Another part of me was saying, *oh shit, oh shit, oh shit.* "Hi!" I said.

"I'm looking for David." She was pissed. Definitely in a disturbed state of mind.

"David who?" I asked. Okay, I was being coy.

"Are you Jake?"

Hell, she even knew who I was. It gave me the willies to think I was part of their pillow talk. "Yeah," I said. "I'm sorry, I don't know—"

She stopped me dead. I take it she didn't show up at our front door to make small talk. She pushed right past me. I mean she shoved me. Where was the Anger Management Lady when you needed her?

I didn't know what to do. Turns out it didn't matter. I didn't need to make any decisions here.

David was talking about his latest case. And right in the middle of his sentence, he eyed Ms. Red Mustang. She walked right up to him, took the drink out of his hand, and downed it. Now, this was my idea of a party. "You never had any intention of leaving her, did you?"

Her finger was pointing at my mom.

"Did you, you bastard? Answer me."

I kept watching my mom whose smile had left her face. Maybe permanently. And then it seemed to me that the room was perfectly still. I mean, this was the silence of a church. Ms. Red Mustang had stopped the show.

And finally, Mom decided to break the silence. "Yes, David, I think she deserves an answer." My mom's voice was shaking. Her lips were quivering.

David was as red as flame. I mean the guy looked like he was on fire. He didn't say a word. I don't know why, but I took pity on the guy. I walked over to the bar, poured him a scotch, and then walked up to him and handed it to him. I was going to say something, but decided I should keep my mouth shut.

Mom shot me a look. Ice cold. I looked at her and shrugged.

The whole damn room was looking at David as Ms. Red Mustang stood in front of him. To tell you the truth she looked like hell. For sure she'd been crying. And it seemed to me that she was a little drunk. Maybe a lot drunk. Or maybe she'd just plain gone over the edge.

"Two years!" she shouted. Or maybe she was shrieking. Certainly she was being very shrill. "Two years. And what have I got. Not even a shitty little raise at your shitty little law firm."

It seemed to me that the audience, at that point, was getting more and more agitated. One of the well-heeled couples headed for the front door and didn't look back. A few other people seemed completely embarrassed by the whole scene. They were too polite to run—so they all just stood or sat there in our lovely living room.

"This isn't about work." Those were the first words out of David's mouth.

"Sleeping with the fucking boss. I'd say it was mixing business with pleasure. More pleasure for you than for me, you bastard." She looked over at me and waved the drink that she'd taken out of David's hand. "Get me another."

She was barking orders at me.

Just then Sally decided to intervene. "Get the hell out of my house," she said.

Ms. Red Mustang just glared at her. She didn't move.

Sally moved toward her and grabbed her by the arm. "Get the hell out of my house before I do something you'll be sorry for." She shoved her toward the door. One of David's law partners finally decided to exercise some leadership. He calmly took Ms. Red Mustang by the arm and led her to the front door. He walked out with her and shut the door behind him.

No doubt about it, he knew her. Look, he was David's law partner. My bet was that he was about to calm her down. Or pay her off. Part of me wanted to go out there and represent her in the negotiations.

But that thought went in and out because just then the whole room decided it was time to leave the party. Most of them didn't bother to say good-bye. They just walked toward

247

the door and didn't look back. They'd had enough for one night. Definitely not their scene. I just stood there and witnessed the mass exodus.

So there were only four people left in the room. Me, Sally, David, and Mrs. Levitz (David's law partner's wife who had no where to go since her husband had escorted Ms. Red Mustang out the door).

There was an awful stillness in the room. I thought that heavy stillness would never leave. That's when Sally lost it. She just started crying hysterically. David tried to pull her toward him and comfort her. But Sally wasn't having any of it. "You need to leave," she gasped through her sobs. "You need to leave right now." She wasn't yelling. She was crying, making it impossible to yell. But it sounded like she meant it. And it also sounded like her heart was breaking. Which really made me sad. She was completely destroyed.

"You better do what she says, David." I just looked at him like maybe I was about to break his nose. I mean, it was something I knew how to do.

"This is my house," he said. But his voice didn't have much fight in it. I mean, it was over for the poor bastard. "My house," he repeated.

That's when Mrs. Levitz decided to exert some leadership skills of her own. "It won't be your house for long," she said. "I suggest you join my husband and Ms. Nesbit."

Mrs. Levitz was a scary lady. She got up from where she was seated, took David's drink out of his hand (the very one I'd poured for him), and pointed toward the door with her chin. I mean, Mrs. Levitz meant business.

David nodded. It's pathetic to watch a man in that kind of defeat.

And Sally, she was wailing at this point. "How could he

have done this? How could he have done this? To me? To me?" At that point she was beating her chest. But when I reached over to hold her—I mean, I didn't know what else to do—she shoved me away. "Don't touch me, you little creep."

I pulled away and raised my hands in the air like I was about to be arrested.

"You're all the same," she yelled. "All of you!" And then I felt a slap right across my face. And then another. And then another. She would have kept slapping me if Mrs. Levitz hadn't stopped her. "I hate you," she said. "I hate all of you."

She ran toward the patio howling like a coyote. "Get out. Everyone get out! This party is over!" She even managed to slap a few other faces. One of the guys was Mark. Oh well, there was bound to be some collateral damage. "Get out! All of you little bastards get out of my house!"

It wasn't exactly the party I'd dreamed of having. It turned out to be Sally's party all along.

Me
(Happy Birthday, Jake)

There I was standing next to Mrs. Levitz in the living room.

She really was a very scary lady. Too many jewels. Too much makeup. A face-lift. A voice that sounded like she'd been chewing on rocks her whole life. But you know something? She just sort of smiled at me. "She's in shock," she said. "She's not herself."

I don't think I reacted much.

"She didn't mean to slap you."

"Maybe she did."

"I think she was slapping David."

"No," I said, "I was there. She was slapping me." I was burning. God, I could feel my cheek burning.

"Don't be so literal, young man. You know what I mean."

"If she wanted to slap David, she should've slapped David. Frankly, I think she thinks this is all my fault."

"She doesn't hate you."

"She might."

"She doesn't."

"Not that you know."

"She's in shock."

"Okay." Yeah, okay. My cheek was burning. It was beginning to swell. I just shrugged at Mrs. Levitz. "So, what are we supposed to do?" Sally was outside chasing people out the gate and yelling at them. For all I knew she was taking a swing at a few people.

"I'm going to take her into one of the bedrooms and calm her down."

I nodded.

"Just tell the caterers to clean everything up. If they

haven't been paid, tell them to leave the bill." She smiled at me. "I'll take care of it." She certainly seemed in control. Practical woman. Scary.

"Okay," I said.

"You're shaking," she said.

"Yeah," I said. I guess I just didn't feel like talking.

I almost didn't even notice when she left the room in search of my mother. I just sort of sat down and gulped down a drink that was just sitting there. At least it was bourbon and not scotch. I don't know how long I sat there. Not long. I mean, I could still hear the last of the partygoers heading out the door.

Mrs. Levitz walked by, holding my mother as she sobbed. They walked up the stairs. I made my way to the patio just in time to see Ram and Alejandra walking out the side gate. "Wait," I said.

Alejandra turned around. She sort of smiled at me. "I'm sorry it turned out like this," she said.

"Don't go," I said. "Stay."

"The party's over, Jacob."

"Yeah," I said, "I guess it is."

I must have looked sad. Because she walked over to me and studied me. "Did she slap you?"

I nodded.

She kissed me. Not on the lips. But on my burning cheek. I think I flinched.

"Did that hurt?"

I nodded.

"Put ice on it." She smiled softly, then walked away.

Ram waved at me. "See ya, Jake."

I nodded. He looked real sorry too.

I didn't want them to go. I didn't know what to do.

Everything hurt. All I could do was wave at them. And watch them leave.

So there I was. Me. Jake. Just Jake. I went out to the back-yard and retrieved my Jack Daniels and I proceeded to take a swig. Right from the bottle. Then I took another swig. Then another.

Not that it did any good.

Look, that's just what I did.

There was no amount of irony that could stop me from feeling all this emptiness. Sincerity? That wouldn't help either.

I hated David.

I felt sorry for Sally. I just didn't know if I loved her.

Hell, what did it matter? I was drunk.

I stumbled to my room. The room was spinning. I closed my eyes. I wanted to sleep. And never wake up again.

I'd never been this destroyed in all my life.

Me
(Fatherless Ramiro)

Sometimes, I guess you just have to accept the life that was
given to you. Not having a father doesn't have to be an effen
tragedy. That's what Tito did, he turned his whole life into a
tragedy. That's not for me.

And Me, Jake
(Sincerely)

The Anger Management Lady told me once that I used my
intelligence like a weapon. "Sometimes like a weapon and
sometimes like armor. Life hurts, Jacob. It hurts like hell." Like
I didn't know that. She had a lot to say about a lot of things.
But on the subject of screwed-up parents? Well, on that subject she had nothing to say. I was on my own on that one.

Me, Ram
(And Her, Alejandra)

It wasn't late. Just after ten thirty. That's when we left Jake's party. That's when we left him there, with his sad face and his breaking heart. I knew something about a breaking heart. Maybe that's the thing I'd seen in Jake all along.

Alejandra and I didn't say much when we made our way to the car. I opened the door for her. She got in. She nodded at me. There was an almost smile on her face, but something sad, too. And something happy. Absolutely. Something had changed. Or maybe it was me.

Maybe it was a season of change. Like the air that was beginning to turn cold. Change. It comes and the funny thing about change is that sometimes we don't stop to notice. Maybe I was just noticing.

She didn't fight me about driving. Not that I would have let her drive if she had fought me. Not in her condition. Not that she was that drunk. She wasn't. But not sober like me. Maybe that was my problem. See, uncool guys like me were too sober. That's the way of the uncool lifestyle. Sober. But, see, the world couldn't do without us types. Who would drive? Yeah. Sure.

"Drive it nice." That's what she told me every time I drove her car. The girl took good care of her things. She almost spoiled that car as much as she spoiled her dog, Sofie. Look, the car was inanimate. I'd told her that once. She said that inanimate things could be very expensive. Okay. What was that?

"Where are you, Ram?"

"Here." I put the key in the ignition.

"Drive it nice," she said. Again.

"Yup," I said, "I'll drive it nice." Of course I always did. I was a much more careful driver than Alejandra. She was always looking around, trying to see stuff. Me, I kept my eyes on the road.

"Strange night," she whispered.

"Yeah," I said. Then I said, "Strange in a good way or strange in a bad way?"

"Both," she said.

"You really like that Jake, huh?"

"Yeah. There's something about him."

"Yeah," I said. There was something about him.

"He's got a really weird mom. And a missing dad."

"Yeah, well, there's a lot of dads who are missing. You're lucky."

"Yeah. Lucky," she said. "Either way, dealing with parents—that's—" She was quiet. Stopped right in the middle of her sentence.

"That's what?"

"Complicated."

"Yeah. Complicated," I said. "The problem with parents is that they're adults."

"Exactly."

We both laughed. When we finished laughing, we both got real quiet.

"Are you jealous?" That's what she asked me.

About one percent of me was jealous. Look, that sort of thing just wasn't me. I had to be careful here. You don't go around telling girls that you're only one percent jealous. Even uncool guys like me know that. I had the feeling that maybe one percent jealousy was a complete and total insult. But I decided that Alejandra and I just needed to tell each other the truth about things. I mean, setting aside her gender-politics thing. "Ten percent of me is jealous." I said. Okay, I lied a little. One percent wasn't going to cut it.

"Only ten percent?"

I'd said the right thing. "Maybe a little more. But not much more."

She laughed.

"Were you trying to make me jealous, is that it?"

"Don't be an idiot. If you got a little jealous, that would only be icing on the cake."

"Jake being the cake?" I smiled. "And I'm not an idiot."

"I only tell people I like that they're idiots. And, yes, Jake being the cake." She almost whispered Jake's name. She was trying to picture him. I could tell by her voice.

"Look, I'm glad you like him. I think he likes you, too. You know, I think he's kind of a lonely guy."

"How did you get to know him?"

"I don't know him, not really. I mean, he hangs out by himself. Likes to smoke. He talks to me. And I sort of like the guy. He's got something, but he's, well, different. But, you know, there's something real about him. I mean, I guessed he was this rich kid. You know, he goes to the magnet school, lives on the Oh-Wow West Side. But I've always gotten this feeling from him. He's real." I smiled. I smiled because I knew I was going to tell Alejandra something nice about herself. "He's like you. Real."

Alejandra got real quiet. Then she reached over and kissed me on the cheek. "That's the nicest thing you've ever said to me."

"You're going to make me wreck your spoiled car."

And then we both just started laughing.

"You know what?" she said. "You're going to be my best friend for all my life."

I nodded. I could do that. It sounded like a great thing. "It's a deal," I said. "Just don't ask me to be your maid of honor when you get married. I don't do that crap."

And then she and I, we just started laughing again. I had to control myself before I got on the freeway. Then we both got real quiet again. I just kept driving. And then she asked me, "Did you like that girl?"

"Katie?"

"Yeah, Katie."

"She seemed nice. Too complicated, though. You know, she has that boyfriend thing going on. I'm not interested in complicated right now. With Tito and everything, you know—" I didn't know what was happening just then. It was as if the whole thing with Tito just came at me like a boxer and punched me right in the stomach. And that boxer, he kept punching and punching me, and I just couldn't breathe. There was an exit just ahead, and I got off the freeway. I couldn't breathe. I couldn't.

Alejandra looked a little scared. I was just trying to hold on. That boxer kept coming at me. I pulled over just as soon as we got off the exit ramp. I was trembling.

I put the car in park. Then I just sat there. I took a deep breath. And then another. And then, there was this storm inside me. And there was thunder and there was rain. God, there was rain.

I cried like I'd never cried in my life.

Tito, Tito, Tito.

I just kept saying his name over and over in between all my sobs.

Alejandra just kept squeezing my hand.

I don't know how long I sat there crying. A long time, I think. And then, you know, the boxer was gone. And I was better. Not great. But better.

It was real quiet in the car. I took a deep breath.

"Better?"

"Yeah," I said. "Better. Let's get something to eat," I said. "I'm starving."

"Crying does that," Alejandra said.

"Crying makes you hungry?"

"Sure it does. Every girl knows that."

"I'm not a girl."

"I noticed." She squeezed my hand again. "Some boys," she whispered, "are perfect shits. And other boys are very, very beautiful."

I didn't say anything.

She put on a CD as I got back on the freeway.

I listened to her voice as she sang along.

Some girls, I thought, were perfect shits. Other girls were very, very beautiful.

Me, Ram
(And Her and Him, My Mom and My Father)

We stopped off at the Good Luck Café. It was a very cool joint. And "joint" was exactly the right word. Not the kind of place you took someone to impress them. This was the kind of joint you took people you knew. I mean, you could count the number of people who were speaking English. I mean, if you brought a certain kind of person here, they might say something like, "Don't they know this is America?" But to me and Alejandra, it was normal. The America we knew. Hell, even Border Patrol guys went there. In fact, just as Alejandra and I sat down at our table, a couple of those jokers walked into the place. Okay, my mom said everyone had to make a living and I should show them respect.

Alejandra rolled her eyes when she saw them walk in. "They make a living by throwing their relatives across the border." That was an old, recycled joke.

"Be quiet," I said, "they'll ask us for our papers."

"That's not funny, Ram."

"That's the way it is."

"I don't have anything to prove to anyone." She'd been so quiet and thoughtful most of the evening, but the other side of her was reappearing. The I-don't-keep-my-mouth-shut-for-anybody side of her.

"Be cool."

"I *am* cool, Ram. I'd like to walk over to their table and shove a jalapeño down their throats." She was raising her voice.

"You don't have to talk so loud."

"Look, if you ever even think of becoming a Border Patrol agent, I swear I'll kick your skinny ass all the way to Buenos Aires."

"Always wanted to go," I said. "It'll be the only way I'll ever be able to afford it."

"Stop with the jokes."

But even she was laughing.

"I have to go pee," she said.

"It's all that booze," I said.

"I didn't have that much."

"You had enough," I said. "You broke the law."

She rolled her eyes. "Yeah, a real felon."

"Maybe you're on your way."

"Be quiet," she said as she got up to walk toward the bathroom. She really was something, Alejandra. And she had all this stuff inside her. It was good stuff, I think. She cared. I mean, she really cared. About everything. That's what made her so effen impossible. Look, maybe she and Jake would make a perfect pair. The first thing he asked us was if we were into politics. That meant he was way into all of that. And Alejandra was way political. When I was seven, she said it was our job to make sure the poor inherited the earth. I didn't know what she was talking about. "How do we do that?" I asked. "Revolution," she said. Sure. Revolution? What was that? We were seven. Where did she get all that stuff? It was her dad. I mean, I'd heard things about him. It was true that he was a good, upstanding business man with his chain of copy stores and business centers. "Coffee with your copy." That was the store's motto. Fresh ground coffee for a better price than anybody else. Smart guy. Successful. Pretty mainstream. Pull-yourself-up-by-the-bootstraps kind of guy. But it was also true that a lot of people questioned his politics. "He's not patriotic." That's what I heard our next-door neighbor say. But our next-door neighbor was always trying to move the property line—so I'd never really trusted anything he had to say.

Besides, who got to say who was patriotic? I knew all about that game. They liked to use it against us all the time. Us. The citizens of Dizzy Land.

When Alejandra came back, we both ordered a bowl of menudo. I mean, that was the Mexican test. It was the SATs of Mexican-hood. That's what we called menudo. See, only real Mexicans ate it. And Alejandra, she loved menudo. Me too. Well, I mean, that's the way it was for the both of us. And you know, the menudo at the Good Luck Café was excellent. Look, the Border Patrol guys were eating menudo too. So, we all lived in the same world. Yeah. Utopia.

"I can drive now." Alejandra said.

"Why risk it," I said.

She rolled her eyes.

I won the argument. I drove.

"Can we stop at the hospital?"

"Think they'll let you in?"

"They might."

"I don't want you to cry anymore."

"I thought you said it was okay if guys cried?"

"It just hurts to see you that way."

"I won't cry," I said. "I'm done with that."

I wasn't surprised when we found my mom there. Sitting. Reading to him. For an instant I thought they were a painting. The saddest, most beautiful painting I had ever seen. More beautiful than the painting of my father I carried around inside.

I was motionless as I watched. As motionless as they were.

I felt Alejandra take my hand and squeeze it. Even without looking at her, I knew there were tears falling down her face. Yeah. Tears. The girl who told me not to cry.

So much rain, I thought. *So much rain inside us.*

Mom looked up at me, then saw Alejandra was with me. She smiled.

"Aren't you tired, Mom?"

She didn't even seem to hear my question.

"We had so little time."

Oh, God, she sounded more than tired. She sounded beat-up and sad. Beyond sad. As sad as I had always imagined my father was.

I wanted to say something. Something that would take all the sadness away. But the words didn't exist.

"We're taking him off the respirator." She just looked at me. Waiting. I'm not sure for what.

"When?"

"Tomorrow. As soon as we reach his doctor. Probably in the afternoon."

I didn't say anything.

"I can't take this," she said.

"I know."

"We have to do this, Ram."

"I know, Mom."

She put the book down. "I'm almost finished reading this to him."

She looked at me. Then at Alejandra. "I want to tell you something." She was whispering and I thought she was going to cry. And I was getting real tired of all that rain inside us. Effen tired.

She got up from sitting beside Tito. Tito. My brother, my brother, the guy I never knew. How can you love someone you never knew? Alejandra and I followed my mother down the hall, past the crowded ER waiting room, and out the doors.

She had her back to us, and it seemed like she was looking

out into the night sky. "The weather's changing," she said.

She was right. There was a chill in the air. Sometimes, in El Paso, it seemed that summer might stay forever. But even here, it never did. She turned around and faced us.

"Maybe I should go." Alejandra sounded unsure of herself.

My mother looked at Alejandra. "No, *amor*, you can stay. Please."

Alejandra looked at me. I nodded at her.

We all looked at each other. I don't know why.

"I talked to your father," she said.

At first my heart stopped beating. Then it sped up and I swear that my heart was a car speeding down a road in the darkness. A mad, crazed car speeding toward a crash. I couldn't speak.

My mother put on that strong face of hers. I knew that look, the one that had learned how to hide all the pain. "He lives in California." She looked into my eyes.

"California," I said. That's where everybody went to disappear. That's where you went if you wanted to forget.

"I have to tell you this. I promised myself I would tell you. I have to tell you now before I lose my nerve, Rammy. *I have to tell you.*" She was shaking. Her lips were trembling.

"It's okay, Mom, you can tell me." I could hear my own words echoing inside me. God, my heart was beating.

"This is so hard." I knew. That's when I knew. Whatever she said was going to hurt me. She hated that. She just didn't want to hurt me. But she'd told herself she wasn't going to hide anything from me anymore. That addiction to silence was killing her. And maybe it was killing me, too. I'd always known that.

"It's okay, Mom."

"I know how much you love your father," she said.

How could she know? How? How? I couldn't speak.

"Your father. He has another life now. He has another family."

I nodded. California.

"He said it was okay to let Tito go. He said he was sorry for everything."

"Is he coming?" God, even I could hear the desperate thing in my voice. I hated myself for that desperate thing.

She shook her head. "He didn't think it was a good idea."

I nodded. Why was I nodding?

She walked up to me and stared into my eyes. She was searching for something.

"Did he ask for me?" I whispered.

She nodded.

"He said you should forget about him."

I smiled. I don't know why.

I don't think I ever knew that human beings were like animals. Until just then. I remember this thing in my throat. In my chest. I remember trembling and my legs couldn't hold me, and I fell to my knees. There was this thing, this chaos inside me. And it had a noise, a howling. That's what it was. I was nothing more than a dog or a coyote or any other animal in pain. And even then I was trying to speak. But my words weren't any use in the face of the terrible wind that was escaping from my heart. I guess it was from my heart. It hurt so bad. Why did it hurt so bad? How could a man I didn't know, a man who was my father, how could he hurt me this bad all the way from California?

I remember my mom and Alejandra picking me up and embracing me.

I remember thinking that I understood Tito perfectly.

I hated God for giving me a heart. What good were they? Hearts? Having one got me exactly where?

Me, Ram
(And the Hurt)

When I woke up, it was raining.

I listened to the rain for a long time.

A hard rain. But the rain was from the sky—so much better than the rain that came from inside me.

I looked at the clock. Ten o'clock. Late. Late for me. Late for an uncool guy who never slept in. I heard voices. My mom and Tía Lisa.

I slipped on a pair of jeans. I walked into the bathroom. I looked at myself in the mirror. *Is he coming?* "Who effen are you?" *He said you should forget about him.* I took an aspirin, then brushed my teeth, then poured cold water on my face. *Did he ask about me?* I swore I had a hangover. Except I hadn't drunk an effen thing. *He said it was okay to let Tito go?* "You never even laid eyes on Tito. Not ever, you son of a bitch." Hearts. They were good for something. They were good for rage. Yeah.

I walked into the kitchen. I tried to smile at Mom and Tía Lisa. I poured myself a cup of coffee and sat at the table.

I wanted everything to be normal. But nothing had ever been normal, not really. But I wanted to say something ordinary. So I did. "Did you go to Mass?"

My mom nodded. She had this Saturday morning Mass thing going. I mean, I never really understood why you would go to Mass on Saturday *and* Sunday. I was a go-to-Mass-once-a-week kind of Catholic.

"Father Rick asked about you."

I'd been an altar boy. Of course I had been. Uncool. "How is he?"

"I told him about Tito."

So much for a normal conversation.

I sipped on my coffee. My mom made good coffee. She ground her own beans. Really good stuff. I drank it black. You know, left out the sugar. Yeah. It was raining. No sugar.

"You okay, Rammy?"

I sort of shrugged at my Tía Lisa. "Yeah, I guess so."

"You look terrible." My Tía Lisa, she didn't bullshit people.

"I'm tired."

My mom was studying me. "I shouldn't have told you."

If she could study me, I could study her. I looked into her face. "I'm like you," I said. "I'm always ready to take all the blame."

She sort of smiled. Sort of.

"All you did was tell me the truth."

"I could've made up a lie."

"To protect him or me?"

It was like I'd slapped her. I could see that.

"I'm sorry," I mumbled. I looked down.

I felt her hand on my chin. "To protect you, *amor*."

"Why do you need to protect me?"

"Because I'm your mother. I shouldn't have told you. I could have told you later."

"When? Ten years from now? Twenty?" I shook my head. "And then what?"

"Rammy, your father, he's—"

"Don't ever talk about him again. Not ever."

"Ram."

"Mom. Just don't. I never want to think about him ever again. Not fucking ever." I cussed. I cussed in front of my mother. I said that word in front of my mother. "I'm sorry," I whispered. "I'm sorry, I'm sorry, I'm sorry." I looked at my Tía Lisa, and then at my mother. "I just don't want to talk about him ever again." I don't know why I kept insisting on that. It wasn't true. And Mom didn't think it was true either.

She reached over and combed my hair with her fingers. "You're all I have."

My poor mom. My poor, poor mom. All she had was me.

I smiled.

Tía Lisa leaned over and kissed me.

"I'm going to the hospital," my mom said. "I want to finish reading the book to Tito."

"Okay." The ending was a little bit sad. In fact, the whole book was a little bit sad.

"I talked to the doctor," she said. "He said we could all be there."

I understood what she was saying.

"He said he'd be there this afternoon. Around four. He can't get to the hospital any sooner."

"Should I dress up?" What a stupid thing to ask. What a stupid, stupid thing to ask.

"Yes," she said. "I'll dress up too. That would be nice, wouldn't it?"

We both nodded.

"Alejandra called. She's worried about you."

"She's pretty great."

"I think so."

"I'll call her later."

She nodded.

I finished my cup of coffee, listened to Mom and Tía Lisa talk. Mom brought out pictures of me and Tito when we were little boys. I was always smiling—but not Tito. He never smiled for a camera. Not ever. Even when he was three, he looked old. I wondered why? When did we learn anything about what it really means to be alive?

Me, Jake
(Shit! Numb)

I stumbled out of bed. Literally. I found myself on the floor. I pulled myself up, then sat on the edge of my bed. At least the room had stopped spinning. Sometime during the night, I'd managed to make my way to the toilet and vomit every drop of anything that had settled in my stomach. I remembered lying there on the floor and falling asleep. I didn't remember crawling back to bed—which I must have done, because that's where I'd woken up.

My first hangover. What a party, huh, Jake!

The stomach was better now, but not the head. Not my head, not my fucking life. That definitely wasn't better. God, the head. Okay, so I deserved it. Have another, Jake! Yeah, that's it. I hated myself. That was the truth. Maybe that had always been the truth. Sarcasm and irony were these blankets I used to cover up the truth. Whatever that was. Sometimes I got the feeling that the truth was like God. It just didn't exist. And if it did exist, it was something you couldn't get at anyway.

I walked into the kitchen, took some aspirin, and drank a gallon of water. Well, maybe not quite a gallon. I felt like someone had been using my head for a drum for most of the night. I took a breath. I looked at the clock. It was only eight. God, eight o'clock in the morning, and I had a hangover and I hated myself and I didn't want to feel anything and why was I awake when all I wanted to do was sleep. This is the thing about life—it gives you the opposite of what you want. You know, I'm going to start to use reverse psychology on life. What am I talking about? God, my head hurt.

And I swear I could feel my cheek still burning.

I went back to bed and waited for my headache to subside. I knew it would. Aspirins worked miracles in my body. I mean those things really worked on me. I would take any miracle I could get. I lay there in my bed and tried not to think of anything. But my mom's slap kept coming back. I kept rerunning the whole scene in my life like a film, and I kept hoping the ending would be different. Ha, ha, frickin' ha, I kept feeling the slap, kept seeing that look on her face. That was hate. That's exactly what it was.

I kept thinking about what Mrs. Levitz had said. "She was slapping David." Why in the hell didn't she slap him? Why? Why had she lashed out at me instead? I had some theories. I always had theories. I didn't want to go there. C'mon, Jake, don't go there.

I put on some music, then got in the shower. I let the cold water pelt my body until I got used to it. I don't know how long I stayed under that cold water, but it must have been a long time.

I put on some clean clothes, then stared at myself in the mirror.

I tried to see what my mom saw when she saw me.

Then I tried to see what Alejandra had seen the night before. What had she seen? I think she'd liked what she saw. But what was it? What? I wanted her to show me. Or even Ram. What had he seen? I mean, the guy came to my party. What did he see when he saw Jake Upthegrove?

I walked into the kitchen and put on some coffee. I liked the smell. There was something so clean and so pure about the smell of coffee.

That's when Sally walked in.

I didn't say anything.

I thought she'd look like hell, but she didn't. She'd taken a shower, cleaned herself up, and had even put on some make-up. She looked like she was ready to go on a picnic or something.

"You look terrible," she said finally.

"Do I?'

"You were drinking last night, weren't you?"

"Yeah, Sally, I was drinking last night."

"That's not permissible."

"You're destroying me, Sally."

"I'm your mother. I don't know who Sally is."

"Sally's the mask my mother wears. That's all she is. A mask. And my mother—I don't have a fucking clue who she is. I really don't."

"I don't want to fight with you this morning. I've decided I'm just not going to fight with anyone anymore. I'm just going to make peace."

"Well, you weren't much in the mood for peace last night."

"I was upset."

"With who?"

"With the whole damn world."

"The whole damn world? That's a switch. I thought you liked the world. 'A nice place to live.' Isn't that what you always say? Why take on the world at this late stage, Mom? Why not just take on David. It's David you should be mad at."

"You've never liked David."

"I like him about as much as he likes me."

"What's that supposed to mean?"

"Nothing. Never mind."

"He's not a bad man."

"Not like me, you mean."

"I didn't mean that at all."

"He's having an affair."

"It's not what it seems. We talked it all through last night."

"He's back?"

"No. We talked on the phone. He called. He begged me, he—"

"You're gonna take him back? You're gonna take that slime back?"

"*He wasn't having an affair. He wasn't.* That woman is crazy. Don Levitz said so himself."

"You believe Don Levitz? They're partners in crime."

"Law partners."

"Same thing."

"That's not fair." Sally didn't know fair from a cloud in the sky.

"David even said we could go to counseling, if that's what I wanted."

Counseling. Shit, Sally was going to be in heaven. Now, she could drop her new therapist. She and David at counseling. Hell, Sally was going to be in dog biscuits. "Counseling?" I said. "And why would you need counseling if he really wasn't having an affair?"

"Well, because this has been a shock to our marriage."

"I see," I said. "I'm destroyed."

"Don't say that, Jacob."

"Well, I am destroyed. So, he's coming back home, I take it."

"This is his house. *Our house.*" I wasn't sure if I was a part of the *our*.

You know, I was in hell. I'd gone to bed drunk and woke up in hell as punishment for all my sins. Hadn't I been dancing with the devil? Hadn't I been? So now I was in hell. Maybe I *would* become a Catholic. Maybe I'd been one all along and just didn't know it.

She kept looking at me.

I was going to ask her if she was sorry for slapping me. But I could tell that already she'd forgotten. I mean, to her, it was nothing. Just *my* face. Just *my* hurt. *Screw it,* I thought. *I'm not going fishing for an apology. Not my kind of sport.*

I poured myself a cup of coffee. Then thought, what the hell, and I poured Sally a cup of coffee too.

She looked at it.

"Go ahead and taste it," I said. "It's not poisoned. See." I took a drink. It wasn't half bad. I mean, it really wasn't.

"Where did you get that attitude?" she said. "Where? Your father, well, he may be the most unreliable man on the planet, but he was always respectful. You're certainly not like him, that's for sure. And you're not like me, either. I don't know who you take after. I really don't."

So I wasn't like Upthegrove and I wasn't like Sally. Not the most disappointing announcement I'd ever heard. I don't know what got into me when I asked, "So, you really love David that much? I mean you're willing to forgive him. Just like that."

"He didn't have an affair. She made it all up. I told you."

"Oh yeah, I keep forgetting. And, of course, you believe him."

"Of course I do."

"Why?"

"Why wouldn't I?"

"Oh, I don't know, because we had this screaming lady in our house."

"She's crazy. She needs help."

"Or maybe she was just angry. And had a right to be angry."

"You're taking her side?"

I heard that tone. It was the same tone she'd used when

she said I was taking Rosie's side. I guess there was only one side. Hers. "No," I said, "I'm just trying to figure out what's going on here."

"This is between me and David."

Yeah, except for the fact that I was the guy getting slapped around. "What do you see in David, anyway?"

"That's a mean thing to ask."

"It's an honest question, Sally."

"Is it?"

"Yes."

"We're good together. We're alike."

I couldn't argue with that one. But I couldn't figure out why the hell you'd want to spend the few short years you had on earth with someone who was as shallow as you were. I mean, didn't it make sense to aim a little higher?

"You have a look on your face," she said.

"I have a hangover."

"It serves you right. You're not of age."

"And that slap last night? No, it was three or four slaps. Those slaps last night, Mom—did they serve me right too?" I didn't want to bring it up and there I was bringing it up. I was getting mad. I could feel it. But my headache was better. Not gone, but better. You know, the anger got worse, and the headache got better.

She looked me right in the eye. "I was in shock."

I didn't know I was going to get serious on her. I didn't plan it. But that's exactly what I did. Got serious. "You hurt me," I said.

I think my tone of voice took her by surprise.

"I didn't know what I was doing. I mean, for God's sakes, that woman in my house, saying all those awful things. And most of it, as it turns out, all made up, and I was just stunned. I just, well, I just must've exploded."

"All made up?" I asked. You know, I could be as cool as an ice cube in a fucking mixed drink. "She made it all up?"

"Look, I keep telling you. What aren't you getting here, Jacob? David and I talked about it. We talked about it all night."

I saw them! That's what I was screaming inside. *I saw them!* I don't know. I could feel the spit in my mouth and I wondered if I was going to throw up again. "Mom." I looked at her and repeated the word. "Mom." Then I looked at her. "I said *you hurt me.* And you just can't bring yourself to say I'm sorry."

"Of course I'm sorry."

Of all the things I could see on her face, remorse wasn't one of them. "I don't think you are," I said. I walked out of the kitchen, walked into my room, grabbed my keys and my cell phone, and walked out the door.

Why didn't I tell her the truth about David? Why? I knew part of the answer. Of course I did. You have to care about someone enough to sit down and talk to them. Right then, I just didn't care enough.

As I drove down Thunderbird and drove onto Mesa Street, something else occurred to me. The truth didn't matter to Sally. It didn't. Someone had removed the truth gene on the day she was born. All she wanted was the nice gene. And wouldn't you know, that was the very gene that was removed from me on the day I was fucking born. Ah, no wonder I was in love with irony.

I found a place to park in an empty parking lot. I noticed it was the parking lot of a church. Church parking lots were always empty on Saturday mornings. Only full on Sundays. And there I was, parked. On the wrong day. The only one there.

I wondered if faith was a genetic trait. Of course it wasn't. Hell, what did I know about faith.

I sat there for a while. There was something comforting about sitting in the rain. In a car. By yourself.

Sitting there was better than being at home.

Look, home didn't feel like home anymore. You know, it had never felt like home. Maybe that was my problem. I didn't have a place where I fit. Yeah, well, Jake, join the fucking universe. Who the hell belongs? Belongs to what? To who?

I found Alejandra's number, the one she'd punched in at my party. I called her.

I heard her voice on the other line.

"You like irony?" I asked.

"Jake?"

Me, Jake
(And Her, Alejandra)

It was good to hear her voice. I don't know why really. Except watching her at my birthday party destroyed the hell out of me. Look, I didn't know her. She was nice, I'll tell you that. Nice in a normal way. You know the problem with me and a lot of my friends, we were sort of addicted to destructive behavior. *We were.* I mean, why was that? What the hell was wrong with us? Or maybe it was just me. But look, Alejandra didn't seem like she was like that at all. I mean, she just seemed stable and beautiful. To me, that was a killer combination. I could use stable. And hell, who couldn't use beauty?

"Jake?"

"Yeah?"

"Do you want to say something?"

I nodded.

"Jake?"

"Yeah, I guess so." It was raining. I was in a church parking lot. And I wanted to talk to a girl. A girl that mattered. But I didn't know what to say.

"Jake?"

"Sorry," I said.

"Sorry about what?"

"About everything. About my party."

"Was it your fault?"

"Well, I mean, she's my mother."

"Jake, don't tell me you're like Ram, always beating up on yourself."

"No. Well, maybe. You know the whole thing sucked last night."

"The whole thing?"

"Well, not the whole thing. You know, I had a good time with you and Ram."

"We had a good time too."

"Until the apocalypse brought the whole thing down on my head and left me in ruins."

"I'm sorry, Jake."

"There's nothing we can do about my mother, I suppose."

"No, mothers can be very strange."

"Your mother like that too?"

"Probably."

"Probably?"

"My dad raised me. My dad and my grandparents. My mom, I met her once. I wasn't that impressed."

That made me laugh. Though I knew that she had to hurt somewhere. Or maybe the hurt had gone away. Look, I didn't know a damn thing about other people's hurts. And my hurt, well, mostly I avoided it. So shoot me.

She told me all about her dad and her grandparents and her dog, Sofie. It all sounded nice. I mean, her father actually took her on vacations and took her out to eat, dinner, stuff like that. David and my mom, well, they liked going out—but just the two of them. I wondered what it was like, to actually know one of your parents. I mean, I knew Sally in a way. But we didn't really talk. We argued. Hell, that was my fault, I guess.

"Does anyone have a normal family?" That's what came out of my mouth. Look, I knew someone had to have one. Okay, so maybe it was all a big lie, this myth about normal.

"What's normal?" I could almost see her smiling.

"Well, I'd be the last one to ask. I mean you were there last night, weren't you? What about Ram?"

"Ram? I don't know," she said. "He's got a great mom. Really great. She's a nurse at a doctor's office. And his uncles and aunts are great too. So, he has a good family. They're great to be around. But Ram doesn't remember his dad. He took off when he was about two. No, three. I don't remember. Anyway, Ram never knew him. And his brother, well, you know, drugs. It kills Ram. I know it does. He's in the hospital, you know?"

"Is he gonna be okay?"

"No."

I didn't know what to say.

"You know," she said, "even though Ram doesn't talk about it, he loves his brother. I mean he really loves him. Ram is, I don't know, he's hard on himself. And hard on other people too, sometimes. He's hard on me, I'll tell you that." She laughed. "But I'm hard on him, too. Anyway, this thing with his brother, I'm afraid for him. It's going to really kill him. It really is."

She sounded like she was about to cry. But then I heard her take a breath. Then she changed the subject. Everyone did that. When something hurt, well, we just changed the subject. Even someone like Alejandra.

"Jake?"

"Yeah?"

"Can I ask you something?"

"Sure."

"Why did your mother slap you?"

"How do you know it was my mother?"

"Who else?"

"Yeah, okay, she slapped me."

"Why?"

"I don't know."

"Take a guess." Alejandra, she really was tough.

"She was upset. I mean, I think she was in shock. That's what Mrs. Levitz said, that she was in shock."

"And so she slapped you?"

"I guess."

"And where was your stepfather?"

"She'd asked him to leave."

"Oh." She was quiet for a long time. And then she said. "It was wrong of her. You know that, don't you?"

"Yeah. I know that."

I don't think I sounded very convincing. And I didn't want to talk about this. So I did what she did. I changed the subject. "You like movies?"

And then she said, "You're changing the subject. Okay."

"Well, you just changed the subject."

"When?"

"You were almost going to cry talking about Ram and his brother. Then you just changed the subject."

"Guess I did. But when I changed the subject we were talking about Ram. And when you changed the subject, it was about you. And movies? Jake, is that the best you can do?" Man, she was so unlike the individuals in my family.

And after that, we talked and talked. Alejandra. She liked to talk. I liked that. And she liked to laugh. Alejandra. Destroy me. Destroy me forever. And she was so tough, too. God, she made me feel, I don't know, like there was hope. Now, there was a word for an ironic guy like me. Hope.

I wondered what it would be like to kiss her.

I told her all about Upthegrove and our nonrelationship. I told her all about Sally and David and I even found myself telling her about the Anger Management Lady. I never talked about her to anybody. Just to my mom. And to myself. I mean, I had long conversations with myself about the Anger Management Lady. And here I was telling Alejandra all about it. I could have stayed there forever.

"You don't hit people anymore, do you?"

"Nah," I said, "I gave it up for Lent."

"Are you Catholic?"

"Nah."

And then we both started laughing.

I wanted to tell her I loved her. But that wasn't too smart. Not a great thing to tell a girl you just met. And besides, you didn't say things like that in Jake land.

There I was.

Sitting in my car.

In the rain.

Talking to Alejandra.

And it felt more like home than the place where I slept.

Me, Jake
(And Sally in My Head)

"Why is it so hard for you to love me?"

"I do love you, Jake."

"Do you, Mom?"

"I do."

"You used to leave me alone."

"Only sometimes."

"It's not as if you had to work. Some mothers, they had to go to work. And they had to leave their kids. But you didn't have to work, Mom."

"There were other things I had to do."

"Did you?"

"Yes. And you were safe. I knew you were safe. I would have never left you if I didn't know you were absolutely safe."

"But I was alone."

"You had your bear and your bed. And the doors were all locked and you were safe. I always kept you safe."

"I didn't like being alone."

"Oh, but you learned to be so independent."

"I guess I did."

God, I wanted to be sick at the conversation I was making up in my head. I did. I could taste the bitterness in my mouth. Why was I doing this? Where exactly was this getting me?

I remembered this one time. I think I was about five years old. She was dating David. They were going out. The babysitter cancelled. My mom was upset. I was studying her face. And then she sort of smiled. She took me into my room, put me to bed, and read me a story. I fell asleep. Later, I woke up. I don't know why, but I was afraid. So I went looking for her—but I couldn't find her. I looked everywhere. In every room.

I don't know why, but I was so panicked. She was gone. I was alone. I started to cry. But then, I don't know, something happened to me. I stopped crying. I just stopped.

I mean, what good was it, to cry?

She was gone.

I watched television until I fell asleep.

I think that was when I stopped expecting anything from her.

The next day, she told me she and David were getting married.

I smiled at her because I knew she wanted me to. That's what she wanted me to do.

Smile.

Me, Jake
(And Her—Mom, Elaine, Sally)

I still had a couple of hours to kill before meeting Alejandra. "I might bring Ram. He might need it." She'd told me all about Ram's brother, how he was brain-dead, how it happened, the whole story. The whole thing made me sad. I thought of that day at the cemetery. I thought of how I'd dropped him off at the hospital. I thought of that sadness in his eyes. It felt like something inside him had died or was dying. Something like that. So what the hell did I have to be sad about? No one in my house was dying. Not that we weren't brain-dead.

I took off in my car and found myself driving back home. Okay, so I was going back home. What was I going to do in the rain?

When I pulled up to the driveway, David's car was sitting there. You know, like it belonged. Of course it belonged. It was his house. It just wasn't mine.

I took a breath and just stood out in the rain. It wasn't raining that hard, not really. Just hard enough to get wet if you stood in it. What the hell. It made me feel something. I wonder if Upthegrove ever stood out in the rain. And why the hell was I thinking about Upthegrove. I made my way inside the house.

David and Sally/Elaine/Mom (yeah, all four of them) were sitting in the den. Since the weather had turned cold, they'd decided to light a fire. Romantic. Yeah. Very nice. Mom smiled at me, then shook her head. Not in a bad way but in a nice way. Look, she was really screwed up, but she wasn't a monster. "Dry off," she whispered. A command. A soft one. She seemed really soft right then. And I felt sorry for her. I waved.

David waved back.

And he seemed soft then too.

"If you want to talk," he said, "we can."

I shrugged. "Let me dry off."

I walked into my bathroom. *My bathroom. My bedroom. My own corner of the world.* My everything. I bet my closet was bigger than Ram's bedroom. I bet it was. I didn't even have to go to his house to know that. I'd always had everything. Having everything was normal. I didn't even know how to fucking iron. I didn't. And I'd never run the washing machine. God, I was so spoiled. Mom had done that. This is the way things were supposed to be. But why?

If you want to talk. I could hear David's voice in my head. I could hear my own voice answering him. *Yeah, baby, I want to talk. Let's talk about you and Ms. Red Mustang. Let's talk about how you and she were making all cozy at McKelligon Canyon where you thought no one could see you. Let's talk about how she just made the whole affair up. Yeah, David, I wanna talk. Oh, God, I wanna talk until my heart beats so fast that it breaks. I want you to pick up the shattered pieces and hand them back to me. I want to take hold of them in my hands and push them back inside me until I start to fucking sing. Did you know that I don't sing? That I never hum? Did you know I don't have any songs inside me?* I took a breath. I would never say that to him. Not ever. Because then he would know everything about me that mattered. I would be giving him something he didn't deserve.

I dried off and changed. I walked back into the living room and sat with David and Mom. My head was pounding again.

"We should watch a movie."

I smiled at David. "Great." I meant it. I was too tired for sarcasm or irony or smartass remarks or anything else that required that I use my mind. That was the beauty of sincerity, see? Sincere people didn't have to work at anything. They could just be. They didn't have to pretend anything.

David put on a movie.

I watched.

She watched. Her. Sally. Elaine. Mom.

He watched.

We all watched.

I wasn't destroyed. I wasn't.

But, God, I felt dead. That's no way for the living to feel.

Me, Jake
(And My Family. Yeah. Sure.)

"Where are you going?"

The movie wasn't over. We'd all seen it. But I guess Mom was in the mood for family time. After last night's storm, I guess she just wanted us all to be together. "I'm meeting some friends. I promised."

"Why don't you just stay in? I'll make a nice dinner."

Not that she could cook. I grew up eating Rosie food. Rosie food was good. "I promised them, Mom." I was trying to lay off the Sally thing. "It's like I want to finish my party. You know, from last night."

What could she say? She gave me a look, but didn't say anything. "Will you be out all day?"

"I'll call."

I felt like crap. You know, just because my headache had gone away didn't mean the hangover had lifted. No way. Hangovers, I decided, liked to hang around all day.

My mom put the movie on pause. She got up and gave me a kiss. That was a really nice thing. She didn't do that too often. Maybe that was an I'm-sorry-for-slapping-you kiss. "Have a nice time." She was trying. I was trying. We were all trying.

I walked into the kitchen and grabbed a bottled water. I drank it all down. Then grabbed another.

I noticed David was standing there.

"You want one?" I asked.

He nodded.

I handed him a bottled water.

He tried to smile.

I tried to smile back. "You love her?" I asked.

"I assume you're talking about your mother."

"Who else would I be talking about?"

"Of course I love her."

"Great," I said. "Love is a great thing." Like I would know.

There was a numbness in my heart. Well, it was a disease. Everyone who lived in this house caught it. I sat in the car and wondered to myself about Mom and David and Upthegrove. They were careless people. And thoughtless and selfish. I was like them too. Careless. Thoughtless. Selfish. They had raised me to be just like them. Only something had gone wrong. And I wasn't just like them. I wasn't. I wanted to be something more. But what?

It started to rain harder.

I drove away. I wondered what it would be like to live somewhere else.

I thought of me when I was a little boy, how I had been so afraid because my mom had left me alone.

But things were different now.

Why would it be so bad if I was alone. I mean what would happen if I lived alone. Maybe I'd be more alive. Yeah. Okay. Sure. Look, no one should do any serious thinking when they have a hangover. You can dig that, yes?

Me, Ram
(And Jake and Alejandra)

I was alone in the house.

I was listening to the rain. I liked doing that.

It wasn't noon yet. I was hungry. I kept opening and shutting the refrigerator. I'd put on my nicest white shirt and a tie. For my brother. For when the time came. A sign of respect.

And then my cell phone rang. I knew who it was. "Hi, Allie," I said. I hadn't called her Allie since I was in fifth grade.

"Hi, Rammy," she said. Allie and Rammy. We were kids again. But not really.

"Today," I said. "Around four."

"I'm so sorry, Ram."

"I know you are."

"How's your mom?"

"She's at the hospital. I think she's going to spend the day there."

"So what are you doing now?"

"Nothing. I think I'm hungry."

"You think?"

"I can't decide. I can't decide about anything."

"You wanna go grab a bite to eat? C'mon. I'll pick you up."

"Okay," I said. I just didn't want to be alone. Imagine that. The king of alone didn't want to be alone.

She didn't look tired at all, didn't look like she'd been drinking. Great. She looked great. "We're meeting Jake," she said.

"Are we?" I said. That made me smile. God, I needed to smile.

It was still raining.

"How is he?"

"He has a hangover. He got drunk. He sounds like crap."

"So what happened? Did he tell you?"

"Short version," she said.

"So he gave you a long version?"

"No, he gave me a very short version. But I ask a lot of questions."

I rolled my eyes. "Poor guy."

"Stop that."

We both sort of laughed.

"Out with it."

"His stepfather's mistress showed up at the party and caused a scene. And his mother, well, she didn't take it well."

"Guess not."

"She slapped him. And then she just kept slapping him."

"Who slapped who?"

"His mother. Jake's mother went crazy and just kept slapping him."

"That doesn't sound fair. I mean, what did he do?"

"Exactly."

"That's screwy."

"You think?"

She knew I was giving her a look even though she was keeping her eyes on the road as she drove in the rain.

"Poor guy."

"Yeah. Anyway, it sounds like he has a helluva hangover."

"Maybe we should take him out for menudo."

We looked at each other. "Give him the test," we both said. At the same time. We laughed.

"We're mean," she said.

"Well, we like him enough to give him the test."

She nodded. Then she got real quiet. She kept her eyes on the road. "You think he might really like me?"

"He called you, didn't he? He told you all about his parents, didn't he?"

He was sitting there looking like an old bone a dog had chewed up and spit out. He waved at us as Alejandra and I walked into the restaurant. Waved. Sad.

The place was completely empty. Just us. The rain. I mean, people in El Paso just didn't like driving in the rain. Desert rats. That's what we were.

"Hey Jake," I said.

"Hey," he said.

Alejandra kissed him on the cheek. Such a Mexican thing to do. Jake lit up for an instant.

We sat down and sort of looked at each other.

"Sorry about your party," I said.

He sort of smiled. It was kind of a crooked smile. "Well, my mom, she just sort of lost it."

"So what are you going to do?" Alejandra sounded mad. She was all business.

"I don't know."

"It's not fair," she said.

He shrugged.

"You should move out."

Jake just looked at her. And then he lit up like a lightbulb on a front porch. He just looked at her.

"You should," she said. "You're eighteen. And you're not poor."

"No, I'm not poor. I mean, I'm not poor at all."

"So you should move out."

"What would Sally do?"

"That's your job? To take care of her?"

"But—"

"You should think about it."

"Where would I go?"

I'll be alone. That's what he was thinking. I knew that was what he was thinking. "Anywhere." I said that. Me, Ram.

Alejandra and Jake just looked at me.

"You can go anywhere you want."

"What if they tried to stop me?"

"Get an attorney," I said. What the effen hell did I know about getting attorneys?

Jake was smiling inside. I could tell. But he was shaking inside too. "Let's get something to eat," he said. "I'm starving." He opened the menu.

I took the menu out of his hands. What was wrong with me? I mean, I just didn't act like this. Maybe it was Tito. Maybe it was because I was tired of being so effen passive. And Jake, he wasn't passive. I knew that. But he seemed frozen. And that wasn't right. Why should he just sit there and pretend he couldn't do anything when he could do a lot. Maybe I should have done more about Tito. But I hadn't. And maybe there wasn't anything I could have done to stop how all of this had ended.

I took the menu out of his hands. "Do you like menudo?" I asked.

Alejandra smiled.

"I've never tried it."

"How long have you lived in El Paso?" I asked.

"All my life."

"And you've never tried menudo?"

He shrugged. "No."

"Do you even know what it is?"

"Sure I do. It's got hominy and tripe in a soup of red chile—sort of like a Mexican soup. Hominy," he repeated and then he said the word in Spanish, *"posole."*

Alejandra and I looked at each other.

"Let's go," Alejandra said. "It's time."

Jake smiled. He actually smiled. It was good, his smile.

So there we were, at the Good Luck Café again. Ordering menudo. Again. But the rain didn't want to stop and it was getting colder and colder. And menudo, wasn't it a soup? Well, sort of. At least according to Jake.

When the bowls of menudo came, Jake stared at them. He watched as Alejandra and I sprinkled oregano into our bowls, then squeezed some lime on top.

"You forgot the onions," Jake said. He pointed at the small bowl of onions on the table.

We both shook our heads. I knew Alejandra always skipped the onions, even though she liked them. She had this thing about good breath. Not that she had to worry, she always carried five or six different kinds of mints. Always had money. Always had mints.

"I don't like onions," Alejandra said.

"I'm skipping them today," I said.

Jake shrugged. He sprinkled the oregano, squeezed the lime, then put a spoonful of chopped onions into his menudo.

Then we all looked at each other.

"You first," Alejandra said.

Jake sort of smiled. He dug into the menudo, tested it for heat, nodded, then put a whole spoonful in his mouth. Then another. Then another. He looked up at us. "Aren't you going to eat?"

"So you like it?"

He laughed. "It's fucking great. I can't believe I've never had it."

Alejandra and I looked at each other. God, she was so happy.

292

Jake ate his bowl of menudo up. Then ordered another. I swear that skinny guy was eating like he hadn't eaten a meal in months. He'd been hungry for a long time.

A long time.

He and Alejandra kept looking at each other.

I opened my cell phone and looked at the time. It was 2:30. "I gotta go," I said.

Alejandra looked at me.

I nodded.

"I can take your car, if you want," I said. "You and Jake can stay."

"No," Alejandra said. "We'll take you." She looked at Jake, then back at me. "I told Jake. I told him all about it."

I nodded. Then shrugged.

"I need to spend some time with him. And then—" I just stopped talking. I just couldn't talk. This thing with words.

"We'll wait," Alejandra said. "We'll be there. In the waiting room. We'll wait." She had this look on her face. She looked like an angel. God, she did.

"Allie," I said. That's all I said. This thing with words. It wasn't like me, to reach over and kiss her on the cheek. I never did things like that. I knew right then that we were going to be friends until we were old. I hoped so. You know when you were losing someone, when someone you really loved was dying, well, then you just hung on to the living. I think that's true.

Me, Jake
(Touch Me)

The ICU waiting room was crowded but quiet. I'd never been in a waiting room in a hospital. Not ever. My mom was an only child and her parents were dead by the time I came along. And my Upthegrove grandparents died when I was a boy—not that I knew them all that well, though I seemed to have been my grandmother's favorite—which is why she left me a bundle. (I think she just wanted to send a message to my father.) I did have cousins and two uncles and an aunt on Upthegrove's side, but I didn't know them. In other words, I've never had any reason to go to an ER waiting room—well, except for the time I was in that famous altercation. And since I was a little bloody, I didn't have to do any waiting.

So there I was, sitting with Alejandra, an inexperienced waiter. I'm not that patient. Another one of the virtues that I seem to lack. Alejandra was very quiet. I knew that wasn't normal for her. I think she was just thinking about things. I didn't know whether I should say something or not. I looked at my watch. It was just three o'clock. I knew the doctor wouldn't arrive until four. That's what Ram had said. And doctors, well, they weren't the kind to arrive any earlier than they said they would. Part of the whole Doctor-I'm-Important thing.

I wanted a cigarette. I only had a few left. And I was thinking maybe I should quit. God, here Ram was with his family, and his brother was about to die, and he was all destroyed over it, and all I could think of was my stupid cigarettes. That's the thing with cigarettes. They take over your life. You know, this was it. I wasn't going to smoke after I'd finished this pack. Time to move on. Look, I didn't know many things about Upthegrove, but I knew he was a heavy smoker. Listen, I just didn't want to follow in his footsteps. This thing about the apple not falling far from the tree—well, this apple was gonna sprout wings and, well, you know, get away from that tree. And maybe that went for Sally, too.

I looked at Alejandra. I noticed there were tears rolling down her face.

"Hey, hey," I whispered. "Let's take a walk."

She nodded. "It's still raining, I think."

"Well, we'll walk in the rain."

She smiled. "I have an umbrella in my car."

I followed her out.

It had stopped raining. But the weather had changed and it was really cold, and I was glad I'd worn a sweater. When we walked out, Alejandra took my hand. God, it was warm. She had small hands. My hands were big. I don't know where I got them. It felt nice. To hold a hand. Her hand.

We looked at each other and smiled.

"Where did you come from?" she whispered.

"I'm not that special," I said. I mean, I just wanted to be honest. I wanted to be real.

"Maybe you are."

"You know, I don't think I'm a very happy person."

"What's happy?"

"You're happy. Ram's happy."

"I don't know about Ram. But, no, well, he is happy. I mean, he is. He's sad right now, but that's because of his brother. And he's sad about his father. And he's always had this idea about him, his father I mean. The thing is, fathers aren't ideas. They're real. And his, well, his father is unavailable. I think that's made him sad. But as a person, Ram's a very decent and good person. And he's not mean. I mean, he's a very sweet human being. And he's very patient." She looked at me. "And

I hate that all these bad things are happening to him."

I nodded. "But what about you?"

"Me? I guess I'm happy. Happy—but I'm never satisfied. I'm always thinking things could be better. And you know, sometimes I don't think that's such a great thing."

"Why?"

"I expect too much."

Maybe she was a little bit like me. "I expect too much too. You know, the thing is I never give anybody any slack. I don't. The Anger Management Lady said I was on the verge of being a misanthrope."

Alejandra laughed. She stopped walking and looked at me. "Kiss me," she said.

I just looked at her. Then I did. I did kiss her. She tasted of mint and something else, something sweeter.

I wanted to stay like that forever.

And then we just looked at each other for a long time. And I wanted to cry. Because I saw something in her eyes that I'd never seen. And I thought, *My God, I've lived without a look like that all my life.* And it made me sad. I had been lonely all my life. I had been. And maybe I'd always known it, but I just refused to tell myself just how empty I had always felt. I'd filled all that emptiness up with clever quips and a superior attitude. But it was just a facade. I was good at facades.

I kissed her again. I kept kissing her until there was more happiness inside me than sadness.

And then she looked at me. "You look happy," she whispered.

"Do I?"

"Yes," she said.

Happy? Happy Jake? I didn't know about that. How would the word "happiness" fit into Jake land?

I was destroyed. I was. But I needed to be, I think. I needed my old self to be gone. I needed me to be someone new.

She wiped a tear that was falling down my face.

"All my favorite boys are crying these days," she said.

We kept walking for a while. We didn't say anything. I didn't care if I ever talked again. But there was this thought inside me. *Alejandra, show me the world. Show me how to look at it. Touch me somewhere where nobody's ever touched me. Please.*

Please.

Me, Ram
(Him. Tito. Gone.)

I walked into the room. My mom was just sitting there. With Tito. I pulled up a chair and sat next to her.

"I finished the book," she said. "Poor Pip. So hard for him to learn."

"Yeah," I said. "He forgot about Joe. That was his problem."

My mother smiled. "Memory can be a terrible thing."

I knew something about that terrible thing.

"We won't ever forget." I looked at Tito.

"No. We can't. We won't."

She squeezed my brother's hand. "He cried all the time when he was a baby. Always crying. I could never comfort him."

I didn't remember. Of course, I was only a little boy. I hardly remembered.

"But not you," she said. "I carried you everywhere. And you just slept. You'd wake up smiling."

I nodded. And then we were quiet. We sat there for a long, long time. And it was peaceful. It was us three again. Just us three. We wouldn't be together anymore. Not ever again.

"Do you have anything to say to him?" My mother's voice was soft and peaceful. She was ready, I think. To let him go. I didn't know if I was ready or not. I was ready to stop being sad. I was ready to begin a new life. But all I knew was the old life, the life with Tito sleeping in the bed next to mine, the world where I worried about him all the time, the world where I got mad at him every day, the world where my heart hurt because I knew he would never love me back. Or maybe he did love me back, only he didn't love me back the way I wanted him to. Or maybe he just couldn't love. People can't give you what they don't have. But that didn't mean that you stopped needing.

"Where are you, Rammy?"

"I'm just thinking."

"What?"

"I don't know what to say. Not to him. Not to you. Not to anyone."

"Then just say good-bye."

"I can't."

"You have to, Rammy."

"I don't want to." I felt like I was five. Telling her I didn't want to finish my milk. I was embarrassed. God. I was so effen embarrassed.

She took my hand and squeezed it. And there she was between us. One hand squeezing Tito's hand, and the other hand squeezing mine, trying to keep us together for as long as she could, but knowing it was time to let go now. But then I figured out I was the kind of guy who wouldn't let go until someone made me. I had to be forced into it. Okay, then. Okay. *I had to let go. I had to.* So I did. I let go of my mother's hand, then got up, looked Tito in the face with his closed eyes, and that tube down his throat. "Good-bye," I whispered. "I always loved you." I wanted to tell him that my heart would have a scar now. And the scar was in the shape of his name. But I didn't. I wanted him to go to heaven in peace. I didn't want him to have any memories of hurt. No hurt. No more.

Please, God, take him to a good place.

I watched my mother sign the paper. The doctor was kind and he mostly spoke with his eyes. Doctor Gómez was there too, my mother's boss. Tía Lisa and all my other uncles and aunts were there.

Father Rick was there. He said a prayer. I didn't hear. I just couldn't hear. I swear I couldn't. When the doctor turned off the respirator, I thought Tito would just die. But the body didn't die so quickly. Slowly, slowly, all of his body began to shut down. It took an hour. Maybe longer. Tito was strong.

When he stopped breathing, the whole world stopped and everything was silent. Tito's breath was extinct. It would never be heard again. And then, all there was in the whole world was my mom's sobbing. That was all there was.

I held her. And I remember thinking of that place in the Bible, that place of no more tears. Maybe that's where Tito had gone. But me and Mom, we still lived here. In the valley of tears.

Her and Him and Me
(Alejandra and Jake and Me [Sad Ram])

They were sitting in the waiting room when I came out. Alejandra. Jake.

Alejandra hugged my Tía Lisa and my mother. I was numb. I just watched. It was as if I couldn't do anything but watch. Not even the floor felt real.

I found myself sitting in Alejandra's car, Alejandra in the driver's seat, Jake sitting in the backseat.

"Ram?" Alejandra was looking at me.

"Yeah?"

"You okay?"

I shook my head.

"I need some air," I said. It wasn't raining anymore but it was cold now. I took a breath, then another, then another. Then another. The cold air felt good in my lungs. I looked up at the clear, cold sky. The clouds were gone.

I felt Alejandra and Jake standing next to me.

"Do you think it would have all been different if he'd stayed?"

Alejandra didn't say anything.

"My dad." I said, "Would it have been different if he had stayed?"

Then I heard Jake's voice. "What makes you think it would have been better?"

I looked at Jake.

He looked back at me. Serious. "I used to think that if my father really knew me, he would love me. My father—" he stopped. Laughed. "If he'd have stayed, I think it would have been worse. I would still be fucking invisible. He and Sally would have fought. Look, some guys are just fucking self-absorbed."

"That's no excuse. I'm his son. He forgot to say good-bye. To me. To Tito. He just forgot."

Jake looked sad. Like me. "Ram. Listen. Fathers forget a lot of things. They don't say good-bye. They don't even say hello. You know. You could fill a whole damn book with all the things our fathers left unsaid."

"Screw him. And screw your father too. Screw all of them that left us."

Jake smiled. "Yeah, screw old man Lopez and screw old man Upthegrove."

I smiled too. "I hate them," I said. "I effen hate them."

"Good," Jake said, "I hate them too."

"And I hate my mother," Alejandra whispered. She was smiling and she was almost glowing.

And then we all just started laughing. We laughed our asses off. But I knew that really, all three of us were crying. And I knew there would be tears inside us all our lives. Because they just left. We weren't even worth a good-bye. Yeah, there would always be tears inside us. Because there was an empty space inside the three of us that would always belong to the parent who had refused to love us.

Me, Ram
(And Alejandra Who Was Now My Family)

I remember what Jake said before he drove off. "You loved him. Maybe that's the only thing that matters." He said that. I thought it was really a great thing to say. And I even think that I knew what he was trying to tell me. You know, we can't be taking on what other people feel, how other people act. Tito was whoever he was. And me, well, I'm Ram. And I loved him. And it did matter.

I went back and waited with my mom until the funeral home came for my brother. My mom had one last moment with him. And me, too. Tía Lisa really cried. She hadn't cried until then—but she really let one loose. I loved her tears and her anger and she was so beautiful. And, best of all, she was so alive. I never wanted her to die. Not ever. I couldn't take that.

When we finally got home, I was really tired. My uncles and aunts were there. And so were Alejandra and her dad, Mike. I'd always called him Mike. Not because I didn't respect him, but because that's what he wanted me to call him. He'd brought in a feast. I mean, the guy had called some caterer and brought some serious food over to our house. I mean, Mexicans like to eat when they grieve.

My mom smiled. And hugged him.

"I'm so sorry, Eva." He called her Eva because that was her middle name. I don't know how he knew that. But Dizzy Land people know a lot about each other. My mom let herself cry on his shoulder. Not a long cry. Just, you know, a moment.

We sat around and ate. The house was full, and all my cousins were there. And I knew that my mom and I were going to live.

We were going to be sadder. That was true.

But we were going to live. And that mattered.

★ ★ ★

Alejandra and I sneaked into my room. I lay down on my bed.
And she lay down in Tito's bed. And we just talked.

"How long do you think I'll miss him?"

"You'll miss him forever."

"And my dad?"

"You'll miss him different. Because he's alive."

"Alive but dead."

"Yeah. Alive but dead."

"You think I'll stop hating him someday?"

"You don't hate him."

"Yes, I do."

"No. Just like I don't hate my mom. You don't hate him.
You're just angry. And then you'll just be permanently disappointed."

"That sounds like fun."

"Look, I know this sounds weird. But a part of you will
always love him. And it will really piss you off because he
doesn't deserve it. You know, there's this poem I really love.
You know, it's called "Those Winter Sundays." Remember? I
e-mailed it to you."

She was always sending me poems. I mean, I swear she
was going to be an English professor when she grew up. Well,
probably not. A lawyer. A well-read lawyer. Yeah, she'd be
good at that. She'd be quoting poems to the jury.

"Ram?"

"Yeah?"

"Are you listening?"

"Yeah."

"Do you remember the poem? It was about a guy who's
remembering all the things his father did for him—even
though his father seemed to be a little bit hard. And in the end,

he accuses himself of knowing nothing about all the sacrifices his father made just so they could survive. And he ends the poem by saying: *What did I know? What did I know of love's austere and lonely offices?"*

I did remember. And I had always loved that last line. And I had really envied the writer because he knew his father and remembered him. "Yeah," I whispered, "I remember."

"Well, you know what? You know how the writer thinks of his father as holding an office. Yeah, well, we hold an office too. And sometimes, the love we have—it's just exactly like he says. Austere and lonely."

I nodded. "Yeah, well, does it have to be so effen austere and lonely? I mean, does it have to be that way?"

"No. My Dad. Your Mom. You know they're beautiful, aren't they?"

I smiled. "Yeah, they are."

"When I grow up, I want to be like your mom."

That made me smile. That really made me smile.

"If you could say something to your dad, what would you tell him?"

"I'd tell him I loved him."

"You would?"

"Yes. Then I'd walk away."

"You'd say that—and then you'd walk away?"

"Yup. It's like you said. He doesn't deserve me."

I think we both wanted to laugh. But we were just too tired. I must've fallen asleep. She must have fallen asleep too.

Somewhere in all that timelessness, I felt her kiss me on the cheek as she left the room. But I couldn't move. I just couldn't.

There's something to being still. There is. Sometimes, you can find something important in the stillness. Something you lost. Or something you didn't know you had.

Me, Jake
(Home)

I found myself singing as I drove home. Me, Jake. Singing. To tell you the truth, I couldn't carry a tune in a bucket. I mean, I had the worst singing voice in the whole state of Texas. But I didn't care. I just sang. Jake Upthegrove had a song in him after all.

When I got home, my mom was reading. She wasn't a big reader, but tonight she had a book open.

The fireplace was still lit.

"Hi," I said.

"Hi," she said.

"Did you have fun?"

"Well," I said, "maybe not fun. But I'm glad I went." And then I just told her the whole story. I actually told her everything—well, I left out the part when I kissed Alejandra. No kissing and telling. No, no, I don't do that. But the thing is, I really just told her about my day. I'd never done that before.

And she listened. She really listened. And she didn't interrupt me. She just let me talk.

"I'm sorry about Ram's brother," she said.

I nodded. I was tired and destroyed.

She placed her hand on my cheek. The same cheek she'd slapped the night before. "Are we going to be okay?"

I nodded. "Yeah, Mom. We are."

We sort of smiled at each other.

I was lying in bed. And I was thinking. You know, Mom and David, they had their own thing. And I wasn't going to interfere. Mom needed him. I wasn't sure whether I knew the difference between love and need. But she needed him. And so I decided right then and there to keep David's secret. I wasn't going to worry about him and Mom. I was tired of worrying about them, judging them, trying to make them into something they were never going to be.

And the same thing with Upthegrove. The hell with Upthegrove. I was going to let my mind rest from thinking about that guy.

I guess I was going to let them go.

And they were going to have to let me go too. Because, hell, I was never going to be their idea of a good son. Look, nothing much had changed. I was still the same. I wasn't going to be better—not in their eyes. I wasn't. I would never have their politics. I would never want the same things they wanted. I didn't want to live my life the way they lived their lives. I didn't. I was still Jake. And I'd always sort of seen myself through their eyes. I had. Even if I didn't want to. You know, I think I was getting to know myself a little bit better. And there were things I needed that Upthegrove and Mom and David could never give me. I was going to have to find those things on my own.

Maybe that's where Ram and Alejandra came in. Maybe Ram would be my friend. I mean, a real friend. And maybe Alejandra might love me someday. It was possible. Why not? I mean, why not?

Maybe David and Mom's house would never be home. Maybe home was something I had to find on my own. And maybe it would take me a long time to find it. So, I'd live here until graduation. What the hell. Then I'd leave. And whatever the hell there was out there, well, I'd taste it. I'd touch it. And maybe someday I would be really happy.

I fell asleep thinking about all these things. See, everything was still the same. Me, staying up thinking about things until I fell asleep. Except I think I fell asleep smiling. That was something new in Jake land.

I don't know what time it was, but the sound of my cell phone ringing woke me up. The room was dark and I was a little confused. And I was so happy when I heard Alejandra's voice.

"Were you asleep?"

"Yes," I said.

"I'm sorry I woke you."

"That's okay. How's Ram?"

"He's sad."

"Well, there's a lot to be sad about."

"Maybe so. But I think he's gonna be okay. What about you?"

"I think I'm okay too. Maybe."

"Maybe? Someday, you're going to be great."

Alejandra. That girl. She had the heart of an optimist. I wanted to tell her that I'd sung a song all the way home. Maybe that was as close to great as I was ever going to be.

Me, Ramiro Lopez

On Monday morning I went with my mom and my Tía Lisa to the funeral home. We took some clothes for Tito. A white shirt that I ironed just for him, and a pair of jeans and his favorite tennis shoes. My mom spoke to the funeral director and they let us clothe Tito. That sounds weird, I know, but Mom was crazy fierce about this thing of clothing Tito for the last time. Crazy. Fierce. When my uncle Celso shook his head and said, "We're not in Mexico," she stopped him cold. She gave him a look and said, "The poor people in Mexico take care of their dead. And here, we think we're so civilized. Civilized? We pay other people to take care of our dead because it's too damn hard for us—is that it? Are we that delicate, Celso? Well, I'm not. He was my son. *Mine*. And I'm not going to have some hired undertaker put on the last shirt he'll ever wear."

Her lecture was something, I'll tell you that. God, she was so fierce and beautiful. Not crazy at all. I didn't know I could love anybody as much as I loved her right then.

She had brought Tito into this world—and she was going to prepare him for the next.

I didn't really help Mom and Tía Lisa clothe Tito. I just watched. My mom was so careful. It was as if she thought he could still feel. She almost broke down crying—but then she made herself strong. She was good at making herself strong. But I was thinking that the business of making yourself strong was an addiction. You know, like not talking was an addiction. And I was thinking that maybe Mom should let that go. Since we were letting Tito go and I was letting my father go, well, we both might as well throw a few other things on that pile, that letting-go pile. You know, start fresh. Travel lighter.

When Mom and Tía Lisa finished dressing Tito, my Mom

straightened out his collar. Then kissed him. She turned around and smiled at me. Such a sad and peaceful smile. This wasn't going to break her. "Never be afraid of the dead, Rammy."

My Tía Lisa added her own editorial. Well, that's what she did. That's why I loved her. "It's the living that should scare the hell out of you."

That made me laugh. That made us all laugh. And you know what? She had a point.

I kissed my brother one last time. That's when I remembered that I used to kiss him all the time. He used to crawl around the house before he learned how to walk. And we played a game. I would chase him as he tried to crawl away from me. He would get so excited that he'd sort of squeal. And when I caught him, I'd kiss him. And we would both laugh as hard as we could.

I wondered if there was laughing and kissing where he was going. I wondered if there was love or happiness or peace. *Please, please let there be peace for Tito.*

My Tía Lisa took my mom out to buy her a black dress. For Tito's funeral. I think she really just wanted to get my mom out of the house. And then they were going to talk to Father Rick about Tito's funeral Mass. Before they left, Mom came into my room. I was lying on my bed and looking up at the ceiling. "Will you be okay?"

I looked at her and nodded. "You know, I always wondered if I was like him." She knew I was talking about my father. Alvaro. "But now I'm wondering if I'm like you."

She kept watching me.

"I hope so," I said.

"I should have named you Angel," she whispered.

"Glad you didn't," I said. "All the Angels I know are pure hell."

It was strange, to be alone at home in the middle of the day. On a Monday. Not that I wanted to be at school. Hell, no.

Around one o'clock I got a call on my cell.

"What are you doing?" It was Alejandra. Who else?

"I'm sitting around," I said. That was exactly what I was doing. "You're not supposed to make nonemergency calls on your cell when you're at school."

"Well, who said I was at school?"

"You're skipping? I can't believe that. You've never skipped."

"That's what you know," she said.

"Mike's gonna kill you."

"Dad knows. He gave me permission."

"What fun is that? It's not really skipping when your dad lets you stay home. How'd you talk him into it?"

"I told him I just needed a day off."

"And he said okay?"

"Well, he said, 'You're seventeen years old and you need a day off?' That's what he said. But then he smiled, shook his head, and said okay. And guess who's over here?"

I knew exactly who was over there. "Jake," I said.

"Jake," she said.

"Does he have permission too?"

"As a matter of fact, he does."

"You guys are gonna give skipping school a bad rap. It's not fun when it's all legal." I knew she was smiling. "Mom would never have let me do that."

"Probably not," she said. "And good for her."

I laughed at that.

"Well," she said, "Jake gets a day off because it's sort of his mother's gift to him on his real birthday."

That was very cool.

"Today's his actual birthday. Eighteen."

"He can buy his own cigarettes."

"He's going to quit."

"Already ordering him around."

"Funny guy. Come over," she said. "Eat cake."

She made good cakes. That's one of the things she was good at. She was better at karate than cakes. But still, her cakes were good. "Don't you guys want to be alone?"

"You think my dad would let me alone with a guy in the house? My grandmother's here. And she's watching us like a hawk." She laughed. I mean, her grandmother was the sweetest lady in all of Dizzy Land. The word "hawk" just didn't fit in the same sentence as her grandmother. "Jake is speaking Spanish to her."

"Yeah?" That made me smile too. That Jake. He wasn't wasting any time. "Sure," I said. "Why not?"

Yeah. Why not? She only lived two blocks away. As I walked out the door, I wondered why I hadn't ever made the time to make more friends. I was going to start making lots more friends. I was. I was going to stop being so uncool. Sure. Sure I was. This is the thing. If you were born uncool, you would probably spend your whole life being uncool. But maybe you could find people in the world that were okay. You know, cats.

Cats. And then I thought of that guy Steve. And I thought maybe Mom should start dating him. Why not? I mean, maybe she'd always liked him. Maybe she didn't see anybody because I had this thing about my father. My ex-father, Alvaro. Definitely my ex-father. And that Steve guy, he was a very cool cat. And I liked him. I did. And maybe my mom needed some-one like him. Because I had the feeling the guy had it in him to love someone. Someone like my mom. That idea made me smile, so I went back into the house and left my mom a note—which I'd forgotten to do. The note thing was a rule. A rule I'd always kept. Tito, he'd never kept it. Tito. He didn't need that rule anymore. But me, well, I didn't mind that I still needed a few rules. Uncool. Definitely.

> Mom—
> I'm at Alejandra's if you need me. Mike let her skip school. Yeah, I know, she's spoiled. Anyway, that's where I am. I have my cell. Oh, and by the way, I think you should start dating Steve. What do you think?
> Ram

I smiled all the way to Alejandra's house. And when she answered the door, she told me I was smirking. Yeah, I said, I'm a guy. That's what we do. We smirk. You know, I was feel-ing light. Maybe a little drunk. Maybe I could be happy. I bet I could be.

Me, Jake. Happy Birthday.

When I woke up, I put on the coffee. I decided it was time that I learned to do things. Real things. You know, take care of myself. I even thought about pressing one of my shirts. You know, it took me a while to find the ironing board, and then, hell, I decided not to tackle everything at once. I didn't have a clue. Ironing? Take off the "ing" and add a "y." That's what I knew. And you couldn't press a shirt with that.

So I made a cup of coffee and I was humming to myself. You know, happy birthday to me, happy birthday to me. Yeah, I was humming that song. And then Mom walks into the kitchen and says, "You're up early."

I nodded.

And then she smiled and said, "Happy birthday."

And I smiled back at her. I wanted to ask her about that day, when I was born. She'd never told me about it. Not ever. I guess she just didn't want to talk about it. I mean, she'd had eighteen years to say something. Guess maybe it was a hard day for her.

She looked at me and asked, "So what do you really want for your birthday since I managed to ruin your party?"

I guess that was the "I'm sorry" I was looking for. That would do. Maybe that was all the gift I wanted.

"I want you to call school and tell them I'm sick." Okay, so I was greedy.

At first, I could tell she wasn't too happy about that request. But then, she sort of smiled, and said, "That's a pretty cheap gift."

"Well, I guess it's the thought that counts."

She shook her head. "Fine. I'll call the school. Just don't drink. And don't hit anybody either."

"About that hitting," I said. "I think I know where I got it from."

She couldn't help herself. She laughed. Sally and I, we were up and down. Today we were up. Okay, so I'd take the up and run with it.

Look, the fact that it was my birthday was only part of the reason I didn't want to go to school. The thing was that I hadn't done an ounce of homework. Not one damn ounce. I mean, I just hadn't. And I didn't even care. The thing about homework was that I hated it. But I always did it. Because I hated getting bad grades. I had this thing about grades. It was as if I really believed they were a measure of my intelligence. Even though I knew better. I sure as hell *did* know better. So why the hell did I want to go to school so that my trig teacher, Mr. Mayes, would look at me and say, "Aha! Finally a reason to flunk your ass!" Not that he'd say that. But he'd think it. He hated me. It was a mutual dis-admiration society. I hated him first. Yeah, Jake, you get a prize for hating first.

And then, in the middle of my one-man discussion about homework, she called. Her. Alejandra.

"Hi," I said.

"Hi," she said. I thought of how I'd kissed her. But really, I thought of how she'd kissed me back. Destroyed. D-E-S-T-R-O-Y-E-D.

"Did you call to wish me a happy birthday?"

"It's your birthday? Today?"

"Yes. Today is the day."

"Happy birthday. Should I sing?"

That made me want to laugh. Not in a sarcastic or ironic or superior way. You know, in a sincere way. In a real way.

"I'm not going to school today." That's what she said.

I wasn't going to school today either. I had plans. Actually, she was part of the plan. A later part of it.

"Me neither," I said.

"Will you get in trouble?"

"Nah. I sort of talked my mom into letting me get out of school for a day."

I thought I heard her smiling. Can you hear a smile?

I spent the morning alone.

I took a walk in the desert. It was a cool day and I liked the breeze on my face. Winter was coming. So, let it come. But right now it was sunny and I could have walked forever. I loved the desert. Mom said Upthegrove had always hated it. How could you hate something so beautiful? Maybe I wasn't sure about God, but I was sure about the sky. I was sure about the smell of creosote. The plants in the desert, they didn't ask for much. Just a little water every few months. With just a little water, they could survive the sun. I liked that. I mean, the trees that grew in a forest? Big deal. They damn well better grow with all that rain. Big deal.

It's funny, I never felt alone when I was taking a walk through all those arroyos. It was the one place in the world where I belonged. The one place in the world where I didn't need words.

I walked. And I walked. And I thought about a few things. So I wound up coming up with a list. I decided on a few things. I wrote them all down in my head and memorized them so that later, I could write the list down on a piece of paper.

1. Upthegrove can go to hell.
2. David can go to hell too.
3. Do not become like Upthegrove or David.
4. Mom and I will never be a good match, but I'm going to love her as best I can. And I will always forgive her.

But she's not going to run my life.

5. Make sure that Rosie and Roman will be all right.
6. Never tell Mom that I saw David with Ms. Red Mustang.
7. Don't send Alejandra away like you did all the others. Just don't.
8. Be a good friend to Ram. You've never been a good friend to anyone.
9. When someone tries to give you a compliment, just say thank you.
10. Anger isn't always a bad thing.

That was the list I made when I was walking around in the desert. I liked the list. It was the best list I'd ever made. The first two things on the list were part of the old me. But you gotta keep something from your old life, yes? I'm sure you can dig that. Sure you can.

I found myself driving to Rosie's house. I mean, she was probably home. At least that's what I figured. I had her number. I could have called. Look, I think I just wanted to see her. I wanted to make sure she was okay. Seeing her face, that would be like giving myself a birthday present. When I got there, I took a deep breath. I knocked at the door.

Nothing happened. So I knocked again.

And then, well, the door opened. There she was. Rosie.

"Hi," I said.

"Hi," she said. She liked saying hi.

"¿Estas bien, Rosie?"

"Sí," she said. And then she motioned me in.

You know, her house was clean and neat. It was nice. A little crowded. But she had a television and a couch and a nice carpet, you know, the normal things. And the walls were painted a real nice color, watermelon. And the house smelled like candles and coffee. Something like that. And she had a statue of Our Lady of Guadalupe and pictures everywhere. Rosie loved pictures.

"No se que decir," I said. I sort of shrugged. Like I said, I was good at that.

She told me that Mr. Armendariz had called and that he was working on Roman's case and that they were going to let him out of the detention center and that he was gathering witnesses that she and Roman were in fact married. You know, the common-law thing. I didn't quite get it all. But she said Mr. Armendariz had told her that he was very optimistic about their case and that Roman would be allowed to get out of the detention center until their hearing came up.

I promised myself I'd be at that hearing. I would be there. The least I could do for a woman who'd washed and ironed my clothes for ten years was stand with her at a hearing. Who knows, maybe I'd even drag Sally along. Okay, maybe I wouldn't push it.

Rosie couldn't stop talking. I mean, I had no idea she was such a talker. She wound up the whole conversation by telling me that Mr. Armendariz had been sent by God and that I had been sent by God too. I think Rosie was really stretching the whole God thing. Look, if I were God, I wouldn't send me to buy a pack of cigarettes.

And then Rosie hit herself on the head, you know, soft, like she'd forgotten to tell me something. She said she'd gotten a job at a restaurant. I told her she worked fast. *"Tengo que comer,"* she said. Yeah, that thing about needing to eat. I got that.

She poured me a cup of coffee and we talked a little bit more and I told her I met a girl I liked named Alejandra and she told me I better be nice to her. But she said it in a very sweet way. Look, in Jake land, sweet didn't exist. But there it all was, all that sweetness in Rosie's voice.

You know something? I'd always been kind of a fuckup. Let's be honest. I was way into myself. Not that the Anger Management Lady hadn't tried to tell me that. I mean, I don't know what I mean. But I did the right thing by finding Mr. Armendariz. Maybe it was the best thing I'd ever done.

When I got to Alejandra's house, she was working on baking a birthday cake. I couldn't believe that.

I kinda got a little choked up. I mean, I was subtle about it. It's not like I was falling apart. But the tears were there. You know, well, shit, it had been a long week.

"*Mira, que lindo.*" That's what her grandmother said. "*Que dulce.*"

I wanted to tell her that when a guy cried it wasn't that beautiful and it wasn't that sweet. It was, well, pathetic. I pulled myself together. "Sorry," I said.

Alejandra smiled. Then laughed. But it wasn't like she was making fun of me. It wasn't like that. "I didn't know you were sentimental. Just like Ram." It looked like she was filing something away in her head. "Well," she said, "I figured you have everything you want. Except someone who'll bake you a cake."

And wasn't that the fucking truth.

A white cake. From scratch. No boxes. None of that. How did she know how to do that? I mean, she had a real kitchen and a real grandmother who seemed so nice. Her grandmother studied me, and held my face between her palms. She was old and her palms were soft and her eyes were dark and even softer than her palms.

And then Alejandra's dog, Sofie, comes wandering into the

room. Calmest dog I'd ever seen. And a very cool dog too. White with brown circles around her eyes. She just sort of came up to me and expected me to pet her, which I did. And then she just plopped herself on the floor—then closed her eyes and went back to sleep.

"She's old," Alejandra said. "I've had her since I was four."

Alejandra walked over to the dog, bent down, and kissed her. She didn't seem like the kind of girl who would do something like that. But she didn't seem like a black belt in karate either. She picked up the phone and called Ram. She told him to come over.

When he walked in the door, Ram looked at me and said, "You should have told me it was your birthday." Like all this crap in his life wasn't happening. He looked a little sad. And tired. But mostly he looked like, well, I don't know what he looked like. He looked older. In a good way. Not like a kid. And I thought that maybe he was beginning to become a man. And I wondered if maybe I was starting to become a man too. I don't know. It's hard to say what's happening when you're in the middle of becoming.

Man. I repeated that word to myself. *Man.* What a strange word. What a beautiful and strange thing.

Ram made the frosting. Chocolate with cream cheese. Excellent. I mean, the guy knew how to do stuff too. I bet he even knew how to iron. Shit, the only resident of Jake land had some catching up to do.

And then Ram got this idea. "Let's look for a gift for Jake on eBay."

Alejandra thought it was a very cool idea.

And so we got on Alejandra's computer as my cake was baking. 350 degrees. That's what cakes baked at. That was one of the things I'd never known. Look, it was a good thing to know. You know, useful. I mean, if you baked cakes.

We spent the afternoon looking at stuff.

We laughed and we talked, and for a little while Ram forgot about Tito and his mother's broken heart and I forgot about how I didn't fit in anywhere and thought that Alejandra seemed like a place called home.

I couldn't decide what I wanted. Finally, we got to bidding on an old Beatles album. *Abbey Road.* Vinyl. In mint condition. Retro city.

When we won the bid, you'd have thought we'd bought the most valuable thing in the entire known universe. Alejandra and Ram paid too much for it.

But they were happy. Because they wanted to give me something.

Happy Birthday, Jacob Upthegrove. I was the richest kid in the effen world. Effen. That was a Ram word.

There were so many words I wanted to get rid of. And so many words I wanted to learn. Okay, maybe "effen" wasn't the best place to start.